"A SUPERIOR MYSTERY."

—*The New Yorker*

"The writing is really first class—a continual delight."

—[London] *Times Literary Supplement*

"As a character novel with a vivid sense of place, it has all the Tey magic and delight."

—*San Francisco Chronicle*

"Miss Tey's style and her knack for creating bizarre characters are among the best in the field."

—*The New Yorker*

Books by Josephine Tey

Published by POCKET BOOKS

THE SINGING SANDS

Josephine Tey

PUBLISHED BY POCKET BOOKS NEW YORK

POCKET BOOKS, a Simon & Schuster division of
GULF & WESTERN CORPORATION
1230 Avenue of the Americas, New York, N.Y. 10020

ISBN: 0-671-43525-6

First Pocket Books printing May, 1977

10   9   8   7   6   5   4   3

POCKET and colophon are trademarks of Simon & Schuster.

Printed in the U.S.A.

1

It was six o'clock of a March morning, and still dark. The long train came sidling through the scattered lights of the yard, clicking gently over the points. Into the glow of the signal cabin and out again. Under the solitary emerald among the rubies on the signal bridge. On toward the empty grey waste of platform that waited under the arcs.

The London mail at the end of its journey.

Five hundred miles of track lay behind it in the darkness all the way to Euston and last night. Five hundred miles of moonlit fields and sleeping villages; of black towns and unsleeping furnaces; rain, fog, and frost; snow flurry and flood; tunnel and viaduct. Now, in the six o'clock bleakness of a March morning the hills had risen round it and it was coming, casual-seeming and quiet, to rest after its long urgency. And only one person in all its crowded length did not sigh with relief at the realisation.

Of those who sighed, two at least sighed with a gladness that bordered on passion. One of these was a passenger, and the other was a railway employee. The passenger was Alan Grant, and the railway employee was Murdo Gallacher.

Murdo Gallacher was a sleeping-car attendant, and the

best-hated living creature between Thurso and Torquay. For twenty years Murdo had browbeaten the travelling public into acquiescence and blackmailed them into tribute. Monetary tribute, that is. Their vocal tribute was voluntary. To first-class passengers far and wide he was known as Yoghourt. (Oh, God, it's Old Yoghourt! they would say as his sour face became visible through the steamy gloom of Euston.) The third-class passengers called him a variety of things, both frank and descriptive. What his colleagues called him is nobody's business. Only three people had ever got the better of Murdo: a cowhand from Texas, a lance-corporal of the Queen's Own Cameron Highlanders, and an unknown little cockney woman in the third-class who had threatened to beat him over his bald head with a lemonade bottle. Neither rank nor achievement impressed Murdo: he hated one and resented the other; but he was greatly afraid of physical pain.

For twenty years Murdo Gallacher had done the absolute minimum. He had been bored by the job before he had been a week at it, but he had found it a rich lode and he had stayed to mine it. If you got morning tea from Murdo, the tea would be weak, the biscuit soft, the sugar dirty, the tray slopped, and the spoon missing; but when Murdo came to collect the tray the protests which you had been rehearsing died on your lips. Now and then an Admiral of the Fleet or something like that would venture an opinion that it was damned awful tea, but the ruck smiled and paid up. For twenty years they had paid up, weary and browbeaten and blackmailed. And Murdo had collected. He was now the owner of a villa at Dunoon, a string of fried-fish shops in Glasgow, and a very nice bank balance. He might have retired years ago but he could not bear the thought of losing his full pension; so he endured the boredom a little longer and evened things up by not bothering with early-morning teas unless passengers suggested the thing themselves; and sometimes, if he was very sleepy, forgetting about the order anyway. He hailed the end of each journey with the relief of a man who is working out his sentence and has only a short time left.

Alan Grant, watching the lights of the yard float past beyond the steamed-up window and listening to the gentle sound of the wheels clicking over the points, was glad because the end of the journey was the end of a night's suffering. Grant had spent the night trying not to open the door into the corridor. Wide awake, he had lain on his

6

expensive pallet and sweated by the hour. He had sweated not because the compartment was too hot—the air-conditioning worked to a marvel—but because (O Misery! O Shame! O Mortification!) the compartment represented A Small Enclosed Space. To the normal eye the compartment was just a neat little room with a bunk, a washbasin, a mirror, luggage racks in assorted sizes, shelves that appeared or disappeared as bidden, a fine little drawer for one's hypothetical valuables, and a hook for one's presumably unhocked watch. But to the initiate, the sad and haunted initiate, it was A Small Enclosed Space.

Overwork, the doctor called it.

"Sit back and browse for a little," the doctor had said, crossing one elegant Wimpole Street leg over the other and admiring the hang of it.

Grant could not imagine himself sitting back, and he considered browsing a loathsome word and a contemptible occupation. Browsing. A fattening-up for the table. A mindless satisfaction of animal desires. Browse, indeed! The very sound of the word was an offense. A snore.

"Have you any hobbies?" the doctor had asked, his admiring glance going on to his shoes.

"No," Grant had said shortly.

"What do you do when you go on holiday?"

"I fish."

"You fish?" said the psychologist, seduced from his Narcissian gazing. "And you don't consider that a hobby?"

"Certainly not."

"What is it, then, would you say?"

"Something between a sport and a religion."

And at that Wimpole Street had smiled and had looked quite human, and assured him that his cure was only a matter of time. Time and relaxation.

Well, at least he had managed not to open the door last night. But the triumph had been dearly bought. He was drained and empty, a walking nothingness. "Don't fight it," the doctor had said. "If you want to be in the open, go into the open." But to have opened the door last night would have meant a defeat so mortal that he felt there would be no recovery. It would have been an unconditional surrender to the forces of Unreason. So he had lain and sweated. And the door had stayed closed.

But now, in the unrewarding dark of early morning, in the bleak, anonymous dark, he was as without virtue as if he had lost. "I suppose this is how women feel after long labour," he thought, with that fundamental detachment which Wimpole Street had noted and approved. "But at least they have a brat to show for it. What have I got?"

His pride, he supposed. Pride that he had not opened a door that there was no reason to open. Oh, God!

He opened the door now. Reluctantly, and appreciating the irony of that reluctance. Loath to face the morning and life. Wishing that he could throw himself back on the rumpled couch and sleep and sleep and sleep.

He picked up the two suitcases which Yoghourt had not offered to do anything about, tucked the bundle of un-read periodicals under his arm, and went out into the corridor. The little vestibule at the end of it was blocked almost to the roof with the luggage of the more lavish tippers, so that the door was nearly invisible; and Grant moved on into the second of the first-class coaches. The forward end of that too was stacked waist-deep with privileged obstacles, and he began to walk down the corridor towards the door at the rear end. As he did so Yoghourt himself came from his cubby-hole at the far end to make sure that Number B Seven was aware that they were nearly at the terminus. It was the acknowledged right of Number B Seven, or of any Number whatever, to leave the train at his leisure after arrival; but Yoghourt had of course no intention of hanging round while some-one had his sleep out. So he knocked loudly on the door of B Seven and went in.

As Grant came level with the open door, Yoghourt was shaking B Seven, who was lying fully dressed on the bunk, by the cloth of his sleeve and saying in choked exaspera-tion: "Come on, sir, come on! We're practically in."

He looked up as Grant's shadow darkened the door and said disgustedly, "Tight as an owl!"

The compartment was so solid with the reek of whisky that you could stand a walking-stick in it, Grant noticed. Automatically he picked up the newspaper that Yoghourt's shaking had dislodged on to the compartment floor, and straightened the man's jacket.

"Can't you recognise a dead man when you see one?" he said. Through the haze of his tiredness he heard his own voice say it: Can't you recognise a dead man when you see one? As if it were a thing of no moment. Can't you recognise a primrose when you see one? Can't you recognise a Rubens when you see one? Can't you recognise the Albert Memorial when—

8

"Dead!" said Yoghourt in a kind of howl. "He can't be! I'm due to go off."

That, Grant noted from his far-away stance, was all that it meant to Mr. Blast His Soul Gallacher. Someone had taken leave of life, had gone out from warmth and feeling and perception to nothingness, and all it meant to Damn His Eyes Gallacher was that he would be late in getting off duty.

"What'll I do?" said Yoghourt. "How was I to know anyone was drinking themselves to death in my coach! What'll I do?"

"Report to the police, of course," Grant said, and for the first time he was conscious of life again as a place where one might have pleasure. It gave him a twisted, macabre pleasure that Yoghourt had at last met his match: the man who would get out of tipping him; and that that man should be the one to put him to more inconvenience than anyone had succeeded in doing in all his twenty years in the railway service.

He looked again at the young face under the rumpled dark hair, and went away down the corridor. Dead men were not his responsibility. He had had his fill of dead men in his time, and although he had never quite lost a heart-contraction at its irrevocability death had no longer power to shock him.

The wheels ceased their clicking, and instead came the long low hollow sound that a train makes coming into a railway station. Grant lowered the window and watched the grey ribbon of the platform run past. The cold struck him like a blow in the face, and he began to shiver uncontrollably.

He dropped the two suitcases on the platform and stood there (chattering like a blasted monkey, he thought resentfully) and wished that it were possible to die temporarily. In some last dim recess of his mind he knew that to dither with cold and nerves on a station platform at six of a winter morning was in the final resort a privilege, a corollary to being alive; but oh, how wonderful it would be to achieve temporary death and pick up life again at some happier moment.

"To the hotel, sir?" the porter said. "Yes, I'll take them over when I've seen to this barrow-load."

He stumbled up the steps and across the bridge. The wood sounded drumlike and hollow under his tread; great bursts of steam billowed up round him from below;

9

noises clanged and echoed from the dark vault about him. They were all wrong about hell, he thought. Hell wasn't a nice cosy place where you fried. Hell was a great cold echoing cave where there was neither past nor future; a black, echoing desolation. Hell was concentrated essence of a winter morning after a sleepless night of self-distaste.

He stepped out into the empty courtyard, and the sudden quiet soothed him. The darkness was cold but clean. A hint of greyness in its quality spoke of morning, and a breath of snow in its cleanness spoke of the "high tops." Presently, when it was daylight, Tommy would come to the hotel and pick him up and they would drive away into the great clean Highland country; away into the wide, unchanging, undemanding Highland world where people died only in their beds and no one bothered to shut a door anyhow because it was too much trouble.

In the hotel dining-room the lights were on only at one end, and into the gloom of the unlit spaces marched ranks of naked baize-topped tables. He had never before, now he came to think of it, seen restaurant tables undressed. They were really very humble shabby things stripped of their white armour. Like waiters without their shirtfronts.

A child in a black uniform dress and a green jersey coat embroidered with flowers poked her head round a screen and seemed startled to see him. He asked what he might have for breakfast. She took a cruet from the sideboard and set it on the cloth in front of him with an air of ringing the curtain up.

"I'll send Mary to you," she said kindly, and went away behind the screen.

Service, he thought, had lost its starch and its high glaze. It had become what housewives call rough-dried. But now and then a promise to send Mary to one made up for embroidered jerseys and similar infelicities.

Mary was a plump calm creature who would inevitably have been a Nannie if Nannies were not out of fashion, and under her ministrations Grant felt himself relaxing as a child does in the presence of a benevolent authority. It was a fine state of affairs, he thought bitterly, when he needed reassurance so badly that a fat hotel waitress could provide it.

But he ate what she put in front of him and began to feel better. Presently she came back, removed the slices of cut bread, and put in their place a plate of morning rolls.

10

"Here's the baps to you," she said. "They've just this minute come. They're poor things nowadays. No chew in them at all. But they're better than that bread."

She pushed the marmalade nearer to his hand, looked to see if he needed more milk, and went away again. Grant, who had had no intention of eating any more, buttered a bap and reached for one of the unread papers from last night's store. What came to his hand was a London evening paper, and he looked at it with a puzzled lack of recognition. Had he bought an evening paper? Surely he had read the evening paper at the normal hour of four o'clock in the afternoon. Why buy another at seven o'clock in the evening? Had buying an evening paper become a reflex action, as automatic as brushing one's teeth? Lighted bookstall: evening paper. Was that the way it worked?

The paper was a *Signal*, the afternoon voice of the morning *Clarion*. Grant looked again at the headlines which he had absorbed yesterday afternoon and thought how constant in kind they were. It was yesterday's paper, but it might equally be last year's or next month's. The headlines would for ever be the ones that he was looking at now: the Cabinet row, the dead body of the blonde in Maida Vale, the Customs prosecution, the hold-up, the arrival of an American actor, the street accident. He pushed the thing away from him, but as he reached out a hand for the next roll in the pile he noticed that the blank space for the Stop Press news bore scribblings in pencil. He turned the paper round so that he could see what someone had been calculating. But it seemed that the scribble was not, after all, some newsboy's hasty reckoning of the odds. It was someone's attempt at verse. That it was an original work and not an attempt to remember some verse already known was apparent in the desultory writing and in the fact that the writer had filled the two missing lines by ticking in the required number of feet, a trick that Grant himself had used in the days when he had been the best sonnet-writer in the sixth form.

But this time the poem was none of his.

And suddenly he knew where the paper had come from. He had acquired it by an action much more automatic than buying an evening paper. He had put it under his arm with the others when he picked it up as it slipped to the floor of compartment B Seven. His conscious-mind

11

—or as much of it as was conscious after last night—was concerned with the disarray that Yoghourt was making of a helpless man. His only deliberate action had been his reproof to Yoghourt in his straightening of the man's jacket, and for that he had needed a hand, and so the paper had gone under his arm with the rest.

So the young man with the tumbled black hair and the reckless eyebrows had been a poet, had he?

Grant looked with interest at the pencilled words. The writer had designed his effort in eight lines, it seemed, but he had not been able to think of the fifth and sixth, so that the scribble read:

> The beasts that talk,
> The streams that stand,
> The stones that walk,
> The singing sand,
> . . . .
> . . . .
> That guard the way
> To Paradise

Well, it was odd enough, in all conscience. The beginnings of delirium tremens?

It was understandable that the owner of that very individual face would see nothing so ordinary in his alcoholic dreams as pink rats. Nature itself would turn cartwheels for the young man with the reckless eyebrows. What was the Paradise that was guarded by so terrifying a strangeness? Oblivion? Why had he needed oblivion so badly that it represented Paradise to him? That he had been prepared to run the known horror of the approaches to it?

Grant ate the fine fresh bap that there was "no chew in" and considered the matter. The writing of an adult who wrote an unformed hand not because his coordination was bad but because he had never quite grown up. Because in essentials he was still the schoolboy who had originally written that way. This theory was confirmed by the shape of the capital letters, which were made in pure copy-book form. Odd that so individual a creature had had no desire to impress his individuality on the form of his letters. Very few people indeed did not adapt the copy-book form to their own liking, to their own unconscious need.

One of Grant's milder interests had for years been the business of handwriting; and in his work he had found the results of his long observation greatly useful. Now and then, of course, he was shaken out of any complacency about his deductions—a multiple murderer who dissolved his victims in acid turned out to have handwriting remarkable only for its extreme logic, which after all was perhaps appropriate enough—but in general, handwriting provided a very good index to a man. And in general a man who continued to use the schoolboy form for his letters did so for one of two reasons: either he was unintelligent, or he wrote so little that the writing had had no chance of absorbing his personality.

Considering the high degree of intelligence that had put into words that nightmare hazard at the gates of Paradise, it was obvious that it was not lack of personality that had kept the young man's writing adolescent. His personality—his vitality and interest—had gone into something else.

Into what?

Something active, something extrovert. Something in which writing was used for messages like: "Meet me Cumberland bar, 6:45, Tony," or for filling up a log.

But he was introvert enough to have analysed and put into words that country-of-the-moon on the way to his Paradise. Introvert enough to have stood apart and looked at it, to have wanted to record it.

Grant sat in a pleasant warm daze, chewing and considering. He noted the tightly joined tops of the *ns* and *ms*. A liar? Or just secretive? A curiously cautious trait to appear in the writing of a man with those eyebrows. It was a strange thing how much the meaning of a countenance depended on eyebrows. One change of degree in the angle this way or that, and the whole effect was different. Film magnates took nice little girls from Balham and Muswell Hill and rubbed out their eyebrows and painted in other ones and they became straightway mysterious creatures from Omsk and Tomsk. He had once been told by Trabb, the cartoonist, that it was his eyebrows that had lost Ernie Price his chance of being Prime Minister. "They didn't like his eyebrows," Trabb had said, blinking owlishly over his beer. "Why? Don't ask me. I just draw. Because they looked bad-tempered, perhaps. They don't like a bad-tempered man. Don't trust him. But that's what lost him his chance, take it from me. His eyebrows. They didn't like 'em." Bad-tempered eyebrows, supercilious eyebrows, calm eyebrows, worried eyebrows —it was the eyebrows that gave a face its keynote. And it was the slant of the black eyebrows that had given that thin white face on the pillow its reckless look even in death.

Well, the man had been sober when he wrote these words, that at least was clear. That toper's oblivion in compartment B Seven—the fugged air, the rucked blankets, the empty bottle rolling about on the floor, the over-turned glass on the shelf—may have been the Paradise he sought, but he was sober when he blue-printed the way to it.

The singing sand.

Uncanny but somehow attractive.

Singing sand. Surely there actually were singing sands somewhere? It had a vaguely familiar sound. Singing sands. They cried out under your feet as you walked. Or the wind did it, or something. A man's forearm in a checked tweed sleeve reached in front of him and took a bap from the plate.

"You seem to be doing yourself very well," Tommy said, pulling out a chair and sitting down. He split the bap and buttered it. "There's no chew in these things at all nowa-days. When I was a boy you sank your teeth in them and pulled. It was evens which came away first, your teeth or the bit of bap. But if your teeth won, you really had something worth having. A nice floury, yeasty mouth-ful that would last you for a couple of minutes. They don't taste of anything nowadays, and you could fold them in two and put the whole thing in your mouth without any danger of choking yourself."

Grant looked at him in silence and with affection. There was no intimacy so close, he thought, as the intimacy that bound you to a man with whom you'd shared a prep-school dorm. They had shared their public school days too, but it was prep school that he remembered each time he encountered Tommy anew. Perhaps because in all essentials that fresh pinky-brown face with the round, ingenuous blue eyes was the same face that used to appear above a crookedly buttoned maroon blazer. Tommy had always buttoned his blazer with a fine insouciance.

It was so like Tommy not to waste time or vitality on conventional inquiries as to his journey and his health. Neither would Laura, of course. They would accept him

14

as he stood, as if he had been there for some time; as if he had never gone away at all but was still on his previous visit. It was an extraordinarily restful atmosphere to sink back into.

"How is Laura?"

"Never better. Putting on a bit of weight. At least that's what she says. Don't see it myself. I never liked skinny women."

There had been a time, when they were both about twenty, when Grant had thought of marrying his cousin Laura; and she, he had been sure, had had thoughts of marrying him. But before any word had been said, the magic had faded and they were back on the old friendly footing. The magic had been part of the long intoxication of a Highland summer. Part of hill mornings smelling of pine needles, and of endless twilights sweet with the scent of clover. For Grant his cousin Laura had always been part of the happiness of summer holidays; they had graduated together from burn-paddling to their first fishing-rods, and together they had first walked the Larig and together had stood for the first time on the top of Braeriach. But it was not until that summer at the end of their adolescence that the happiness had crystallised into Laura herself; that the whole of summer was focused into the person of Laura Grant. He still had a slight lifting of the heart when he thought of that summer. It had the light perfection, the iridescence, of a bubble. And because no word had been said, the bubble would never now be broken. It stayed light and perfect and iridescent and poised, where they had left it. They had both gone on to other things, to other people. Laura, indeed, had skipped from one person to the next one with the bright indifference of a child playing hop-scotch. And then he had taken her to that Old Boys' dance. And she had met Tommy Rankin. And that had been that.

"What's the fuss at the station?" Tommy asked. "Ambulances and things."

"A man died on the train. I expect it is that."

"Oh," said Tommy, dismissing it. "Not your funeral this time," he added in a congratulatory way.

"No. Not my funeral, thank Heaven."

"They'll miss you on the Embankment."

"I doubt it."

"Mary," said Tommy, "I could do with a pot of good strong tea." He flicked the plate that held the baps with

15

a contemptuous forefinger. "And another couple of these poor bargains." He turned his serious childlike gaze on Grant and said: "They'll have to miss you. They'll be one short, won't they?"

Grant expelled his breath in the nearest he had come to a laugh for months. Tommy had been commiserating with Headquarters, not on the loss of his genius, but on the lack of his presence. His "family" attitude had been almost identical with the professional reaction of his Chief. "Sick leave!" Bryce had said, his little elephant eyes running over Grant's healthy looking frame and coming back to his face with disgust. "Well, well! What is the Force coming to! In my young days you stayed on duty until you fell over. And you went on writing up your notes until the ambulance carted you away off the floor." It had not been easy to tell Bryce what the doctor had said, and Bryce had not made it any easier. Bryce had never had a nerve of any sort in his body; he was mere physical force animated by a shrewd if limited brain. There had been neither comprehension nor sympathy in his reception of Grant's news. Indeed, there had been a subtle suggestion, a mere whiff of an implication, that Grant was malingering; that this so-strange breakdown that left him so markedly well and fit in appearance had something to do with the spring run in Highland rivers; that he had already arranged his fishing flies before going to Wimpole Street.

"What will they do to fill the gap?" Tommy asked.

"Promote Sergeant Williams, probably. His promotion is long overdue anyhow."

It had been no easier to tell the faithful Williams. When your subordinate has openly hero-worshipped you for years, it is not pleasant to have to appear before him as a poor nerve-ridden creature at the mercy of non-existent demons. Williams, too, had never had a nerve in his body. He took everything as it came, placid and unquestioning. It had not been easy to tell Williams and see the admiration change to concern. To—pity?

"Push over the marmalade," Tommy said.

2

The peace induced by Tommy's matter-of-fact acceptance of him deepened as they drove into the hills. These two accepted him; standing around in a detached benevolence, watching him come in a familiar quiet. It was a grey morning, and still. The landscape was tidy and bare. Tidy grey walls round bare fields, bare fences along the tidy ditches. Nothing had begun to grow yet in the waiting countryside. Only a willow here and there by a culvert side showed live and green in the half-shades.

It was going to be all right. This was what he had needed, this wide silence, this space, this serenity. He had forgotten how benevolent the place was, how satisfying. The near hills were round and green and kind; beyond them were farther ones, stained blue by the distance. And behind all stood the long rampart by the Highland line, white and remote against the calm sky.

"The river is very low, isn't it?" he said, as they came down into the valley of the Turlie. And was invaded by panic.

That was the way it always happened. One moment a sane, free, self-possessed human being, and the next a helpless creature in the grip of unreason. He pressed his hands together to keep himself from flinging the door open and tried to listen to what Tommy was saying. No rain for weeks. They had had no rain for weeks. Let him think about the lack of rain. It was important, the lack of rain. It spoiled the fishing. It was to fish he had come to Clune. If they didn't have rain, there would be no run of fish. No water for them. Oh, God, help me not to make Tommy stop! No water. Think intelligently about fishing. If they had had no rain for weeks, then rain must be due, mustn't it? Why could you ask a friend to stop the car and let you be sick and yet not ask him to stop the car so that you could get out of its small shut-in-ness? Look at the river. *Look* at it. Remember things about it. That was where you caught your best fish last year. That was where Pat slipped down when he was sitting on the rock and was left hanging by the seat of his pants.

"As nice a clean-run fish as ever you saw," Tommy was saying.

The hazels by the river made a bright mauve smudge in the grey-green of the moor. Presently, when it was summer-time, the cold clattering of their leaves would make an obbligato to the river's song, but just now they stood in a pink, silent huddle along the bank.

Tommy, looking at the state of the water, also noticed the bare hazel twigs, but being a parent he was not moved to think of summer afternoons. "Pat has discovered that he is a diviner," he said.

That was better. Think about Pat. Talk about Pat.

"The house is strewn with twigs of all shapes and sizes."

"Has he discovered anything?" If he could keep his mind on Pat, it might be all right.

"He has discovered gold under the sitting-room hearth, a body under the what-you-may-call-'em in the downstairs bathroom, and two wells."

"Where are the wells?" It couldn't be so very long now. Five miles to the head of the glen and Clune.

"One under the dining-room floor and one under the kitchen passage."

"I take it that you haven't dug up the sitting-room hearth." The window was wide open. What was there to worry about? It wasn't really a closed space, not a closed space at all.

"We have not. He is very peeved about that. Said I was a once-born."

"Once-born?"

"Yes. It's his latest word. It ranks just one degree below a stinker, I understand."

"Where did he get the word?" He would hang on till they got to that birch wood at the corner. Then he would ask Tommy to stop.

"Don't know. From some Theosophist woman who talked to the W.R.I. last autumn, I should think."

Why should he mind Tommy's knowing? There was nothing shameful about it. If he were a paralysed syphilitic, he would accept Tommy's help and sympathy. Why should he want to keep from Tommy's knowledge the fact that he was sweating with terror because of something that didn't exist? Perhaps he could cheat? Perhaps he could just ask Tommy to stop for a little while he admired the view?

Here was the birch wood. At least he had lasted that far.

He would make it the bit of road level with the bend of the river. He would make the excuse of having a look at the water. Much more plausible than looking at the view. Tommy would look with alacrity at a river and only with passive protest at a view.

About fifty seconds more. One, two, three, four . . .

Now.

"We lost two sheep in that pool this winter," Tommy said, sweeping past the bend.

Too late.

What other excuse could he make? He was too near Clune now for excuses to be easy to find.

He could not even light a cigarette for fear his hands were shaking too much.

Perhaps if he did something, however trivial . . .

He took the bundle of papers from the seat by his side, rearranging them, shuffling them busily and without point. He noticed that the *Signal* was not among them. He had meant to take it with him because of the odd little tentative verse in the Stop Press, but he must have left it in the hotel dining-room. Oh, well. It didn't matter. It had served its turn in giving interest to his breakfast. And the owner certainly would not want it again. He had achieved his Paradise, his oblivion; if that was what he had wanted. Not for him the privilege of uncontrolled hands and sweating skin. The privilege of wrestling with demons. Not for him the clean morning, the kind earth, the loveliness of the Highland line against the sky.

19

For the first time it occurred to him to wonder what had brought the young man to the North.

He had not, presumably, engaged a first-class sleeping compartment just to drink himself insensible in. He had had an intended destination. He had had business and desire. A purpose.

Why had he come to the North at this bleak, unfashionable season? To fish? To climb? The compartment as he remembered it had been given an impression of bareness, but the heavy luggage might have been under the bunk. Or, indeed, in the van. Apart from sport what was there?

Official business?

Not with that face, no.

An actor? An artist? Just possibly.

A sailor going to join his ship? Going to some naval base beyond Inverness? That was possible. The face would look very well on the bridge of a ship. A small ship; very fast; and hellish in any kind of sea.

What else was there? What would bring a dark, thin young man with reckless eyebrows and a passion for alcohol to the Highlands at the beginning of March? Unless in these days of whisky shortage he had had thoughts of starting an illicit still?

It was a pleasant idea, at that. How easy would it be? Not as easy as in Ireland, because the will to lawlessness was lacking; but once you had achieved it the whisky would be a great deal better. He almost wished that he could have put the idea to the young man. Could have sat opposite him at dinner last night, perhaps, and watched the gleam come into his eye at the thought of such delicious flouting of the Law. He wished that he could have talked to him anyway; exchanged ideas with him; found out about him. If someone had talked with him last night, he might now be part of this living morning, of this fine gracious world with its gifts and its promise, instead of—

"And gaffed him in the pool below the footbridge," said Tommy, finishing a story.

Grant looked down at his hands, and found that they were still.

The dead young man, who could not save himself, had saved him.

He looked up and saw in front of him the white house of Clune. It lay in the green cup of the hill, alone except for its attendant slab of sheltering fir-wood stuck like some dark green wool-work on the bare landscape. A blue curl of smoke rose up from the chimney into the still air. It was the fine essence of peace.

As they drove up the sandy track from the road, he saw Laura come out of the door and stand waiting for them. She waved to them, and as her arm came down from its wave she tucked in the strand of hair that fell on to her forehead. The familiar gesture warmed his chilled being. Just so she used to be waiting on the little Badenoch platform for him when she was a child, with just that wave and that tucking-in of a strand of hair. The same strand of hair.

"Damn," said Tommy, "I forgot to post her letters. Don't mention it unless she asks."

Laura kissed him on both cheeks, took one look at him, and said:

"I have a lovely bird for your lunch, but you look as if a good long sleep would do you more good. So go straight up and have it and forget about food until you waken. We have weeks to gossip in, so we don't have to start right now."

Only Laura, he thought, would have streamlined her hostess role to a guest's need so neatly. No subtle touting of the beautifully planned luncheon, no concealed blackmail. She did not even ply one with unwanted cups of tea, nor pointedly recommend her fine hot bath-water. She did not even demand the small-chat of arrival, the polite hanging around. She supplied without question and without hesitation the thing that he needed. A pillow.

He wondered whether it was that he looked a wreck or whether it was just that Laura knew him so well. It occurred to him that he would not mind Laura's knowing about his bondage of fear. It was odd that where he had shrunk from exhibiting his weakness to Tommy he should not care that Laura might learn about it. It should have been the other way about.

"I have put you in the other bedroom this time," she said, preceding him up the stairs, "because the west one has been done up and it still stinks a bit."

She was in truth putting on weight a little, he noticed; but her ankles were as good as ever. And then, with that native detachment that never quite deserted him, he realised that his lack of any desire to conceal from Laura his childish fits of panic was proof that no small remote part of him was still in love with her. The need of the male to look well in the eyes of the beloved one was no part of his relation with Laura.

"People always say about east bedrooms that they get the morning sun," she said, standing in the middle of the east bedroom and looking at it as if she had never seen it before. "As if it were a recommendation. I think myself it's much nicer to be able to look out on a sunny landscape. Which you can't do with the sun in your eyes." She stuck her thumbs in her waistband and eased the belt that was growing too tight. "But the west room will be habitable in a day or two, so you can change over then if you want to. How is my dear Sergeant Williams?"

"Pink and clean."

He had an instant picture of Williams, sitting solid and shy at the tea-table in the lounge of Westmorland. He had been on his way out after a session with the manager and had come across Laura and Grant having tea, and had been persuaded to join them. He had made a great success with Laura.

"You know, whenever this country is in one of its periodic messes, I think of Sergeant Williams and am quite sure on the instant that everything is going to be all right."

"I suppose *I* don't reassure you at all," Grant said, busy unstrapping luggage.

"Not noticeably. Not that way, anyway. You'd only be a comfort if everything *wasn't* going to be all right." With which cryptic statement she left him. "Don't come down until you want to. Don't come down at all, if it comes to that. Just ring when you waken."

Her footsteps went away down the passage, and the silence flooded in behind her.

He stripped off his clothes and without bothering to pull a curtain over the light he fell into bed. Presently he thought: I'd better draw those curtains or the light may waken me too soon. He opened his eyes reluctantly, to gauge the degree of light, and found that the light was no longer coming in at the window at all. It was lying on the out-of-doors instead. He lifted his head from the pillow to consider this oddity, and realised that it was late afternoon.

Relaxed and amused, he turned on to his back and lay listening to the quiet. The immemorial quiet. He savored it, and luxuriated in his long reprieve. Not an enclosed space between this and the Pentland Firth. Between this

22

and the North Pole, if it came to that. Through the wide-open window he could see the evening sky, still grey but faintly luminous and streaked with level cloud. No rain in that sky; only an echo of the peace that held the world in this contented quiet. Oh, well, if he could not fish he could walk. If the worst came to the worst, he could shoot rabbits.

He watched the level clouds darken against their background and wondered whom Laura would have got for him to marry this time. It was an extraordinary thing how all married women were banded together against the state of singleness in man. If the women were happily married, like Laura, they considered marriage the only satisfactory state for an adult not suffering from any marked incapacity or relevant hindrance. If they were unhappily yoked, then they were filled with resentment of anyone who had escaped such punishment. Each time that he came to Clune, Laura was in the habit of producing some carefully vetted female for his consideration. Nothing was ever said about their desirable qualities, of course; they were just trotted up and down in front of him so that he might view their paces. Nor, when he showed no particular interest in a candidate, was there any overt regret in the atmosphere, any suggestion of reproof. All that happened was that next time Laura had a new idea.

Somewhere, far away, was a sound that was either the lazy clucking of a hen or the clash of teacups being assembled. He listened for a little, hoping that it was a hen, but decided with regret that it was tea in preparation. He must get up. Pat would be home from school, and Bridget awake from her afternoon nap. It was quite typically Laura that she should not even have demanded from him a due admiration of her daughter; that he had not been asked to exclaim over her growth in the last year, her intelligence, her looks. Bridget had not been mentioned at all. She was merely a young creature somewhere out of sight, like the rest of the farm animals.

He got up and went to have a bath. And twenty minutes later he went downstairs conscious that he was hungry for the first time for months.

The family picture upon which the sitting-room door opened was pure Zoffany, he thought. The sitting-room at Clune occupied almost the whole of what had been the original farmhouse and was now a small wing to the main building. Because it had once been several rooms instead of one, it had more windows than usual in its kind; because it had thick walls it was warm and safe-feeling; and because it had a south-west outlook it was brighter than most. All the traffic of the house was concentrated there, as in the hall of some medieval manor. Only at luncheon and supper was any other room used by the family. A large round table by the fire ensured the comforts of "dining-room" meals at tea and breakfast, and the rest of the room was a fine free mixture of office, drawing-room, music-room, schoolroom and greenhouse. Johan, Grant thought, would have have had to alter one detail. It was all there already, even to the cadging terrier at the table and Bridget splay-legged on the hearthrug.

Bridget was a blonde, silent child of three who spent her days endlessly rearranging the same few objects into new patterns. "I can't make up my mind whether she is mentally deficient or a genius," Laura said. But Grant thought that the two-second glance with which Bridget favored him on introduction entirely justified the cheerfulness of Laura's tone; there was nothing wrong with the intelligence of The Child, as Patrick called her. This epithet as used by Pat had no sense of opprobium, nor even any marked condescension; it merely emphasised his own inclusion in the adult group, to which his six years of seniority in his own estimation entitled him.

Pat had red hair, and a bleak and intimidating grey eye. He was wearing a tattered green tartan kilt, smoke-blue stockings, and a much-darned grey jersey. His greeting to Grant was offhand but reassuringly uncouth. Pat spoke from choice what his mother called "clotted Perth-shire," his bosom friend at the village school being the shepherd's son, who hailed from Killin. He could, of course, when he had a mind, speak faultless English, but it was always a bad sign. When Pat was "not speaking" to you, he was always not speaking in the best English.

Over tea, Grant asked him if he had yet made up his mind what he was going to be, Pat's invariable answer to the question from the age of four having been, "A'm taking it into avizandum." A phrase borrowed from his J.P. Father.

"Ay," said Pat, spreading jam with a liberal hand. "A've made up muh mind."

"You have? That's fine. What are you going to be?"

"A revolutionary."

"I hope I never have to arrest you."

24

"Yu couldna," said Pat simply.

"Why not?"

"A'll be *good,* man," said Pat, dipping the spoon again.

"I'm sure that's the sense Queen Victoria used the word in," Laura said, removing the jam from her son's possession.

It was for that sort of thing that he had loved her. The odd glinting detachment that shot the texture of her maternalism.

"I have a fish for you," Pat said, scraping the jam to one side of the slice of bread so that it would, over at least half the surface, achieve the required depth. (What he actually said was, "Ah hiv a fush forrya," but Pat's phonetics are no pleasanter to the eye than they are on the ear, and may be left to the imagination.) "Under the ledge in the Cuddy Pool. You can have a len' of my fly, if you like."

Since Pat possessed a large tin box full of assorted invitations to slaughter, "my fly" in the singular could only mean "the fly I have invented."

"What is Pat's lure like?" Grant asked when Pat had taken himself off.

"Actionable, I should say," said his mother. "A fearsome object."

"Does he catch anything with it?"

"Oddly enough, yes," Tommy said. "I suppose there are suckers in the fish world just the same as in any other."

"The poor things just gape with astonishment at sight of it," Laura said, "and before they have time to shut their mouths the current has swept it in. Tomorrow's Saturday, so you can see it in operation. But I don't think that anything, even Pat's unholy creation, will lure that six-pounder in the Cuddy Pool to the surface with the water the way it is just now."

And of course Laura was right. Saturday morning was bright and rainless, and the six-pounder in the Cuddy Pool was far too dismayed by his imprisonment, far too obsessed with his desire to go higher up the river, to be interested in surface distractions. So it was suggested that Grant should go trout fishing in the loch, with Pat as gillie. The loch was two miles away in the hills, a flat pool on a bleak bit of moor. When it was windy on Lochan Dhu, the gale took your line out of the water at right angles and held it stiff as a telephone wire. When it was calm the midges made a meal of you while the trout came to the surface and openly laughed. But if trout fishing was not Grant's idea of the perfect occupation, being gillie was obviously Patrick's idea of heaven. There was nothing, from riding the black bull down at Dalmore to demanding threepence-worth of sweets from Mrs. Mair at the post-office with the aid of a ha'penny and menaces, that Pat was not capable of. But the joy of messing about in a boat was still something that he could not provide for himself. The boat at the loch was padlocked.

So Grant set off up the sandy path through the dry heather, with Pat at his side and one pace in the rear like a gun dog on its best behaviour. And as he went he was conscious of his own reluctance, and wondered at it.

Why should there be any qualification in his pleasure this morning, in his delight in going fishing? Brown trout might not be his idea of a sporting contest, but he was glad enough to be spending the day with a rod in his hand even if he caught nothing whatever. He was supremely glad to be out in the open, alive and at leisure, with the familiar spring of peaty turf under his feet, and the hills before him. Why the small unwillingness at the back of his mind? Why, instead of taking a boat out for the day on Lochan Dhu, did he want to hang round the farm?

They had walked for a mile before he had flushed the reason from the cover of his subconscious. He had wanted to stay at Clune today so that he could see the daily paper when it arrived.

He had wanted to find out about B Seven.

His conscious mind had dropped B Seven behind, with the tribulations of the journey and the memory of his humiliation. He had not consciously remembered him from the moment when he fell into bed on arrival until now, nearly twenty-four hours later. But B Seven was still with him, it would seem.

"When does the daily paper arrive at Clune these days?" he asked Pat, still silent and on his best behaviour one pace in the rear.

"If it's Johnny it comes at twelve, but if it's Kenny it's often near one before it comes." And Pat added, as if glad to have conversation introduced into the expeditionary routine, "Kenny stops to have a cup at Dalmore, east the road. He's gone on the MacFadyean's Kirsty."

A world where the news of the nations' clamour waited

while Kenny had a cup from the MacFadyean's Kirsty was a very pleasant one, Grant thought. In the days before radio it must have bordered on Paradise.

"That guard the way to Paradise."
The singing sands.

> *The beasts that talk,*
> *The streams that stand,*
> *The stones that walk,*
> *The singing sand . . .*

What had it stood for? *Was* it just a country of the mind?

Out here in the open, in this elemental land, it had an appropriateness that somehow lessened its stangeness. It was quite possible to believe this morning that there were places on this earth where stones might walk. Were there not places, known places, even in the Highlands, where a man alone in the bright sunlight of a summer day could be invaded by the knowledge of unseen watchers, so that he was filled with a great fear and ran panic-stricken from the place? Yes, and without any previous interviews in Wimpole Street, either. In the "old" places anything was possible. Even beasts that talked.

Where had B Seven got his idea of strangeness?

They launched the light boat from its wooden runway, and Grant pulled out into the loch and made for the windward end. It was much too bright, but there was a breath of air that might lift to a breeze strong enough to put a ripple on the surface. He watched Pat put his rod together and bend a fly on the line, and thought that if he could not have the felicity of possessing a son then a small redheaded cousin made a very good substitute.

"Did you ever present a bouquet, Alan?" asked Pat, busy with the fly. He called it a "bookey."

"Not that I can remember," Grant said carefully. "Why?"

"They're at me to present a bookey to a Viscountess that's coming to open the Dalmore hall."

"Hall?"

"That shed place at the cross-roads," Pat said bitterly. He was silent a moment, evidently mulling it over. "It's an awful jessie-like thing to present a bookey."

Grant, bound in duty to the absent Laura, searched his mind. "It's a great honour," he said.

"Then let The Child have the honour."

"She is a little young yet for such responsibility."

"Well, if she's too young for such responsibility I'm too old for such capers. So they'll have to get some other family to do it. It's all havers anyway. The hall's been open for months."

To this disillusioned contempt for adult pretence Grant had no answer.

They fished turn-about, in a fine male amity, Grant flicking his line with a lazy indifference, Pat with the incurable optimism of his kind. By noon they had drifted back to a point level with the little jetty, and they turned inshore to make tea on the primus in the little bothy. As Grant was paddling last few yards, he saw Pat's eye fixed on something along the shore, and turned to see what occasioned such marked distaste. Having looked at the advancing figure with its shoggly body and inappropriate magnificance, he asked who that might be.

"That's Wee Archie," said Pat.

Wee Archie was wielding a shepherd's crook that, as Tommy remarked later, no shepherd would be found dead with, and he was wearing a kilt that no Highlander would dream of being found alive in. The crook stood nearly two feet above his head, and the kilt hung down at the back from his non-existent hips like a draggled petticoat. But it was obvious that the wearer was conscious of no lack. The tartan of his sad little skirt screamed like a peacock, raucous and alien against the moor. His small dark eel's head was crowned by a pale blue Balmoral with a diced band, the bonnet being pulled down sideways at such a dashing angle that the slack covered his right ear. On the upper side a large piece of vegetation sprouted from the crest on the band. The socks on the hairpin legs were a brilliant blue, and so hairy in texture that they gave the effect of some unfortunate growth. Round the meagre ankles the thongs of the brogues were cross-gartered with a verve that even Malvolio had never achieved.

"What is he doing round here?" Grant asked, fascinated.

"Oh. What does he do?"

"He's a revolutionary."

"Really? Is that the same revolution as yours?"

"Nah!" said Pat in great scorn. "Oh, I'm not saying maybe he didn't put the idea in my head. But no one would take heed of the likes of him. He writes pomes."

28

"I take it that he is a once-born."

"Him! He's not born at all, man. He's a—a—a *egg*."

Grant concluded that the word Pat had sought was amoeba, but that knowledge had not reached so far. The lowest form of life he knew of was the egg.

The "egg" came blithely towards them along the stony beach, swinging the tail of his deplorable petticoat with a fine swagger that went ill with his hirpling movement over the stones. Grant was suddenly convinced that he had corns. Corns on thin pink feet that sweated easily. The kind of feet people were always writing to medical columns in the Press about. (Wash every evening without fail and dry thoroughly, especially between the toes. Dust well with talcum powder and put on fresh socks each morning.)

"Cia mar tha si?" he called as he came within hailing distance.

Was it just chance, Grant wondered, that all cranky people had that thin bodiless voice: Or was it that thin bodiless voices belonged to the failures and the frustrated and that frustration and failure bred the desire to repudiate the herd?

He had not heard the Gaelic phrase since he was a child, and the affectation of it cooled his welcome. He bade the man good-morning.

"Patrick should have told you that it was too bright to fish today," he said, swinging up to them. Grant did not know which displeased him more: the vile Glasgow speech or the unwarranted patronage.

The freckles on Pat's fair skin were lost in a red tide. Speech trembled on his lips.

"I expect he didn't want to do me out of my pleasure," Grant said smoothly, and watched the tide recede and a slow appreciation dawn. Pat had discovered that there were more effective ways of dealing with folly than direct attack. It was a quite new idea, and he was trying the taste of it, rolling it on his tongue.

"You've come ashore for your elevenses, I take it," Wee Archie said brightly. "I'll be glad to join you if you've no objection."

So they made tea for Wee Archie, glum and polite. He produced his own sandwiches, and while they. ate he lectured them on the glory of Scotland, its mighty past and dazzling future. He had not asked Grant's name and was betrayed by his speech into taking him for an Englishman. Surprised, Grant heard of England's iniquities to a captive and helpless Scotland. (Anything less captive or less helpless than the Scotland he had known would be difficult to imagine.) England, it seemed, was a bloodsucker, a vampire, draining the good blood of Scotland and leaving her limp and white. Scotland had groaned under the foreign yoke; she had come staggering behind the conqueror's chariot; she had paid tribute and prostituted her talents to the tyrant's needs. But she was about to throw off the yoke, to unloose the bands; the fiery cross was about to be sent out once more, and soon the heather could be alight. There was no cliché that Wee Archie spared them.

Grant watched him with the interest one accords to a new exhibit in a collection. He decided that the man was older than he had thought. Forty-five at least; probably nearer fifty. Too old to be curable. Whatever success he had coveted had passed him by; there would never be anything for him but his pitiable fancy-dress and his clichés.

He looked across to see what effect this perversion of patriotism was having on Young Scotland, and rejoiced in his heart. Young Scotland was sitting facing the loch, as if even the sight of Wee Archie was too much for him. He was chewing in a dogged detachment, and his eye reminded Grant of Flurry Knox: "an eye like a stone wall with broken glass on top." The revolutionaries would want heavier guns than Archie to make any impression on their countrymen.

Grant wondered what the creature lived on. "Pomes" did not provide a living. Nor did free-lance journalism; or, rather, the kind of journalism that Archie was likely to write. Perhaps he scraped a living from "criticism." It was from the tanks of the ineffective that the minor critics were recruited. There was always the chance, of course, that he was subsidised; if not by some native malcontent with a thirst for power, then by some foreign agency with an interest in trouble-making. He was of a type very familiar to the Special Branch: the failure, sick of a curdled vanity.

Grant, still hankering after the midday newspaper that Johnny or Kenny was due to deliver at Clune, had had thoughts of suggesting to Pat that they call it a day, and give up enticing fish that had no intention of biting. But if they went now they would have to walk back in Wee Archie's company, and that was something to be avoided. He prepared to resume his idle flicking of the loch water.

But Archie, it seemed, was anxious to make one of the fishing party. If there was room in the boat for a third passenger, he said, he would be glad to accompany them.

Again speech trembled on Pat's lips.

"Yes," said Grant, "do come. You can help to bale."

"Bale?" said the saviour of Scotland, blenching.

"Yes. Her seams are not too good. She makes a lot of water."

On second thoughts Archie decided that perhaps after all it was time that he was wending his way (Archie never went anywhere he always wended his way) towards Moymore. The post would be in, and there would be his mail to deal with. And then, lest it might cross their minds that he was unused to boats, he told them how good he was in a boat. It was thanks only to his skill in a boat that he and four others had reached a Hebridean beach alive last summer. He told the tale with a growing verve that gave rise to a base suspicion that he was making it up as he went along, and having finished he switched hastily from the subject, as if afraid of questions, and asked if Grant knew the islands.

Grant, locking up the bothy and pocketing the key, said that he did not. Whereupon Archie made him free of them with a proprietor's generosity: the herring fleets of Lewis, the cliffs of Mingulay, the songs of Barra, the hills of Harris, the wild flowers of Benbecula, and the sands, the endless wonderful white sand, of Berneray.

"The sands don't sing, I suppose," Grant said, putting bounds to the boasting. He stepped into the boat, and pushed off.

"No," said Wee Archie, "no. They're in Cladda."

"What are?" asked Grant, startled.

"The singing sands. Well, good fishing to you, but it's not a day for fishing, you know. Much too bright."

And with this kindly pat on the head he re-erected his shepherd's crook, and swung away along the shore towards Moymore and his letters. Grant stood motionless in the boat, watching him go. When he was nearly beyond earshot he called to him suddenly:

"Are there any walking stones on Cladda?"

"What?" said Archie's inadequate pipe.

"Are there *any walking stones on Cladda?*"

"No. They're in Lewis."

And the dragonfly creature with its mosquito voice went away into the brown distance.

3

They came home at tea-time with five unimpressive-looking trout and large appetites. Pat, excusing the thin trout, pointed out that on such a day you couldn't expect to catch any but what he called "the sillies"; the respect-worthy fish had more sense than to be caught in such weather. They came down the last half-mile to Clune like homing horses, Pat skipping from turf to turf like a young goat, and as voluble as he had been silent on the way out. The world and London River seemed the width of stellar space away, and Grant would not have called the King his cousin.

But as they scraped their shoes at the flagged doorway of Clune, he became aware of his unreasonable impatience to see the newspaper. And since he resented un-reason in anyone and abominated it in himself, he carefully scraped his shoes all over a second time.

"Man, you're awfully particular," said Pat, giving his footgear a rudimentary wipe on the twin scraper.

"It's a boorish thing to go into a house with mud on one's shoes."

"Boorish?" asked Pat, who, as Grant suspected, held it a "jessie-like" thing to be clean.

"Yes. Slovenly and un-grown-up."

"Huh," said Pat, and surreptitiously scraped his shoes again. "It's a poor house that can't stand a few dollops of mud," he said, reasserting his independence, and went storming into the sitting-room like an invading army.

In the sitting-room Tommy was dripping honey on to a hot scone, Laura was pouring tea, Bridget was arranging a new set of objects in a design on the floor, and the terrier was on the make round the table. Except that sunlight had been added to firelight, it was the same picture as last night. With one difference. Somewhere in the room there was a daily paper that mattered.

Laura, seeing his searching eye, asked him if he was looking for something.

"Yes, the daily paper."

"Oh, Bella has it." Bella was the cook. "I'll get it from her after tea if you want to see it."

He had a moment of stinging impatience with her. She was far too complacent. She was far too happy, here in her fastness, with her laden tea-table, and her little roll of fat above the belt, and her healthy children, and her nice Tommy, and her security. It would do her good to have some demons to fight, to be swung out in space and held over some bottomless pit now and then. But his own absurdity rescued him, and he knew that it was not so. There was no complacence in Laura's happiness, nor was Clune any refuge from the realities. The two young sheep-dogs who had welcomed them at the road gate in a swirl of black-and-white bodies and lashing tails would once upon a time have been called Moss or Glen or Trim or something like that. Today, he had noticed, they answered to Tong and Zang. The waters of the Chindwin had long ago flowed into the Turlie. There were no Ivory Towers any more.

"There is *The Times,* of course," Laura said; "but it is always yesterday's, so you will have seen it."

"Who is Wee Archie?" he asked, sitting down at the table.

"So you've met Archie Brown, have you?" Tommy said, clapping the top half of his hot scone, and licking the honey that oozed from it.

"Is that his name?"

"It used to be. Since he elected himself the champion of Gaeldom, he calls himself Gilleasbuig Mac-a'-Bruithainn. He's frightfully unpopular at hotels."

"Why?"

34

How would *you* like to page someone called Gilleasbuig Mac-a'-Bruithainn?"

"I wouldn't like to have him under my roof at all. What is he doing here?"

"He's writing an epic poem in Gaelic, so he says. He didn't know any Gaelic until about two years ago, so I don't think the poem can be up to much. He used to belong to the cleesh-clavers-clatter school. You know, the Lowland-Scots boys. He was one of them for years. But he didn't get anywhere very much. The competition was too keen. So he decided that Lowland Scots was just debased English and very reprehensible, and that there was nothing like a return to the 'old tongue,' to a real language. So he 'sat under' a bank clerk in Glasgow, a chap from Uist, and swotted up some Gaelic. He comes to the back door and talks to Bella now and then, but she says she doesn't understand a word. She thinks he's 'not right in the head.' "

"There's nothing wrong with Archie Brown's head," Laura said tartly. "If he hadn't had the wit to think up this role for himself, he would be teaching school in some God-forsaken backwater and even the school inspector wouldn't have known his name."

"He's very conspicuous on a moor, anyhow," Grant said.

"He's even worse on a platform. Like one of those awful souvenir dolls that tourists take home, and just about as Scottish."

"Isn't he Scots?"

"No. He hasn't a drop of Scottish blood in him. His father came from Liverpool and his mother was an O'Hanrahan."

"Odd how all the most bigoted patriots are Auslanders," Grant said. "I don't think he'll get very far with those xenophobes, the Gaels."

"He has a much worse handicap than that," Laura said.

"What is that?"

"His Glasgow accent."

"Yes. It is pretty repellent."

"I didn't mean that. I mean, every time he opens his mouth his audience is reminded of the possibility of being ruled from Glasgow: a fate worse than death."

"When he was talking about the beauty of the Islands, he mentioned some sands that 'sing.' Do you know anything about them?"

"I seem to," said Tommy, not interested. "On Barra or Berneray or somehwere."

"On Cladda, he said."

"Yes, perhaps it's Cladda. Do you think that boat at Lochan Dhu will last a season or two yet?"

"Can I go and get the *Clarion* from the Bella now?" asked Pat, having wolfed four scones and a slab of cake with the neat speed of a sheep-dog consuming a stolen tit-bit.

"If she has finished with it," his mother said.

"Uch, she'll have finished with it this long time," Pat said. "She only reads the bits about the stars."

"Stars?" said Grant, as the door closed behind Pat. "Film stars?"

"No," Laura said, "the Great Bear and Co."

"Oh. The day as arranged by Sirius, Vega, and Capella."

"Yes. In Lewis they have to wait for the second-sight, she says. It's a fine convenient thing to have the future in the paper every day."

"What does Pat want with the *Clarion?*"

"The strip, of course. Two objects called Tolly and Snib. I can't remember whether they are ducks or rabbits."

So Grant had to wait until Pat had finished with Tolly and Snib, and by that time both Laura and Tommy had taken themselves off, the one to the kitchen and the other to out-of-doors, so that he was left alone with the silent child on the mat, endlessly rearranging her treasures. He took the tidily folded paper from Pat ceremoniously, and as Pat went away he unfolded it with controlled interest. It was a Scottish edition, and apart from the "middles" the paper was crammed with the most parochial of news, but there seemed to be nothing about yesterday's railway event in it. To and fro he went, through the jungle of unimportances, like a terrier routing through bracken, and at last he came on it: a tiny paragraph at the bottom of a column, down among the bicycle accidents and the centenarians. MAN DIES IN TRAIN, said the inconspicuous heading. And under the heading was a succinct statement:

On the arrival of the *Flying Highlander* at its destination yesterday morning it was found that one of the passengers, a young Frenchman, Charles Martin, had died during the night. It is understood that the death

36

was due to natural causes, but since the death occurred in England, the body is being returned to London for an inquest.

"French!" he said aloud, and Bridget looked up from her playthings to watch him.

French? Surely not! Surely not?

The face yes. Perhaps. The face quite likely. But not that writing. That very English schoolboy writing.

Had the paper not belonged to B Seven at all?

Had he just picked it up? In a restaurant where he was having a meal before boarding the train, perhaps. The chairs of station dining-rooms were habitually strewn with the discarded papers of those who had eaten there. Or in his home for that matter: or his rooms or wherever he lived. He might have come by the paper in a score of casual ways.

Or, of course, he might be a Frenchman who was educated in England, so that the round untidy script was substituted for the slanting elegant spidery handwriting of his inheritance. There was nothing fundamentally incompatible with B Seven having been the author of those pencilled lines.

All the same, it was an oddity.

And in cases of sudden death, however natural, oddities have importance when he first came in contact with B Seven, he was so divorced from his professional self, so detached from the world at large, that he had considered the matter as any other sleep-sodden civilian would. B Seven had been for him merely the young dead occupant of a whisky-sodden compartment who was being mauled about by a furiously impatient sleeping-car attendant. Now he became something quite different; he became The Subject of an Inquest. A professional matter; a matter bound by rules and regulations; a matter to be proceeded with circumspectly, with due decorum and by the book. And it occurred to Grant for the first time that his abstraction of that newspaper might be held, if orthodoxy must be pushed to its furthest point, to be a little irregular. It had been an entirely unintended abstraction, an accidental purloining. But it had, if one had to be analytical about it, been a removal of evidence.

While Grant was debating the matter, Laura came back from the kitchen and said, "Alan, I want you to do something for me."

She took her mending basket and brought it over to a chair beside him.

"Anything I can do."

"Pat is sticking in his toes about someting that he has to do and I want you to talk him into it. You're his hero, and he will listen to you."

"It isn't about presenting a bouquet, by any chance?"

"How did you know? Has he talked about it to you already?"

"He just mentioned it this morning on the loch."

"You didn't take his side, did you?"

"With you in the background! No. I expressed the opinion that it was a great honour."

"Was he convinced?"

"No. He thinks the whole thing is 'havers.' "

"So it is. The hall has been in unofficial use for weeks. But the glen people spent a lot of money and energy on getting that thing put up, and it is only right that it should be opened with a 'splash.' "

"But does it have to be Pat who presents the bouquet?"

"Yes. If he doesn't do it, the MacFadyean's Willie will."

"Laura, you shock me."

"I wouldn't if you could see the MacFadyean's Willie. He looks like a frog with elephantiasis. And his socks are always falling down. It should be a little girl's business, but there is no female child of the right age in the glen. So it rests between Pat and the MacFadyean's Willie. And quite apart from Pat's looking nicer, it is right that someone from Clune should do it. And don't say 'Why?' and don't say I shock you. You just see what you can do to talk Pat into it."

"I'll try," Grant said, smiling at her. "Who is his Viscountess?"

"Lady Kentallen."

"The dowager?"

"The widow, you mean. There is only one, so far. Her boy isn't old enough yet to be married."

"How did you get her?"

"She was at school with me. At St. Louisa's."

"Oh: blackmail. The tyranny of auld lang syne."

"Tyranny nothing," said Laura. "She was glad to come and do the chore. She's a darling."

"The best way to bring Pat up to his bit would be to make her attractive in his eyes."

"She's ragingly attractive."

"I don't mean that way. I mean, make her good at something he admires."

"She's an expert with a fly," Laura said doubtfully, "but I don't know that Pat would find that very impressive. He just thinks that someone who can't fish is abnormal."

"I suppose you couldn't endow her with a few revolutionary tendencies."

"Revolutionary!" said Laura, her eye brightening. "Now that's an idea. Revolutionary. She used to be a little on the pink side. She did it 'to annoy Miles and Georgiana,' she used to say. They are her parents. She was never very serious about it; she was much too good-looking to need anything like that. But I might build something on that foundation. Yes. We might make her a revolutionary."

The quirks that women are reduced to! thought Grant, watching her needle flicker through the wool of the sock she was darning, and went back to considering his own problem. He was still considering it when he went to bed. But before he went to sleep, he decided that he would write to Bryce in the morning. It would be to all intents a letter reporting his arrival in these healthful surroundings and his hope to be better in less time than the doctor had given him, but in the course of it he would take the opportunity of putting himself in the right by passing the knowledge of the newspaper's presence on to those whom it might concern.

He slept the deep, uninterrupetd sleep induced by fresh air and an unsullied conscience, and woke to an immense silence. The silence was not only out-of-doors; the house itself was in a trance. And Grant suddenly remembered that it was Sunday. There would be no post out of the glen today. He would have to go all the way to Scoone with his letter.

He asked Tommy at breakfast if he might borrow the car to go to Scoone to post an important letter, and Laura offered to drive him. As soon as breakfast was over, he went back to his room to compose the letter, and in the end was very pleased with it. He brought the matter of B Seven into the texture of it as neatly as an invisible mender fits an unbelonging piece to the over-all pattern. He had not been able to shake the memory of work from him as soon as he might, he said, because the first thing he had been confronted with at the end of the journey was a dead body. The body was being furiously shaken by an enraged sleeping-car attendant who thought that the man was just sleeping it off. However, it had been none of his business, thank Heaven. His only part in the affair had been to purloin unintentionally a newspaper from the compartment. He had found it among his own when he was having breakfast. It was a *Signal,* and he would have taken it for granted that it was his own property if it had not been that in the Stop-Press space someone had been pencilling a scribbled attempt at verse. The verse was in English and in English writing, and might not have been written by the dead man at all. He understood that the inquest was being held in London. If Bryce thought that it was of any importance, he might hand on the small item of information to the relevant authority.

He came downstairs again to find the Sabbath atmosphere shattered. The house rocked with war and rebellion. Pat had discovered that someone was going in to Scoone (which in his country eyes was even on a Sunday a metropolis of delectable variety) and he wanted to go too. His mother, on the other hand, was determined that he was going to Sunday school as usual.

"You ought to be very glad of the lift," she was saying, "instead of grumbling about not wanting to go."

Grant thought that "grumbling" was a highly inadequate word to describe the blazing opposition that lighted Pat like a torch. He throbbed with it, like a car at rest with the engine running.

"If we didn't happen to be going in to Scoone, you would have to walk to the church as usual," she reminded him.

"Huch, who ever minds walking! We have fine talks when we're walking, Duggie and me." Duggie was the shepherd's son. "It's wasting time at Sunday school when I might be going to Scoone that's a fact. It's not fair."

"Pat, I will not have you referring to Sunday school as a waste of time."

"You won't have me at all if you're not careful. I'll die of a decline."

"Oh. What would bring that on?"

"Lack of fresh air."

She began to laugh. "Pat, you're wonderful." But it was always the wrong thing to laugh at Pat. He took himself as seriously as an animal does.

"All right, laugh!" he said bitterly. "You'll be going to

church on Sundays to put wreaths on my grave, that's what you'll be doing on Sundays, not going into Scoone!"

"I shouldn't dream of doing anything so extravagant. A few dog-daisies now and then when I'm passing is as much as you'll get from me. Go and get your scarf; you'll need it."

"A gravat! It's March!"

"It's also cold. Get your scarf. It will help to keep off the decline."

"A lot you care about my decline, you and your daisies. A mean family the Grants always were. A poor mean lot. I'm very glad I'm a Rankin, and I'm very glad I don't have to wear their horrible red tartan." Pat's tattered green kilt was Macintyre, which went better with his red hair than the gay Grant. It had been part of Tommy's mother's web, and she, as a good Macintyre, had been glad to see her grandson in what she called a civilised cloth.

He stumped his way into the back of the car and sat there simmering, the despised "gravat" flung in a limp disavowed heap at the far end of the seat.

"Heathen aren't supposed to go to church," he offered, as they slipped down the sandy road to the gate, the loose stones spurting from under the tires.

"Who is heathen?" his mother asked, her mind on the road.

"I am. I'm a Mohammedan."

"Then you have a great need to go to a Christian church and be converted. Open the gate, Pat."

"I've no wish to be converted. I'm fine as I am." He held the gate open for them and shut it behind them. "I disapprove of the Bible," he said, as he got in again.

"Then you can't be a good Mohammedan."

"What for no?"

"They have some of the Bible too."

"I bet they don't have David!"

"Don't you approve of David?" Grant asked.

"A poor soppy thing, dancing and singing like a lassie. There's not a soul in the Old Testament I'd trust to go to a sheep sale."

He sat erect in the middle of the back seat, too alive with rebellion to relax, his bleak eye watching the road ahead in absent-minded fury. And it occurred to Grant that he might equally have slumped in a corner and sulked. He was glad that this cousin of his was a rude and erect flame of resentment and not a small, collapsed bundle of self-pity.

The injured heathen got out at the church, still rude and erect, and walked away, without a backward glance, to join the small group of children by the side door.

"Will he behave, now he is there?" Grant asked as Laura set the car in motion again.

"Oh, yes. He really likes it, you know. And of course Douglas will be there: his Jonathan. A day when he couldn't spend part of it laying down the law to Duggie would be a day wasted. He didn't really believe that I would let him come to Scoone instead. It was just a try-on."

"It was a very effective try-on."

"Yes. There's a lot of the actor in Pat."

They had gone another two miles before the thought of Pat faded from his mind. And then, quite suddenly, into the blank that Pat's departure left, came the realisation that he was in a car. That he was shut into a car. He ceased on the instant to be an adult watching, tolerant, and amused, the unreasonable antics of a child, and became a child watching, gibbering and aghast, the hostile advance of giants.

He let down the window on his side to its fullest extent. "Let me know if you feel that too much," he said.

"You've been too long in London," she said.

"How?"

"Only people who live in towns are fresh-air fiends. Country people like a nice fug as a change from unlimited out-of-doors."

"I'll put it up, if you like," he said, although his mouth was stiff with effort as he said the words.

"No, of course not," she said, and began to talk about a car they had ordered.

So the old battle started. The old arguments, the old tricks, the old cajoling. The pointing out of the open windows, the reminding himself that it was only a car and could be stopped at any moment, the willing himself to consider a subject far removed from the present, the self-persuading that he was lucky to be alive at all. But the tide of his panic rose with a slow abominable menace. A black evil tide, scummy and revolting. Now it was round his chest, pressing and holding, so that he could hardly breathe. Now it was up to his throat, feeling round his

42

windpipe, clutching his neck in a pincer embrace. In a moment it would be over his mouth.

"Lalla, stop!"

"Stop the car?" she asked, surprised.

"Yes."

She brought the car to a standstill, and he got out on trembling legs and hung over the dry-stone dyke sucking in great mouthfuls of the clean air.

"Are you feeling ill, Alan?" she asked anxiously.

"No, I just wanted to get out of the car."

"Oh," she said in a relieved tone. "Is that all!"

"Is that *all?*"

"Yes: claustrophobia. I was afraid you were ill."

"And you don't call that being ill?" he said bitterly.

"Of course not. I nearly died of terror once, when I was taken to see the Cheddar caves. I had never been in a cave before." She had switched off the motor and now she sat down on a roadside boulder with her back half-turned to him. "Except those rabbit burrows that we called caves in our youth." She held up her cigarette case to him. "I'd never been really underground before, and I didn't mind going in the least. I went all eager and delighted. I was a good half-mile from the entrance when it struck me. I sweated with terror. Do you have it often?"

"Yes."

"Do you know that you're the only person who still calls me Lalla sometimes? We are getting very old."

He looked round and down at her, the strain fading from his expression.

"I didn't know you had any terrors other than rats."

"Oh, yes. I have a fine variety. Everyone has, I think. At least everyone who is not just a clod. I keep placid because I lead a placid life and collect adipose tissue. If I overworked the way you do, I'd be a raving maniac. I'd probably have claustrophobia *and* agoraphobia, and make medical history. One would have the enormous consolation of being something in the *Lancet*, of course."

He turned from leaning over the wall and sat down beside her. "Look," he said, and held out the shaking hand that held his cigarette for her to see.

"Poor Alan."

"Poor Alan, indeed," he agreed. "That came not from being half a mile underground in the dark, but from be-

43

ing a passenger in a car with wide-open windows in an open countryside on a fine Sunday in a free country."

"It didn't, of course."

"It didn't?"

"It came from four years of consistent overwork and an overgrown conscience. You always were a demon where conscience was concerned. Quite tiresome you could be. Would you rather have a spot of claustrophobia or a stroke?"

"A stroke?"

"If you work yourself half to death you have to pay in some manner or other. Would you rather pay in the more usual physical manner with high blood-pressure or a strained heart? It's better to be scared of being shut into a car than to be pushed about in a bath-chair. At least you have time off from being scared. If you hate the thought of getting back into the car, by the way, I can go on to Scoone with your letter and pick you up on the way back."

"Oh, no, I'll go on."

"I thought it was better not to fight it?"

"Did *you* scream and yell half a mile underground in the Cheddar Gorge?"

"No. But I wasn't a pathological specimen suffering from overwork."

He smiled suddenly. "It's extraordinary how comforting it is to be called a pathological specimen. Or rather, to be called a pathological specimen in just those tones."

"Do you remember the day at Varese when it rained and we went to the museum and saw those specimens in bottles?"

"Yes; you were sick on the pavement outisde."

"Well, you were sick when we had sheep's heart for lunch because you had watched it being stuffed," she said instantly.

"Lalla, darling," he said, beginning to laugh, *"you* haven't grown up at all."

"Well, it's nice that you can still laugh, even if it's only at me," she said, caught out in that flash of childhood rivalry. "Say when you want to go on."

"Now."

"Now? Are you sure?"

"Quite sure. Being called a pathological specimen has wonderfully curative qualities, I find."

"Well, next time don't wait until you are on the point of suffocation," she said matter-of-factly.

He did not know which he found more reassuring: her awareness that the thing was a sort of suffocation or her matter-of-fact acceptance of unreason.

4

If Grant had imagined that his chief would be gratified either by the possibility of his earlier recovery or by his punctiliousness in the matter of the newspaper, he was wrong. Bryce was still antagonist rather than colleague. And his reply contained a right-and-left that was typically Bryce. Reading it, Grant thought that only Bryce could manage to have his cake and eat it so successfully. In the first paragraph he rebuked Grant for his unprofessional conduct in abstracting any article from the vicinity of sudden and unexplained death. In the second paragraph he was surprised that Grant should have thought of bothering a busy Department with any matter as trivial as that of the purloined paper, but supposed that no doubt his divorce from workaday surroundings had contributed to a lack of judgment and proportion. There was no third paragraph.

What came off the familiar thin office paper was a strong impression that he had been put, not in his place, but outside. What the letter really said was: "I can't imagine why you, Alan Grant, should be bothering us, either to report on your health or to take an interest in our business. We are not interested in the one and you have no concern with the other." He was an outsider. A renegade.

And it was only now, reading the snubbing letter and having the door banged in his face, that he became aware that beyond his conscientious need to put himself straight with the Department over the purloined paper had been the desire to hang on to B Seven. His letter, as well as an apology, had been a way to information. There was no longer hope of obtaining information from the Press. B Seven was not news. Every day people died in trains. There was nothing to interest the lieges in that. As far as the Press was concerned B Seven was dead twice over, once in fact and once as news. But he had wanted to know more about B Seven, and he had hoped, without knowing it, that his colleagues might be chatty on the subject.

He might have known Bryce better, he thought, tearing up the sheet of paper and dropping it into the wastepaper basket. However, there was always Sergeant Williams, thank Heaven; the faithful Williams. Williams would wonder why someone of his rank and experience should be interested in an unknown dead body seen once for a moment or two, but he would probably put it down to boredom. In any case there would be no lack of chat about Williams. So to Williams he wrote. Would Williams find out what the result of the inquest had been on a young man, Charles Martin, who had died on Thursday night a week ago on the night train to the Highlands, and anything else about the young man that might have transpired in the course of the inquiry? And kind regards to Mrs. Williams and Angela and Leonard.

And for two days he settled back in a sort of happy impatience to wait for Williams's reply. He inspected the unfishable Turlie, pool by pool; he caulked the boat at Lochan Dhu; he walked the hill in the company of Graham the shepherd with Tong and Zang more or less at heel; and he listened to Tommy's plan for a nine-hole private golf course between the house and the hillside. And on the third day he went homing at post time with an eagerness he had not known since he was nineteen and used to send his poems to magazines.

Nor was his blank unbelief when there was nothing for him any less poignant than it had been in those callow years.

He reminded himself that he was being unreasonable (the unforgivable sin, always, in Grant's estimation). The inquest had nothing to do with the Department. He did not even know which Division might have been landed with the job. Williams would have to find out. Williams had work of his own; twenty-four-hours-a-day work. It was unreasonable to expect him to drop everything to satisfy some holiday-making colleague's frivolous questions.

For two more days he waited, and then it came.

Williams hoped that Grant wasn't hankering after work. He was supposed to be having a rest, and everyone in the Department hoped that he was getting it (not everyone! thought Grant, remembering Bryce) and feeling the better for it. They missed him very badly. As to Charles Martin, there was no mystery about him. Or about his death, if that is what Grant had been thinking. He had hit the back of his head against the edge of the porcelain wash-hand basin, and although able to crawl around for a little on his hands and knees and eventually reach the bed, he had died from internal haemorrhage very shortly after falling over. The fact that he had fallen backwards at all was due to amount of neat whisky he had consumed. Not enough to make him drunk but quite enough to make him muzzy, and the tilt of the coach as it changed direction had done the rest. There was no mystery, either, about the man himself. He had had the usual bundle of French identity papers in his possession, and his people were still living at his home address, near Marseilles. They had not seen him for some years—he had left home after being in trouble for stabbing his girl in a fit of jealousy—but they had sent money to bury him so that he should not be buried in a pauper's grave.

This left Grant with an appetite whetted rather than assuaged.

He waited until, according to his reckoning, Williams would be happily settled down with his pipe and his paper, while Mrs. Williams mended and Angela and Leonard did their homework, and put in a personal call to him. There was always the chance that Williams was out pursuing the ill-doer through the devious ways of inhabiting, but there was, too, the chance that he was at home.

He was at home.

When he had been duly thanked for his letter, Grant said: "You said his people sent money to bury him. Didn't anyone come to identify him?"

"No; they identified a photograph."

"A live photograph?"

"No, no. A photograph of the body."

"Didn't anyone turn up to identify him in London?"

"Not a soul, it seems."

"That's odd."

"Not so odd if he was a wide boy. Wide boys don't want trouble."

"Was there any suggestion that he was wide?"

"No, I don't think so."

"What was his profession?"

"Mechanic."

"Did he have a passport?"

"No. Just the usual papers. And letters."

"Oh, he had letters?"

"Yes; the usual odd two or three that people carry. One was from a girl saying she would wait for him. She's going to wait some time."

"Were the letters in French?"

"Yes."

"What money had he?"

"Wait a minute till I find my notes. Um-m-m. Twenty-two, ten, in mixed notes; eighteen and tuppence ha-penny in silver and copper."

"All English?"

"Yes."

"Between the lack of passport and the English currency, it looks as if he had been in England a good long time. I wonder why no one came to claim him."

"They may not know yet that he is dead. It didn't get much publicity."

"Didn't he have any address in Britain?"

"He had no address on him. The letters were not in envelopes: just in his wallet. His friends will probably turn up yet."

"Does anyone know where he was going? Or why?"

"No; seemingly not."

"What luggage had he?"

"An overnight case. Shirt, socks, pyjamas, and bedroom slippers. No laundry marks."

"*What?* Why? Were the things new?"

"No, oh, no." Williams sounded amused at Grant's overt suspicion. "Very well worn."

"Maker's name in the slippers?"

"No; those hand-made thick leather things you find in

North African bazaars and in the Mediterranean ports."

"What else?"

"In the case? A New Testament in French, and a yellow paper-backed novel, also in French. Both well worn."

"Your three minutes are up," said the operator.

Grant had another three minutes, but he got no nearer an explanation of B Seven. Apart from the fact that he had no record, either in France (the stabbing had been merely a domestic incident, it seemed) or in Britain, nothing was known of him. It was indeed typical that the one positive thing about him should be a negation.

"By the way," Williams said, "when I was writing I quite forgot to answer your postscript."

"What postscript?" Grant asked, and then remembered that he had written as an afterthought:

"If you ever have nothing better to do you might ask the Special Branch if they are interested at all in a man called Archibald Brown. Scottish patriot. Ask for Ted Hanna and tell him I was asking."

"Oh, yes, of course. About the patriot. Did you have time to do anything about it? It wasn't important."

"Well, as it happened, I met your reference on a Whitehall bus, day before yesterday. He says he has nothing against your bird but they would very much like to know who the ravens are. Do you know what he was talking about?"

"I think I do," Grant said, amused. "I'll do my best to find out for them. Just as a piece of holiday homework, tell him."

"You keep your mind off your work, if you please, and get well enough to be back here before the place falls to pieces without you."

"The shoes he was wearing: where were *they* made?"

"Who was wearing? Oh. Yes. Karachi."

"*Where?*"

"Karachi."

"Yes, that's what I thought you said. He seems to have got around. No name on the fly-leaf of the Testament?"

"Don't think so. I don't think I made any note of that when I read the evidence. Just a minute. Oh, yes, I did. No name."

"And no one in 'missing persons' that fits him?"

"No. No one. No one even approximately like him, it seems. He isn't 'missing' from anywhere."

"Well, it was wonderful of you to go to all that trouble

for me instead of telling me to go fish in my burn. I'll do as much for you some day."

"Are the fish in your burn biting?"

"There's hardly any burn, and the fish are cowering in the deepest recesses of the remaining pools. That is why I am reduced to taking an interest in cases that aren't worth a flicker of real interest in busy places like South-West One."

But he knew that that was not so. It was not boredom that had driven him to this interest in B Seven, this—he had almost said—alliance. He had a curious feeling of identification with B Seven. Not in the sense of being one, but in the sense of having an identity of interests. This, in view of the fact that he had seen him only once and knew nothing whatever about him, was highly unreasonable. Was it perhaps that he had thought of B Seven as also wrestling with demons? Had the feeling of personal interest, the championship, begun in that?

He had supposed that B Seven's Paradise had been oblivion. He had supposed that because of the whisky-sodden fug in the compartment. But the young man had not after all been sodden. He had not, indeed been very drunk. Just tipsy. His backwards fall against the solid round bulk of the basin had been the kind of thing that might happen to anyone. His so strangely guarded Paradise had not after all been oblivion.

He caught his attention back to what Williams was saying.

"What's that?"

"I forgot to say that the sleeping-car attendant is of the opinion that Martin was seen off by someone at Euston."

"Why is this an afterthought?"

"Well, I gather that he wasn't much of a help anyway, the sleeping-car chap. He seemed to treat the whole thing as a personal insult, the sergeant who was there said."

Old Yoghourt seemed to have run very true to form.

"What *did* he say?"

"He said that when he walked through the corridor, at Euston, Martin had someone with him in the compartment. Another man. He didn't see the man because Martin was facing him and the door was half open, so that all he noticed was that Martin was talking to another man. They seemed very happy and friendly. They were talking about robbing a hotel."

"What!"

"You see what I mean? The coroner said 'What!' too. The railway chap said that they were talking about 'robbing the Caley,' and since no one could rob a football team it must have been a hotel. It seems that all the hotels in Scotland that are not called Waverley are called Caledonian. Popularly known as 'Caley.' They weren't serious about it, he said."

"And that was all he saw of the seer-off?"

"Yes, that was all."

"He mightn't have been a seer-off at all. He might have been just a friend who came across him on the train. Saw his name on the sleeper list, or noticed him in passing."

"Yes; except that you'd expect a friend to turn up again in the morning."

"Not necessarily. Especially if he was far down the train. And the removal of the body would have been so discreet that I doubt if any passengers knew that someone had died. The station was clear of passengers long before the ambulance arrived. I know, because the ambulance fuss was taking place when I had nearly finished breakfast."

"Yes. The sleeping-car chap said he took it for granted that the other man was a seer-off because he was standing in hat and coat. Mostly, he says, when people go coffee-housing along the train they take their hats off. It's the first thing they do, he says: throw their hat on a rack. When they get to their compartment, I mean."

"Talking of names on the sleeper list, how was the berth booked?"

"By phone; but he picked up the ticket himself. At least, it was picked up by a thin dark man. Booked a week in advance."

"All right. Go on about Yoghourt."

"About who?"

"About the sleeping-car attendant."

"Oh. Well. He said that when he came down the train collecting tickets, about twenty minutes out from Euston, Martin had gone to the lavatory, but his sleeper ticket and the outward half of his ticket to Scoone were lying ready on the little shelf below the mirror. He took them and marked them off in his book, and as he was passing the lavatory he knocked at the door and said, 'Are you in B Seven, sir?' Martin said Yes. The attendant said, 'I've taken your tickets, thank you, sir. Will you be wanting tea in the morning?' And Martin said, 'No, thank you; good-night.'"

"So he had a return ticket?"

"Yes. The return half was in his wallet."

"Well, it's all straightforward enough, it seems. Even the lack of anyone to make inquiries about him, or to claim his body, may be due to the fact that he was off on a trip and people didn't expect to hear from him."

"That and the lack of publicity. I don't suppose his people even bothered to put an announcement in an English paper; they would just announce it in their own local affair, where people knew him."

"What did the P.M. say?"

"Oh, the usual. Light meal about an hour before death, large quantity of whisky in stomach and a fair amount in the blood. Quite enough to make him tight."

"No suggestion that he was a soak?"

"Oh, no. No degeneration of any kind. Head and shoulder injuries at some earlier period, but otherwise good healthy specimen. Not to say tough."

"So he had some earlier injury?"

"Yes, but a long time ago. I mean, nothing to do with this. He had at some time had a fractured skull and a broken collar-bone. Would it be very bad-mannered or very indiscreet of me to ask why all this interest in a simple case?"

"So help me, Sergeant, if I knew I would tell you. I think I must be getting childish."

"It's more likely that you're just bored," Williams said sympathetically. "Me, I was brought up in the country and I was never a one for watching the grass grow. An over-rated place, the country. Everything's too far away. Once that burn of yours starts flowing, you'll forget about Mr. Martin. It's pouring stair-rods here, so you probably won't have long to wait for rain now."

It did not, in fact, rain that night in the Turlie valley, but something else happened. The cold bright stillness gave place to a light wind. The wind was soft and warm; the air hung damp and heavy between gusts; the earth was moist and slippery; and down from the high tops came the snow water, filling the river bed from bank to bank. And up the brown racing water came the fish, flashing silver in the light as they leaped over the broken ledges of rock and up the narrow sluicing current between the boulders. Pat took his precious invention from his fly case (where it had a special compartment of its own) and presented it to Grant with the formal benevolence of a headmaster handing over a certificate. "You'll take care of it, won't you?" he said. "It took me a long time to make." The thing was, as his mother had said, a fearsome object. Grant thought that it was rather like something for a woman's hat; but he was aware that he was being singled out among men as the sole recipient worthy of such an honour and he accepted it with due gratification. He put it safely away in his own case and hoped that Pat would not supervise his efforts to the extent of making him use it. But each time he chose a new fly in the days that followed, he caught sight of the fearsome object and was warmed by his small cousin's approval of him.

He spent his days by the Turlie, happy and relaxed about the brown swirling water. The water was clear as beer and its foam froth-white; it filled his ears with music and his days with delight. The damp soft air smurred his tweed with fine dew, and water from the hazel twigs dripped down the back of his neck.

For nearly a week he thought fish, talked fish, and ate fish.

And then, one evening, on his pet pool below the swing bridge, he was startled out of his complacence.

He saw a man's face in the water.

There was time for his heart to come up into his mouth before he realised that the face was not under the surface of the water but at the back of his eyes. It was the dead white face with the reckless eyebrows.

He swore, and sent his Jock Scott singing viciously to the far side of the pool. He was finished with B Seven. He had grown interested in B Seven under a complete misunderstanding of the situation. He had thought that B Seven, too, had been hounded by demons. He had built up for himself an entirely fallacious picture of B Seven. The toper's Paradise in B Seven's compartment boiled down to an overturned whisky bottle. He was no longer interested in B Seven: a very ordinary young man, bursting with rude health to the point of toughness, who had had one over the eight on a night journey and ended his life in the highly undignified manner of falling backwards and then crawling about on his hands and knees until he stopped breathing.

"But he wrote those lines about Paradise," a voice in him said.

"He didn't," he said to the voice. "There's not the slightest evidence that he did any such thing."

"There's his face. No ordinary face. It was the face that you first succumbed to. Long before you began to think of his Paradise at all."

"I have *not* succumbed," he said. "In my job you take an automatic interest in people."

"Yes? You mean, if the occupant of that whisky-sodden compartment had been a fat commercial traveller with a moustache like a badly kept hedge and a face like a boiled pudding, you would still have been interested?"

"I might."

"You lying dishonest bastard. You were B Seven's champion the minute you saw his face and noticed the way that Yoghourt was mauling him about. You snatched him from Yoghourt's grip and straightened his jacket like a mother pulling a shawl over her baby."

"Shut up."

"You wanted to know about him not because you thought there was anything odd about his death but because, quite simply, you wanted to know about him. He was young and dead, and he had been reckless and alive. You wanted to know what he had been like when he was reckless and alive."

"All right, I wanted to know. I also want to know who is going to ride the Lincolnshire favourite, and what my shares are quoted at in today's market, and what June Kaye's next picture is going to be; but I'm not losing my sleep about any of them."

"No, and you don't see June Kaye's face between you and the water, either."

"I have no intention of seeing anyone's face between me and the river. *Nothing* is going to come between me and the river. I came here to fish, and nothing is going to muck up that for me."

"B Seven came North to do something too. I wonder what it was?"

"How should I know?"

"It couldn't be fishing, anyhow."

"Why couldn't it?"

"No one who was going five or six hundred miles to fish would be without tackle of some kind. If he was as keen as that, he would at least have his own pet lures with him, even if he was going to be let a rod."

"Yes."

"Perhaps his Paradise was Tir nan Og. You know, the Gaelic one. That would fit."

"How would it fit?"

"Tir nan Og is supposed to be away out to the west, beyond the outermost islands. The Land of the Young. The land of eternal youth, that's the Gaelic Paradise. And what 'guards the way' to it? Islands with singing sands, it seems. Islands with stones that stand up like men walking."

"And beasts that talk? Do you find them too in the Outer Isles."

"You do."

"You do? What are they?"

"Seals."

"Oh, go away and leave me alone. I'm busy. I'm fishing."

"You may be fishing, but you're not catching a damned thing. Your Jock Scott might as well be stuck in your hat. Now you listen to me."

"I will *not* listen to you. All *right*, there are singing sands in the Islands! All *right*, there are walking stones! *All right*, there are gabby seals! It has nothing to do with me. And I don't suppose it had anything to do with B Seven."

"No? What was he going North for?"

"To bury a relation, to sleep with a woman, to climb a rock! How should I know? And why should I care?"

"He was going to stay at a Caledonian Hotel somewhere."

"He was not."

"How do *you* know where he was going to stay?"

"I don't. Nobody does."

"Why should one of them be all facetious about 'robbing the Caley' if he was going to stay at a Waverley?"

"If he was going to Cladda—and I'll bet there's no inn on Cladda called anything as reeking of the mainland as the Caledonian—if he was going to Cladda he would have gone via Glasgow and Oban."

"Not necessarily. It's just as short and just as comfortable via Scoone. He probably loathed Glasgow. A lot of people do. Why not ring up the Caledonian in Scoone when you go back to the house tonight and find out if a Charles Martin was expected there?"

"I shall do no such thing."

"If you slap the water like that, you'll frighten every fish in the river."

He went back to the house at supper time in a very bad mood. He had caught nothing and had lost his peace.

And in the somnolent hush that filled the sitting-room when work was over for the day and the children in bed, he caught his eye wandering from his book to the telephone at the other end of the room. It stood on Tommy's desk, provocative in its suggestion of latent power, in the infinite promise of its silent presence. He had only to lift that receiver and he could speak to a man on the Pacific coast of America, he could speak to a man in the wastes of the Atlantic Ocean, he could speak to a man two miles above the earth.

He could speak to a man in the Caledonian Hotel in Scoone.

He resisted this thought, with growing annoyance, for an hour. Then Laura went to get bed-time drinks, and Tommy went to let the dogs out, and Grant reached the telephone in a dive that was nearer a rugby tackle than any civilised method of crossing a room.

He had lifted the receiver before he realised that he did not know the number. He put the receiver back in its cradle and felt that he had been saved. He turned to go back to his book but picked up the telephone book instead. He would have no peace until he had talked to the Caledonian in Scoone; it was cheap enough to have peace at the cost of being a little silly.

"Scoone 1460 . . . Caledonian Hotel? Can you tell me: Did a Mr. Charles Martin book accommodation with you any time in the last fortnight? . . . Yes, thank you, I'll wait . . . No? No one of that name . . . Oh . . . Thank you very much. So sorry to have bothered you."

And that was that, he thought, slamming the receiver down. That, as far as he was concerned, was definitely the end of B Seven.

He drank his nice soothing bed-time drink, and went to bed, and lay wide awake staring at the ceiling. He put the light out, and resorted to his own cure for insomnia: pretending to himself that he had to stay awake. He had evolved this long ago from the simple premise that human nature wants to do the thing it is forbidden to do. And so far it had never failed him. He had only to begin pretending that he was not allowed to go to sleep for his eyelids to droop. The pretence eliminated in one move the great-

57

est barrier to sleep: the fear that one is not going to, and so left the beach clear for the invading tide.

Tonight his eyelids dropped as usual, but a jingle ran round and round in his head like a rat in a cage:

> The beasts that talk,
> The streams that stand,
> The stones that walk,
> The singing sand . . .

What were the streams that stand? Was there something in the Islands that corresponded to that?

Not frozen streams. There was little snow or frost in the Islands. Then, what? Streams that ran into the sand and stood still? No. Fanciful. Streams that stand. Streams that stand?

Perhaps a librarian might know. There must be a goodish public library in Scoone.

"I thought you weren't interested any more?" said the voice.

"You go to hell."

A mechanic, he was. What did that mean? *Mechanicien*. It involved an endless range of possibilities.

Whatever he did, he was successful enough to be able to travel first class on a British railway. Which in these days made one practically a millionaire. And he had spent all that money on what, to judge by his overnight case, was a flying visit.

A girl, perhaps? The girl who had promised to wait? But she had been French.

A woman? No Englishman would go five hundred miles for a woman, but a Frenchman might. Especially a Frenchman who had knifed his girl for letting her glance stray.

> The beasts that talk
> The streams that stand . . .

Oh, God! Not again. Little Miss Muffet sat on a tuffet eating her curds and whey. Hickory, dickory, dock. Simple Simon met a pieman going to the fair; said Simple Simon to the pieman Let me taste your ware. Ride a cock horse to Banbury Cross— Your imagination had to be caught before you were fired by the need to write down a thing. You could, if your imagination was vivid, get to a stage when you were in bondage to an idea. When it became an *idée fixe*. You could become so enraptured by the pictured grace of a temple's flight of steps that you would work for years to earn the money and gain the leisure to take you there. In extreme cases it became a compulsion, and you dropped everything and went to the thing that had seduced you: a mountain, a green stone head in a museum, an uncharted river, a bit of sail-cloth.

How far had B Seven's vision ridden him? Enough to send him searching? Or just enough to make him write it down?

Because he *had* written those pencilled words.

Of course he had written them.

They belonged to B Seven as much as his eyebrows did. As much as those schoolboy capital letters did.

"Those *English* capital letters?" said the voice, provocative.

"*Yes,* those English letters."

"But he was a native of Marseilles."

"He could have been educated in England, couldn't he?"

"In two shakes you'll be telling me that he wasn't a Frenchman at all."

"In two shakes I will."

But that, of course, was to enter the realm of fantasy. There was no mystery about B Seven. He had an identity, a home and people, a girl who was waiting for him. He was demonstrably a Frenchman, and the fact that he wrote English verse in English handwriting was entirely by the way.

"He probably went to school in Clapham," he said nastily to the voice, and fell instantly asleep.

5

In the morning he woke with rheumatism in his right shoulder. He lay considering this in slow amusement. There was no end to what your subconscious and your body could achieve between them. They would provide you with any alibi you wanted. A perfectly good honest alibi. He had known husbands who developed high temperatures and the symptoms of 'flu each time their wives were on the point of departure to visit relations. He had known women who were so tough that they could watch a razor fight unmoved and yet would pass out in the deadest of dead faints when asked an awkward question. ("Was the accused so persecuted by police cross-examination that she was unconscious for fifteen minutes?" "She fainted, certainly." "There was no question of a simulated faint, was there? The doctor says that he saw her at the material time and there was great difficulty in reviving her. And that collapse was a direct result of the police cross-examination to which she was being—" and so on.) Oh, yes. There was no limit to what your subconscious and your body could cook up together. And today they had cooked up something that would keep him off the river. His subconscious had wanted to go in to Scoone today and talk to the librarian at the public library. His subconscious had remembered, moreover, that it was market day and that Tommy would be taking the car into Scoone. So his subconscious had set to work on the eternally sycophantic body and between them they had made a tired shoulder muscle into an unworkable joint.

Very neat.

He got up and dressed, wincing each time he lifted an arm, and went down to cadge a lift from Tommy. Tommy was heart-broken at his disablement but delighted by his company, and they were so gay together, this warm spring morning, and Grant was so filled with the pleasure that ferreting out information always provided for him, that they were running through the outer suburbs of Scoone before he remembered that he was in a car. That he was shut into a car.

He was enormously gratified.

He promised to meet Tommy for lunch at the Caledonian, and went away to find the public library. But before he had gone far, a new idea struck him. The *Flying Highlander* would have come clicking over the points at Scoone only a few hours ago. Every twenty-four hours, from year's end to year's end, the *Flying Highlander* made that night journey and came into Scoone in the morning. And since the train crews habitually stuck to the same run, alternating time on and time off, there was just the chance that one of the staff who had come into Scoone on the *Flying Highlander* this morning was Murdo Gallacher.

So he changed direction and went to the station instead.

"Were you on duty when the London mail arrived this morning?" he asked a porter.

"No, but Lachie was," said the porter. He stretched his mouth into a line, let out a whistle that would have done credit to an engine, tilted his head back an inch to summon a distant colleague, and went back to reading the racing page of the *Clarion*.

Grant went to meet the slowly advancing Lachie and asked him the same question.

Yes, Lachie had been on duty.

"Can you tell me if Murdo Gallacher was one of the sleeping-car attendants?"

Lachie said that Yes, Old Sourpuss was on her.

Could Lachie say where Old Sourpuss could be found now?

Lachie glanced up at the station clock. It was after eleven.

Yes, Lachie could say where he would be. He would be in the Eagle Bar waiting for someone to stand him a drink.

So to the Eagle Bar at the back of Scoone Station Grant went, and found that Lachie had been, in the main, right. Yoghourt was indeed there, mooning over a half-pint. Grant ordered a whisky for himself and saw Yoghourt's ears prick.

"Good-morning," he said amiably to Yoghourt. "I've had some very good fishing since I saw you last." He was pleased to notice the hope grow on Yoghourt's face.

"I'm glad of that, sir, very glad," he said, pretending to remember Grant. "The Tay, is it?"

"No, the Turlie. By the way, what did your dead young man die of? The one I left you trying to waken." Antagonism began to wither the eagerness on Yoghourt's face. "Won't you join me?" Grant added. "A whisky?" Yoghourt relaxed.

After that it was easy. Yoghourt was still prickled with resentment at the inconvenience that he had been caused. He had even had to attend the inquest in his spare time. It was, Grant thought, as easy as dealing with a toddler who had just learned to run. It needed only a touch to steer him in any required direction.

Yoghourt had not only hated having to attend the inquest, he had hated the inquest and he had hated every single soul connected with the inquest. Between his hatred and two double whiskies he provided Grant with the most detailed account of everyone and everything. He was the best value for money that Grant had ever had. He had been "on" in the affair from first to last; from the first appearance of B Seven at Euston to the coroner's verdict. As a source of information he was pure horse's mouth, and he "gave" like a beer tap.

"Had he travelled with you before?" Grant asked.

No, Yoghourt had never seen him before and was glad that he was never going to again.

This was where Grant's satisfaction suddenly changed to satiation. One more half-minute of Yoghourt and he would be sick. He pushed himself off the counter of the Eagle Bar and went to look for the public library.

The library was frightful beyond description: a monstrosity in liver-coloured stone; but after Yoghourt it seemed the fine flower of civilisation. The assistants were charming, and the librarian was a thin little piece of faded elegance with a tie no broader than the black silk ribbon of his eyeglasses. As an antidote to too much Murdo Gallacher, it could not have been better.

Little Mr. Tallisker was a Scot from Orkney—which, he pointed out, was not being a Scot at all—and he was both interested in and knowledgeable about the Islands. He knew all about the singing sands on Cladda. There were other alleged singing sands, too (every Island wanted to have what its neighbours had as soon as they heard about any new possession, whether it was a pier or a legend), but the Cladda ones were the original. They lay, like most of the Island sands, on the Atlantic side, facing the unbroken ocean, looking out to Tir nan Og. Which, as Mr. Grant might know, was the Gaelic heaven. The land of the eternally young. It was interesting, wasn't it, how each people evolved its own idea of Heaven? One as a feast of lovely women, one as forgetfulness, one as continuous music and no work, one as good hunting grounds. The Gaels, Mr. Tallisker thought, had had the loveliest idea. The land of youth.

What sang? Grant asked, interrupting the dissection of comparative bliss.

It was a moot point, Mr. Tallisker said. Indeed, you could have it either way. He had walked them himself. Endless miles of pure white sand by a brilliant sea. They did "sing" as one trod on them, but he himself held that "squeak" would be a better description. On the other hand, on any day that provided a steady wind—and such days were of no unusual occurrence in the Islands—the fine, almost invisible, surface sand was swept along the wide beaches so that hey did in fact "sing."

From sand Grant led him to seals (the Islands were full of seal stories, it seemed; the translation of seals into men and vice versa; if they were to be believed half the population of the Islands had some seal blood in them) and from seals to walking stones, and on all Mr. Tallisker was interesting and informative. But on streams he fell down. Streams seemed to be the only things on Cladda that were exactly like their counterpart anywhere else. Except that they too often spread into little lochs or lost themselves in bog, the streams of Cladda were just streams; water in the process of finding its own level.

Well, thought Grant, going away to meet Tommy for

lunch, that in a way was "standing." Running into standing water, into bog. B Seven might have used the word because he needed a rhyme. He had wanted something to rhyme with sand.

He listened with only half an ear to the talk of the two fellow sheep-farmers that Tommy brought to lunch, and envied them their untroubled eyes and their air of unlimited leisure. Nothing hounded these large *rangé* creatures. Their flocks were decimated every now and then by strokes of fate: great snowstorms or swift disease. But they themselves stayed quiet and sane, like the hills that bred them. Big slow men, full of little jokes and pleased with small things. Grant was very conscious that his obsession with B Seven was an unreasonable thing, abnormal; that it was part of his illness; that in his sober mind he would not have thought a second time about B Seven. He resented his obsession and clung to it. It was at once his bane and refuge.

But he drove home with Tommy even more cheerful than when he had set out. There was practically nothing about the inquest on Charles Martin, French mechanic, that he did not now know. He was that much to the good. And that was a lot.

After supper that night he discarded the book on European politics which had shared with Tommy's telephone his interest on the previous evening and went hunting along the bookshelves for something about the Islands.

"Are you looking for anything in particular, Alan?" Laura asked, looking up from *The Times*.

"I'm looking for something about the Islands."

"The Hebrides?"

"Yes. I suppose there is a book about them."

"Hah!" said Laura, mock amused. "Is there a book about them! There's a whole literature, my dear. It's a distinction in Scotland not to have written a book about the Islands."

"Have you any of them?"

"We have practically all of them. Everyone who has ever come to stay here has brought one."

"Why didn't they take them away with them?"

"You'll see why when you have a taste of them. You'll find them on the bottom shelf. A whole row of them."

He began to go through the row, gutting the books with a swift practised eye.

"Why this sudden interest in the Hebrides?" Laura asked.

"Those singing sands that Wee Archie talked about stuck in my mind."

"That must be the first time Wee Archie has ever said anything that stuck in someone's mind."

"I expect his mother remembers his first word," Tommy put in from behind the *Clarion*.

"It seems that Tir nan Og is just one jump west from the singing sands."

"So is America," said Laura. "Which is much nearer the Islanders' idea of Heaven that Tir nan Og is."

Grant, repeating Mr. Tallisker's speech on comparative heavens, said that the Gaels were the only race who visualised Heaven as a country of the young, which was endearing of them.

"They are the only known race who have no word for No," Laura said drily. "That is a much more revealing characteristic than their notions of eternity."

Grant came back to the fire with an armful of books and began to go through them at leisure.

"It is difficult to imagine a mind that has never evolved a word for No, isn't it?" Laura said musingly, and went back to *The Times*.

The books varied from the scientific, through the sentimental, to the purely fantastic. From kelp-burning to the saints and heroes. From bird-watching to soul's pilgrimages. They varied, too, from the admirable but dull to the unbelievably bad. It seemed that no one who had ever visited the Islands had refrained from writing about them. The bibliographies at the end of the soberer books would have done justice to the Roman Empire. On one thing all were agreed, however: the Islands were magic. The Islands were the last refuge of civilisation in a world gone mad. The Islands were beautiful beyond imagining, a world carpeted with wild flowers and bounded by a sea that broke in sapphire on silver beaches. A land of brilliant sunlight, of good-looking people and heart-searching music. Wild, lovely music handed down from the beginning of time, from an age when the gods were young. And if you wanted to go there, see MacBrayne's timetable on Page 3 of the Appendix.

The books lasted Grant very happily until bed-time. And while they drank their nightcaps, he said, "I'd like to have a look at the Islands."

"Make a plan for next year," Tommy said, agreeing. "There's quite good fishing on Lewis."

"No, I mean now."

"Go now!" Laura said. "I never heard anything so daft."

"Why? I can't fish until my shoulder is better, so I might as well go exploring."

"Your shoulder will be better in two days with my treatment."

"How does one get to Cladda?"

"From Oban, I should think," Tommy said.

"Alan Grant, don't be absurd. If you can't fish for a day or two, there are a hundred other things you can do instead of being bucketed about on a Minch crossing in March."

"Spring comes early to the Islands, they say."

"It doesn't to the Minch, believe me."

"You could fly, of course," Tommy said, considering the subject as he considered everything that was put in front of him, with a kind sobriety. "You could fly one day and come back the next, if you liked. It's quite a good service."

There was a little silence while Grant met his cousin's eye. She knew that he could not fly, and why.

"Give it up, Alan," she said, in a kinder tone. "There are much nicer things to do than being stood on one's head in the middle of the Minch in March. If you just want to get away from Clune for a bit, why don't you hire a car—there's a very good garage in Scoone—and go exploring on the mainland for a week or so? Now that the weather is soft, it will be getting green in the West."

"It isn't that I want to get away from Clune. Quite the contrary. If I could take Clune *en bloc* with me, I would. It is just that I have got bitten with the idea of those sands."

He saw Laura begin to consider the idea from a new angle, and he could follow her thought quite well. If this was what his sick mind wanted, then it would be wrong to try to dissuade him. The interest of a place he had never seen before should be an ideal counteraction to self-conscious brooding.

"Oh, well, what you want is a Bradshaw, I suppose. We do have one, but it's mostly used as a door-stop or a step for the top book-shelf, so it's a little out of date."

"As far as the services to the Outer Islands are concerned, it won't matter what the date of it is," said Tommy. "The Laws of the Medes and the Persians are not more unchangeable than MacBrayne's schedules. As someone has remarked, they don't exactly encroach on eternity but they very nearly outlast time."

So Grant found the Bradshaw and took it to bed with him.

And in the morning he borrowed a small case from Tommy, and packed into it the bare necessities of existence for a week or so. He had always had a passion for travelling light, and it always pleased him to be getting away by himself, even from people he loved (a trait that had done much to keep him single), and he caught himself whistling under his breath as he put the few things into the small space. He had not whistled to himself since the shadow of unreason had reached out and taken the sunlight from him.

He was going to be foot-loose again. Foot-loose: it was a beautiful thought.

Laura had promised to drive him into Scoone in time to catch the train to Oban, but Graham was late in coming back with the car from Moymore village, so that it was touch-and-go whether he caught the train at all. They made it with thirty seconds to spare, and a breathless Laura pushed a bundle of papers into the open window as the train pulled out, and gasped: "Enjoy yourself, my dear. Seasickness does wonders for the liver."

He sat, alone in the compartment, in a daze of contentment with the magazines unheeded on the seat beside him. He watched the bare empty landscape trundle by and grow slowly greener as they went west. He had no idea why he was going to Cladda. It was certainly not to gather information in the police sense. He was going—to find B Seven. That is as near as it could be put into words. He wanted to go and see the place which so nearly reproduced the landscape of the poem. He wondered, sunk in sleepy bliss, whether B Seven had ever talked to anyone about his Paradise. He remembered the writing and thought not. Those tightly arcaded *ms* and *ns* were too defensive to have been made by a talker. In any case, it didn't matter how many people he had talked to about the thing, since there was no way of making contact with them. He could hardly put an advertisement in the papers saying: Read this poem and tell me if you recognise it.

Or—why couldn't he?

His sleepiness fell from him while he considered this new angle.

He considered it all the way to Oban.

In Oban he went to a hotel, ordered a self-congratulatory drink, and while he consumed it he wrote to each of the London daily papers, enclosing a cheque and asking them to print an identical notice in their personal column. The notice said:

The beasts that talk, the streams that stand, the stones that walk, the singing sand. . . . Anyone recognising please communicate with A. Grant, c/o P.O., Moymore, Comrieshire.

The only daily papers to which he did not send his appeal were the *Clarion* and *The Times*. He did not want Clune to think that he had taken leave of his senses altogether.

As he made his way along the front to the cockleshell in which he was due to brave the Minch, he thought: It will serve me right if someone writes to say that the thing is one of the best-known lines of some Xanadu concoction of Coleridge's, and that I must be illiterate not to have known it!

6

The wallpaper consisted of far too heavy roses hanging from a far too slender trellis-work, and the insecure character of the whole thing was increased by the fact that the paper not only hung away from the wall but moved about in the draught. It was not readily obvious where the draught came from because the small window was not only tightly shut but had patently been tightly shut since its manufacture and original insertion in the house structure about the beginning of the century. The little swing mirror on the chest of drawers lived up to its promise in the first respect but not in the second. It would swing with ease amounting to abandon through the whole circle of 360 degrees, but it did not reflect anything to any noticeable degree. A last year's cardboard calendar folded in four kept its gyratory talents in check, but nothing, of course, could be done to increase its powers of reflection.

Two of the four drawers in the chest were capable of being opened. The third would not open because it had lost its knob, and the fourth because it had lost the will. Above the black iron fireplace with its frill of red crinkled paper brown with age was an engraving of a partially clothed Venus comforting a quite unclothed Cupid. If the cold had not already eaten into his bones, Grant thought that the picture would have finished the process.

He looked from the little window down on the small harbour with its collection of fishing-boats, at the grey sea slapping drearily against the breakwater, and the grey rain beating on the cobbles, and he thought of the log fire in the sitting-room at Clune. He toyed with the idea of going to bed as the quickest way of getting warm, but a second glance at the bed dissuaded him. Its plate-like thinness was made even more plate-like by the meagre covering of a white honeycomb cotton cover. At the foot, a turkey-red cotton quilt suitable for a doll's perambulator was folded into an elaborate pattern. Above it brooded the finest collection of unmatching brass knobs that it had ever been Grant's fortune to meet.

Cladda Hotel. The gateway to Tir nan Og.

He went downstairs and poked the smoky fire in the sitting-room. Someone had banked the fire with the potato peelings from lunch, so his efforts were not very successful. Rage came to his rescue and he rang the bell with all his might. The wires jangled in a crazy dance somewhere in the walls, but no bell rang. He went out into the lobby where the wind was coming soughing in under the front door and shouted. Never, even in his best form on the "square," had he used his voice with so passionate a determination to produce results. A young female creature came from the back regions and stared at him. She had a face like a rather practical Madonna and legs the same length as her body.

"Wis yu bawling?" she asked.

"No, I wasn't bawling. That sound you heard was my teeth chattering. In my country a sitting-room fire is designed to give out heat, not to consume refuse."

She looked at him a little longer, as if translating his speech into a more understandable idiom, and then moved past him to look at the fire.

"*Oh, Dé,*" she said, "that will never do. Stop you and I'll get you a bit of fire."

She went away and came back with what seemed to be most of the kitchen fire blazing on a shovel. Before he could remove some of the packed dross and vegetable matter from the grate, she had dumped the flaming mass on top of all.

"I'll be getting some tea to warm you," she said. "Mr.

Todd is down at the pier seeing did the things come on the boat. He'll be back in no time at all."

She said it comfortingly, as if the presence of the proprietor would automatically be warming. Grant took it for granted that she was apologising for the absence of an official welcome to a guest.

He sat and watched the kitchen fire gradually lose heart as it became conscious of the bed of potato peelings on which it had been cast away. He did his best to rake out some of the damp black mass from underneath so as to provide an encouraging draught, but the thing merely settled down in a sad heap. He watched the glow fade until only little red worms of incandescence ran to and fro across the surface of the blackened coals as the passing wind sucked the air from the room into the chimney. He thought of putting on his waterproof and walking in the rain; walking in the rain could be a delightful thing. But the thought of hot tea held him where he was.

After nearly an hour of fire-watching, no tea had come. But "N. Todd, Prop.," came back from the harbour, accompanied by a boy in a navy-blue jersey pushing a wheelbarrow laden with large cardboard cartons, and came in to welcome his guest. They did not expect guests at this time of the year, he said; he thought when he had seen him come off the boat that he would be staying with someone on the island. Gathering songs, or something.

There was something in the way he said "gathering songs"—a detached tone bordering on comment—that made Grant sure that he was no native.

No, said Mr. Todd, when asked, he did not belong to the place. He had had a good little commercial hotel in the Lowlands, but this was more to his taste. And, seeing the surprise on his guest's face he added: "To tell you the truth, Mr. Grant, I was tired of counter-rappers. You know, the kind of chap who can't wait a minute. Out here no one ever thinks of rapping on a counter. Today, tomorrow, or next week is all the same to an Islander. It's a bit maddening now and then, when you want something done, but for most of the time it's fine and restful. My blood pressure's away down." He noticed the fire. "That's a poor sort of fire Katie-Ann's given you. You'd better come in to my office and warm yourself."

At this moment Katie-Ann put her head in at the door and said that it had taken all this time to boil the kettle because the kitchen fire had gone out on her, and would

71

Mr. Grant now think it a good thing to have his tea and his high-tea at one and the same time. Grand did indeed think it a good thing, and as she went away to prepare this evening repast he asked his host for a drink.

"The magistrates took away the licence from my predecessor, and I haven't yet got it back. I'll get it back at the next Licensing Court. So I can't sell you a drink. There isn't a licence on the island. But if you'll come in to my office, I'll be glad to stand you a whisky."

The office was a tiny place, tropical in its breathless heat. Grant savoured the oven atmosphere gratefully, and drank the bad whisky neat, as it was proffered. He took the indicated chair and stretched out his feet to the blaze.

"You're not an authority on the island, then," he said.

Mr. Todd grinned. "In one way I am," he said wickedly. "But probably not the way you mean it."

"To whom should I go to learn about the place?"

"Well, there's two authorities. Father Heslop and the Reverend Mr. MacKay. On the whole perhaps Father Heslop would be better."

"You think he is the more knowledgeable?"

"No; they're about fifty-fifty as far as that goes. But two-thirds of the islanders are R.C. If you go to the priest, you'll only have a third of the population against you, instead of two-thirds. Of course the Presbyterian third are much nastier customers to be up against, but if numbers count with you then you'd better see Father Heslop. Better see Father Heslop anyway. I'm a heathen myself, so I'm an outcast from both flocks; but Father Heslop is for a license and Mr. MacKay dead against it." He grinned again and refilled Grant's glass.

"I take it the priest would rather see the stuff sold openly than a drunk on the sly."

"That's it."

"Did you ever have a visitor called Charles Martin staying here?"

"Martin? No. Not in my time. But if you'd like to look through the visitors' book, it's on the table in the lobby."

"If a visitor doesn't stay at the hotel, where would he be likely to stay? In rooms?"

"No, no one lets rooms on the island. The houses are too small for that. They'd stay either with Father Heslop or at the manse."

By the time that Katie-Ann came to say that his tea was waiting on him in the sitting room, the blood was flowing freely again through Grant's once-moribund body and he was hungry. He looked forward to his first meal in his "tiny oasis of civilisation in a barbarous world" (see *Dream Islands* by H. G. F. Pynche-Maxwell, Beal and Batter, 15/6). He rather hoped that it might not be either salmon or sea-trout, having had an elegant sufficiency of both in the last eight or nine days. He would not turn up his nose at a piece of grilled sea-trout if it happened to be that. Grilled with some local butter. But he hoped for lobster—the island was famous for its lobsters—and failing that some herring fresh from the sea, split, and fried after being dipped in oatmeal.

His first meal in the isles of delight consisted of a couple of bright orange kippers inadequately cured and liberally dyed in Aberdeen, bread made in Glasgow, oatcakes baked by a factory in Edinburgh and never toasted since, jam manufactured in Dundee, and butter made in Canada. The only local produce was a pallid, haggis-shaped mound of crowdie, a white crumbly by-product without smell or taste.

The sitting-room in unshaded lamplight was even less appetising than it had been in the grey light of afternoon, and Grant fled to his freezing little bedroom. He demanded two hot-water bottles and suggested to Katie-Ann that since he was the sole guest she should filch the quilts from every other bedroom in the house and dedicate them to his use. She did this with all her native Celt pleasure in the irregular, heaping his bed with borrowed luxury and suffocating with giggles.

He lay under the five meagre bits of wadding, topped off with his own coat and Burberry, and pretended that the whole thing was one good English eiderdown. As he grew warm, he became conscious of the cold stuffiness of the room. That was the last straw, and quite suddenly he began to laugh. He lay there and laughed as he had not laughed for nearly a year. Laughed till the tears came, laughed until he was so exhausted that he could no more, and lay spent and purged and happy under his fine variety of bedclothes.

Laughter must do untold things for one's endocrine glands, he thought, feeling the well-being flood through him in a life-giving tide. More especially, perhaps, when it is laughter at oneself. At the fine, glorious absurdity of oneself in relation to the world. To set out for the threshold of Tir nan Og and fetch up at the Cladda Hotel had an

73

exquisite ridiculousness. If the Islands provided him with nothing but this, he would consider himself well rewarded.

He ceased to care that the room was airless and the covers insecure. He lay looking at the rose-heavy wallpaper and wished that he could show it to Laura. He remembered that he had not yet been transferred into that newly decorated bedroom at Clune which, up till now, had always been his. Was Laura expecting another visitor? Was it possible that her latest candidate for his affections was to be housed under the same roof? So far he had been happily free of female society; the evenings at Clune had been family evenings, peaceful and long-breathing. Had Laura been merely holding her hand until he was, so to speak, able to sit up and take notice? She had been suspiciously regretful that he was going to miss the opening of the new hall at Moymore. A ceremony that she would have in her normal mind not expected him to attend at all. Had she expected a guest for the opening? The bedroom could not be meant for Lady Kentallen, because she would come over from Angus and go back the same afternoon. Then for whom was the bedroom redecorated and kept empty?

He was still turning the small question over in his mind when he fell asleep. And it was only in the morning that it occurred to him that he had hated the closed window because it made the room stuffy and not because it was closed.

He washed in the two pints of tepid water that Katie-Ann brought him and went downstairs rejoicing. He felt on top of the world. He ate the Glasgow bread, still another day older this morning, and the Edinburgh oatcakes, and the Dundee jam, and the Canadian butter, together with some sausages from the English midlands, and enjoyed them. Having given up his expectation of primitive elegance, he was prepared to accept primitive existence.

He was gratified to find that in spite of cold wind and wet weather and thinly covered hard beds his rheumatism had entirely gone, being no longer needed by his subconscious to provide an alibi. The wind was still howling in the chimney and the water spouting up from the break-water, but the rain had stopped. He put on his Burberry and tacked round the harbour front to the shop. There were only two places of business in the row of houses that fringed the harbour: a post-office and a provision merchant. The two between them supplied the island with all that it needed. The post-office was also a newsagent; and the provision merchant was a combination of grocer, ironmonger, chemist, draper, shoe-shop, tobacconist, china-merchant, and ship's chandler. Bolts of sprigged cotton for curtains or dresses lay on shelves alongside the biscuit tins, and hams hung from the roof among strings of locknit undergarments. Today, Grant noticed, there was also a large wooden tray of tuppenny buns baked, if the paper round the queen cakes was to be believed, in Oban. They were crumby and depressed-looking, as if they had been tumbled about in one of the cardboard cartons that were such an indispensable part of island life, and they smelled very faintly of paraffin, but he supposed that they made a change from the Glasgow bread.

In the shop were several men from the fishing-boats in the harbour and a little round man in a black raincoat who could be nothing but a priest. This was a fortunate thing. Even the Presbyterian third, he felt, could hardly hold against him a fortuitous meeting in a public store. He edged in beside His Reverence and waited with him while the fishermen were being served. After that it was plain sailing. The priest "picked him up" and he had five witnesses to it. Moreover, Father Heslop deftly included the proprietor, one Duncan Tavish, in the conversation, and, from the fact that Father Heslop called him Mr. Tavish and not Duncan, Grant deduced that the proprietor was not one of his flock. So he was very happily parcelled out among the islanders over the paraffiny buns and the margarine, and there would be no internecine war over the possession of his person.

He went out into the gale with Father Heslop and strolled home with him. Or rather they beat up against the wind together, staggering a few steps forward at a time, and shouting remarks to each other above the noise of their flapping garments. Grant had the advantage of his companion in that he wore no hat, but Father Heslop was not only lower on the ground but had a figure ideally streamlined for life in a gale. He had no angles anywhere.

It was good to go in from the blast to a warm turf fire and silence.

"Morag!" called Father Heslop, into the further end of the house, "Some tea for me and my friend here. And a scone maybe, like a good girl."

But Morag had not baked, any more than Katie-Ann

75

had. They were given Marie biscuits, a little soft in the island dampness. But the tea was wonderful.

Because he knew that he was an object of curiosity to Father Heslop, as he was to everyone on the island, he said that he had been fishing with relations in Scotland, but had to stop owing to a bad shoulder. And because he had been bitten with the idea of the Islands, and more especially with the singing sands on Cladda, he had taken the chance of coming to see them, a chance he might never have presented to him again. He supposed that Father Heslop was well acquainted with the sands?

Oh, yes, of course Father Heslop knew the sands. He had been fifteen years on the island. They were on the west side of the island, facing the Atlantic. It was no distance across the island. Grant could walk there this afternoon.

"I would rather wait for fine weather. It would be better to see them in sunlight, wouldn't it?"

"At this time of year you might wait for weeks before you'd see them in sunlight."

"I thought spring came early to the Islands?"

"Oh, I think, myself, that's just an idea of the people who write books about them. This is my sixteenth spring on Cladda, and I have yet to catch one here before its time. The spring's an Islander too," he added with a little smile.

They talked of the weather, the winter gales (which made today, according to Father Heslop, a thing of zephyrs), the penetrating damp, the occasionally idyllic summer days.

Why had a place of so few attractions captured the imagination of so many people, Grant wanted to know.

Well, partly it was that they saw it only at high summer, and partly it was that those who came and were disappointed were reluctant to admit their disappointment either to themselves or the friends they had left behind. They compensated themselves by talking big. But it was Father Heslop's own theory that most people who came were unconsciously running away from life, and they found what their imaginations prepared for them. Through their eyes the Islands were beautiful.

Grant thought this over, and then asked him if he had ever known a Charles Martin, who had been interested in singing sands.

No; Father Heslop had never met a Charles Martin, as far as he could remember. Had he come to Cladda?

Grant did not know.

He went out into the blast, and was blown back to the hotel at an undignified trot, teetering on his toes like a elderly toper. The bare lobby at the hotel smelled of unidentifiable hot food and sang like a choir as the wind came shrieking in under the outside door. But they had managed a fire that looked like a fire, in the sitting-room. To the scream of wind in the passage and the yowling of wind in the chimney he ate beef from South America, carrots tinned in Lincolnshire, potatoes grown in Moray, milk pudding packaged in North London, and fruit bottled in the Vale of Evesham. Now that he was no longer conditioned to magic, he filled his stomach thankfully with what was put in front of him. If Cladda had denied him spiritual joy, it had provided him with a fine physical appetite.

"Don't you ever bake scones, Katie-Ann?" he said, when he was arranging the time of his high tea.

"Is it scones you'll be wanting?" she said surprised. "Indeed, yes, I'll bake you some. But we have baker's cakes for your tea. And biscuits and ginger-snaps. Would you rather be having scones than them?"

Remembering the "baker's cakes" Grant said enthusiastically that he would, he would indeed.

"Well, then," she said kindly, "of course I'll bake you a scone."

For an hour he walked, along a flat grey road through a flat grey desolation. To his right, distinct in the mist, was a hill, the only visible height. The whole thing was as inspiring as the fens on a wet January day. Every now and then the wind on his left flank would send him spinning sideways off the road altogether, and he struggled back half amused, half irritated. At long distances odd cottages lay cowering close to the earth, blind and limpet-like, without any sign of human habitation. Some had stones slung from the roof by ropes to weight the structure against the wind's importunity. None of them had fence, outhouse, garden, or bush. It was living at its most primitive; inside four walls; everything under hatches and battened down.

And then, suddenly, the wind smelt salt.

And in less than half an hour he came on it. He came on it without warning, across a great waste of wet green

77

grass that in summer-time must be starred with flowers. There had been no visible reason why the long levels of grassy land should not go on for ever to the horizon; it was all part of this flat grey endless world of bog. He had been prepared to go on walking to the horizon, so that he was startled to find that the horizon was ten miles out at sea. There it lay in front of him, the Atlantic; and if it was not beautiful it was, nevertheless, impressive in its sweep and simplicity. The green water, dirty and ragged, roared on to the beach and broke in a flash of white that was vicious. To right and left, as far as eye could see, were the long lines of breaking water and the pale sands. There was nothing else in all the world but the green torn sea and the sands.

He stood there looking at it, and remembering that the nearest land was America. Not since he had stood in the North African desert had he known the uncanny feeling that is born of unlimited space, the feeling of human diminution.

So sudden had been the presence of the sea, and its rage and extent so overwhelming, that he had hung there motionless for several moments before realising that here were the sands that had brought him to the fringe of the western world in March. These were the singing sands.

Nothing sang today but the wind and the Atlantic. Together they made a Wagnerian tumult that buffeted one almost as physically as did the gale and the spray. The whole world was one mad uproar of grey-green and white and wild noise.

He walked down over the fine white sand to the edge of the water, and let the tumult roar over him. At close quarters it had a senseless quality that dissolved his uncomfortable sense of diminution and made him feel human and superior. He turned his back on it almost contemptuously, as one would on a bad-mannered child who was making an exhibition of himself. He felt warm and alive and master of himself; admirably intelligent and gratifyingly sentient. He walked back up the sand, absurdly and extravagantly glad to be a human being and alive. The air that came off the land when he had turned his back on the salt sterile wind from the sea was gentle and warm. It was like opening the door of a house. He went on across the grassy levels without once looking back. The wind hounded him along the flat bogs, but it was no longer in his face and the salt was no longer in his nostrils. His nostrils were full of the good smell of damp earth, the smell of growing things.

He was happy.

As he came at last down the slope to the harbour, he looked up at the hill in the mist and decided that tomorrow he would climb it.

He came back to the hotel ravenous, and was gratified to be given no fewer than two items of local manufacture for his high tea. One was a plate of Katie-Ann's scones, and the other was "sleeshacks": a delicacy he had known of old. Sleeshacks were mashed potatoes fried in slices; and they certainly helped to make appetising the remains of cold beef from lunch which was the *piece de résistance* of the meal. But as he ate his first course, he kept smelling something more evocative of those early Stathspey days than even sleeshacks could be. An aroma both sharp and subtle it was, floating and circling about his brain in a nostalgic tantalisation. It was not until he had put his knife into one of Katie-Ann's scones that he knew what it was. The scone was yellow with soda and quite uneatable. With a regretful salute to her for the memory (platefuls of yellow soda-laden scones laid out in the farmhouse kitchen table for the farm-hands' tea: Oh, Tir nan Og!), he buried two of Katie-Ann's scones under the glowing coals in the grate and made do with the Glasgow bread.

And that night he fell asleep without looking at the wallpaper and without remembering the closed window at all.

7

In the morning he ran into the Reverend Mr. MacKay in the post-office and felt that he was distributing his favours very successfully. Mr. MacKay was on his way down to the harbour to see if the crew of a Swedish fishing-boat that was lying there would like to come to church if they were still there the day after tomorrow. There was also, he undersood, a Dutch vessel that might be presumed to be of a Presbyterian persuasion. If they showed signs of wanting to come, he would prepare a sermon in the English for them.

He condoled with Grant about the rough weather. It was early in the year for the Islands, but he supposed that one had to take holidays when one was given them.

"You'll be a schoolmaster, maybe, Mr. Grant."

No, Grant said, he was a Civil Servant. Which was his normal answer to questions about his profession. People were prepared to believe that Civil Servants were human beings; no one ever believed that a policeman was one. They were two-dimensional characters with silver buttons and a notebook.

"You'd be amazed, now, you that has not been here before, if you could see what the Islands are like in June,

Mr. Grant. Not a cloud in the sky, day after day, and the air so hot that ye'll see it dancing before you. And the mirage as mad as ever it was in the desert."

"Were you in North Africa?"

Och, yes; Mr. MacKay had been in North Africa with the Jocks. "And believe me, Mr. Grant, I've seen odder things from my window up in the manse there than ever I did between Alamein and Tripoli. I've seen the lighthouse on the point there standing up in the air. Yes, halfway up the sky. I've seen the hill there change shape till it looked like a great mushroom. And as for the rocks by the sea, those great pillars of stone, they can turn light and transparent and move about as if they were walking through a set of the Lancers."

Grant considered this with interest, and ceased to listen to the rest of Mr. MacKay's discourse. As he parted from him alongside the *Ann Loefquist* of Goteborg, Mr. MacKay hoped that he was coming to the *ceilidh* tonight. All the island would be there and he would hear some fine singing.

When he asked his host about the *ceilidh* and where it was being held, Mr. Todd said that it would be the usual mixture of song and talk, that it would end up with the usual dance, and that it would be held in the only place on the island suitable for such a gathering—the Peregrine Hall.

"Why Peregrine?"

"That is the name of the lady who gave it. She used to come to the island in the summer and she was all for improving trade and making the islanders self-supporting, so she built a fine long hut with big windows and skylights so that they could weave in company and not be ruining their eyes over looms in tiny dark rooms. They should get together, she said, and have a Cladda mark for their tweed and make it sought-after, like Harris. She could have saved her breath and her bawbees, poor lady. No islander would walk a yard to work. They would rather go blind than move out of their own light. But the hut is very useful for island gatherings. Why don't you have a look in tonight when it gets going?"

Grant said that he would do that, and went away to spend the rest of the day climbing Cladda's solitary hill. There was no mist, although the wind was still moisture-laden, and as he went upward the seas opened under him, scattered with islands and streaked with the tides. Here and there a single line, unnaturally straight in that arrangement of nature, marked the track of a ship. From the top he had the whole Hebridean world at his feet. He sat there and considered it, the barren, water-logged universe, and it seemed to him the ultimate in desolation. A world half-emerged from chaos, formless and void. Looking down on Cladda itself, it was impossible to tell, so mixed were sea and land, whether one was looking at a land full of lochs or a sea full of islands. It was a place best left to the grey geese and the seals.

He was happy up there, however, watching the changing patterns on the sea floor, violet and grey and green; watching the sea birds soar to inspect him and the flutter of nesting plovers to the low ground. Thinking about Mr. MacKay's mirages and the stones that walked. Thinking, as he never ceased for any length of time to think, about B Seven. Here was B Seven's world, according to specifications. The singing sands, the talking beasts, the walking stones, the streams that ceased to run. What had B Seven intended to do here? Just to come, as he himself had done, and look?

A flying dash, with an overnight case. That surely portended one of two things: a meeting or an inspection. Since no one had yet missed him, then it could not have been a rendezvous. Therefore it was an inspection. One could go to inspect many things: a house, a prospect, a painting. But if one was driven to write verse *en route*, then the verse was surely a pointer to the subject for inspection.

What had held B Seven in bondage to this bleak world? Had he been reading too many books by H.G.F. Pynche-Maxwell and his like? Had he forgotten that the silver sands and the wild flowers and the sapphire seas were strictly seasonal?

From the top of the hill at Cladda, Grant sent B Seven a salute and a blessing. But for B Seven he would not be sitting above this sodden world feeling like a king, newborn and self-owning. He was something more than B Seven's champion now: he was his debtor, his servant.

As he left the shelter he had found for himself, the wind caught him in the chest, and he leaned on it as he went downhill as he used to when he was a boy, so that it supported him and he could almost fall downhill in the most surprising manner and still be safe.

"How long do gales usually last in this part of the

world?" he asked his host as they staggered through the darkness after supper towards the *ceilidh*.

"Three days is the minimum," Mr. Todd said, "but that doesn't happen often. Last winter it blew for a month on end. You got so used to the roar of it that if it died away for a moment you thought you'd gone deaf. You'd be better to fly back, when you go, than cross the Minch in this weather. Most people fly nowadays, even the old people who've never seen a train. They take aeroplanes for granted."

It occurred to Grant that he might indeed fly back; that if he waited another few days, if he had a little longer to grow accustomed to his new-found well-being, he might use the air journey as a test. It would be a pretty severe test, the severest he could subject himself to. To any claustrophobe the prospect of being boxed into a small space and hung helplessly in the air was sheer horror. If he faced it without wincing, and accomplished it without disaster, then he could pronounce himself cured. He would be a man again.

But he would wait a little; it was too early yet to ask himself the question.

The *ceilidh* had been in progress for some twenty minutes when they arrived, and they stood with the rest of the male population at the back. Only the women and the ancients occupied the chairs in the hall. Except for a row of male heads in the very front, where the Importances of the island sat (Duncan Tavish, the merchant, who was uncrowned king of Cladda, the two Churches, and some lesser lights), the male population lined the walls at the back and clustered round the entrance. It was an abnormally cosmopolitan gathering, Grant noticed, as the outsiders made way for them; both the Swedes and the Hollanders had come in force, and there were accents that belonged to the Aberdeenshire coast.

A girl was singing in a thin soprano. Her voice was sweet and true but without expression. It was like someone trying over an air on a flute. She was succeeded by a self-confident youngish man who received an ovation, on which he plumed himself so obviously that it was funny; one waited for him to bill his breast feathers like a bird. He was a great favourite, it seemed, with audiences of exiled Gaels on the mainland, and he spent more time being encored there than he did on his neglected croft. He sang a hearty ditty in a rough over-worked tenor and was cheered to the echo. It surprised Grant a little that he had never bothered to learn the rudiments of singing. He must, in his jaunts to the mainland, have met real singers, who had been taught how to use their voices; even in the case of someone so vain it was astonishing that he had not been moved to learn the basis of the art he professed.

Another woman sang another expressionless song, contralto, and a man recited a funny story. Except for the few phrases that he had learned from the old folk in Strathspey when he was a child, Grant understood no Gaelic, and he listened as he would have listened to an entertainment in Italian or Tamil. Except for the delight of the people themselves in the thing, it was a sufficiently dull affair. The songs were musically negligible; some of them deplorable. If this was the kind of thing that people came to the Hebrides to "gather," then they were hardly worth the gathering. The few inspired songs had, like all products of inspiration, gone over the world on their own wings. It was better that these feeble imitations should be left to die.

Throughout the concert there was a continuous coming and going among the men at the back of the hall, but Grant had been aware of it only as an obbligato until his arm was pressed and a voice said in his ear, "Could you be doing with a wee drop yourself, perhaps?" and he realised that Island hospitality was offering him a share of the scarcest commodity known to Island economy. Since it would have been ungracious to refuse, he thanked his benefactor and followed him out into the darkness. Against the lee wall of the meeting-place leaned a representative minority of the male population of Cladda in a contented silence. A flat two-gill bottle was thrust into his hands. *"Slainte!"* he said, and took a swig of it. A hand, guided by an eye more acclimatised to the dark than his own, took the bottle back from him and a voice wished him health in return. Then he followed his unknown friend back to the lighted hall. Presently he saw Mr. Todd being surreptitiously tapped on the arm, and Mr. Todd too went out into the darkness to be sustained with something out of the bottle. It could happen nowhere else, Grant thought. Unless in the States during prohibition. Not much wonder that the Scots were silly and arch and coy about whisky. (Except, of course, in Strathspey, where the stuff was made. In Strathspey they put the bottle in the middle of the table, as matter-of-factly as an Englishman would, if a little more proudly.) Not much wonder that they behaved as if there was something very dashing, not to say daring, about having a drink of whisky. The surprising, the knowing leer with which the ordinary Scot referred to his national drink could only come from inherited knowledge of prohibition: either the Kirk's or the Law's.

Warmed by his mouthful out of the flat bottle, he listened tolerantly to Duncan Tavish being confident and long-winded in Gaelic. He was introducing a guest who had come a long way to speak to them, a guest who needed no introduction from him or from anyone; whose own achievements spoke for themselves. (Nevertheless Duncan spoke for them at length.) Grant did not catch the Gaelic name of the guest, but he was aware that the renegades from outside came pressing in at the sound of the cheering that greeted Mr. Tavish's peroration. Either the speaker was the real interest of the evening or the whisky had given out.

He watched in idle curiosity the small figure detach itself from the front row, clamber up on to the platform with the aid of the piano, and stride into the middle of it.

It was Wee Archie.

Wee Archie looked even odder in Cladda than he had on Clune moor; his stature more inadequate, his cockatoo brightness more startling. The kilt was not the dress of the islands, and among all these sober-coloured males in their thick, stiff clothes he looked more than ever "a souvenir doll." Without his dashing bonnet with its sprouting greenery, he looked somehow undressed, like a policeman without his helmet. His hair was very scanty, and was drawn in thin strings across the top of his head to hide the bare patch. He was like something out of a not very expensive Christmas stocking.

However, there was no qualification to the welcome he was given. Apart from the Royal Family, in person and *in toto,* Grant could think of no one who could be guaranteed the equivalent of the reception the Wee Archie was now being accorded. Even discounting the effect of libations at the lee end, it was surprising. And the silence that succeeded it when he began to talk was flattering. Grant wished that he could see the faces. He remembered that Bella from Lewis had had no use for his back-door

85

proselytising; and what Pat Rankin thought of him would not go through the post. But what did these Islanders, cut off from the world and from the variety that alone could teach a man to judge between this and that, what did these Islanders think of him? Here was the material of his dreams; innocent, acquisitive, self-conscious, egotistical. They could not be subverted to another rule, the Islanders, because no one had ever ruled them in any real sense. A Government was there, as far as the Islanders were concerned, to be milked of benefits and diddled out of its dues. But their separateness could be played upon to alienate sympathy; their opportunism could be sharpened by dangled benefits. In Cladda, Wee Archie was not the embarrassing nonenity he had been at Lochan Dhu; in Cladda he was a possible power. Cladda and all its attendant islands represented, in the ultimate reckoning, submarine bases, smuggling points, stepping-off places, watch-towers, airfields, patrol bases. What did the Islanders think of Gilleasbuig Mac-a'-Bruithainn and his creed? He wished that he could see the faces.

For half an hour Wee Archie spoke to them in his thin, angry voice, with passion and without pause, and they listened without a sound. And then Grant, casting a glance, at the rows of seats in front of him, thought that they looked less full than they had been at the beginning of the evening. This was so unlikely that he took his attention from Archie to consider the matter. He caught a stealthy movement along the trough between Row 5 and Row 6 and followed it with his eye until it reached the end of the row. There it stood upright and materialised into the person of Katie-Ann. With no fuss at all Katie-Ann, still with demure eyes fixed on the speaker, faded backwards through the standing rows of males and disappeared into the outer air.

Grant watched a little longer and found that this melting process was continuous, both among the seated audience and among the males standing round the walls. The audience was melting away invisibly under Archie's very nose. This was so unusual—a country audience will always wait to the end however boring an entertainment—that Grant turned to Mr. Todd and whispered, "Why are they leaving?"

"They're going to watch the ballet."

"The *ballet?*"

"Television. It's their great treat. Everything else they

see on television is just a version of something they've seen already. Plays, and singing, and what not. But ballet is something they've never seen before. They wouldn't miss ballet for anything or anyone. . . . What is so amusing about that?"

But Grant was not amused by Cladda's passion for ballet. He was enjoying Archie's so unlikely disarming. Poor Archie. Poor wee deluded Archie. He had been overthrown by an arabesque, foiled by an *entrechat,* defeated by a plié. It was fantastically appropriate.

"Have they gone for good?"

"Oh, no, they'll be back for the dance."

And back they were, in force. Every soul on the island was at the dance; the ancients sitting round, and the active taking the roof off with their wild yelling. It was less agile dancing than Grant was used to on the mainland, less graceful; for Highland dancing one needed the kilt, and the soft thonged shoes that made no sound on the floor and let a man dance like a flame among the sword points. The Island dancing had much of the Irish in it; much of the sad Irish immobility that left the dancing a matter of footwork only, and not an uprush of joy that filled a man to the last finger-tip of his up-flung hands. But if the dancing itself lacked art and gaiety, there was a fine wholesale merriment in its stamping performance. There was room, with some squeezing, for three eightsomes, and sooner or later everyone, including the Swedes and the Hollanders, was dragged into this orgy of exercise. A fiddle and a piano gave out the lovely floating rhythm (for that one needed a regimental band, thought Grant as he swung Katie-Ann into the arms of a delighted Swede; one needed that double drumbeat and pause; it might not be purist but it certainly was effective) and the hands of those at rest beat time. The wind howled along the skylights on the roof, the dancers yelled, the fiddle sawed, and the piano thumped, and a wonderful time was had by all.

Including Alan Grant.

He swayed home through the stinging lash of hail wielded by a pitiless south-wester, and dropped into bed drunk with exercise and fresh air. It had been a delightful day.

It had also been a profitable one. He would have something to tell Ted Hanna when he got back to town. He knew now who Archie Brown's "ravens" were.

Tonight he did not look at the closed window with misgiving. Nor tonight did he forget it altogether. He looked at the closed window and was glad of it. He had absorbed the Island point of view that a window is there to keep out the weather.

He burrowed into his cotton-quilt nest, out of the wind and the weather, and fell into dreamless depths of sleep.

8

Wee Archie departed next morning when "the boat" called, on his way to spread light throughout all the other dark places of the archipelago. He had been staying with the Reverend Mr. MacKay, it transpired; and Grant wondered what that blameless padre to a Highland regiment would think if he knew what he had been sheltering under his roof. Or was the Reverend Mr. MacKay, too, sick of Archie Brown's disease?"

On the whole Grant thought not.

Mr. MacKay had all the authority that mortal man could crave; he had a satisfaction for his vanity every Sunday morning; he had seen the world, and life and death, and men's souls in relation to both, and he was not likely to hanker after esoteric glories. He had merely been host to a Scottish celebrity. For in a small country like Scotland Archie ranked as a celebrity, and Mr. MacKay was no doubt greatly pleased to entertain him.

So Grant had the island to himself, and for five days in the company of the whooping wind he quartered his bleak kingdom. It was rather like walking with a bad-mannered dog; a dog that rushes past you on narrow paths, leaps on you in ecstasy so that you are nearly knocked over, and drags you from the direction in which you want to go. He spent his evenings with his legs stretched out to the office fire listening to Mr. Todd's tales of pub-owning in the Lowlands. He ate enormously. He put on weight visibly. He slept as soon as his head touched the pillow, and he woke only when it was morning. And by the end of the fifth day he was ready to face a hundred air journeys rather than spend another twelve hours in the place.

So on the sixth morning he stood on the great flat of white sand waiting for the little plane to pick him up on its way back from Stornoway. And the small misgiving somewhere in the depths of him was nothing like the pervading apprehension with which he had expected to be filled at this moment. Mr. Todd stood with him, and beside them on the sand was his small case. Up on the grass, where the road ended, was the Cladda Hotel car, the only one on the island and the only one of its class anywhere in the world. They stood there, four tiny dark objects in the shining waste, watching the small bird-like thing in the sky drop down to them.

This, Grant thought, was as near to the original idea of flight as one was likely to get nowadays. As someone had pointed out, when man first dreamed of flying he had seen himself rising on his own silver wings into the blue empyrean, but it hadn't turned out at all like that. First he was trundled to a field, then he was shut in a box, then he was terrified, then he was sick, then he was in Paris. Being picked up from the sands on the sea-ward fringe of the world by a casual-alighting bird was as near as one would ever come to the free soaring of man's original vision.

The great bird idled up to them along the sand, and for a moment Grant panicked. It was, when all was said, a box. A tight-closed trap of a thing. But the casualness of everything loosened his rigid muscles almost as soon as they had stiffened. In the clinical order of an airport, shepherded and compelled, panic might have conquered. But here, on the open sand, with the pilot draped about the top step as he gossiped with Mr. Todd, and the crying of gulls and the smell of the sea, it was a thing one could take or leave. There was no compulsion to be afraid of.

So when the moment came he put his foot over the last step with nothing more than a slight heart-quickening. And before he could analyse his reaction to the closing

90

door, a nearer interest caught his mind. In front of him, on the other side of the gangway, was Wee Archie.

Wee Archie looked as if he had just got out of bed, and as if he had done that getting-out in some hurry. His dishevelled splendour looked more than ever as if they were someone's else's clothes altogether. He looked like a discarded armature with some studio props flung on top of it. He greeted Grant like an old friend, condescended to him about his ignorance of the Islands, recommended Gaelic to him as a language it would pay him to study, and went back to sleep. Grant sat and looked at him.

The little bastard, he thought. The vain, worthless little bastard.

Archie's mouth had fallen open, and the strands of black hair no longer covered the thin patch. The knees above the fat brilliant socks were more like anatomical specimens than any mechanism designed for the propulsion of a living being. They weren't knees; they were "the knee joint." The articulation of the fibula was particularly interesting.

The vain, vicious little bastard. He had had a profession that would give him his bread and butter, a profession that would have given him a certain standing, a profession that would have brought him spiritual reward. But that had not satisfied his egotistical soul. He had needed the limelight. And as long as he could strut in the light, he did not care who paid for the illumination.

Grant was still considering the fundamental part that vanity played in the make-up of the criminal when a geometrical pattern opened below him like a Japanese flower in water. He took his thoughts from psychological matters in order to consider this Euclidean phenomenon in a world of nature and found that they were circling the mainland airport. He had flown back from Cladda and had hardly been aware of it.

He climbed down on to the tarmac and wondered what would happen if he did a war-dance of joy there and then. He wanted to go whooping and prancing round the aerodrome like a child on his first hobby-horse. Instead he went to the telephone booths and asked Tommy if he could pick him up at the Caledonian in Scoone in about two hours. Tommy could and would.

The food at the airport restaurant tasted like Lucas-Carton, the Tour d'Argent, and La Crémaillière all rolled into one. The man at the next table was complaining bitterly about it. But he, of course, had not just been reborn after five months of hell and seven days of Katie-Ann.

Tommy's round kind face in the lounge of the Caledonian looked rounder and kinder than even Tommy's face had ever looked before.

There was no wind.

No wind at all.

It was a beautiful world.

What a frightful anticlimax it would be, he thought, if when he got into the car with Tommy the old horror overcame him. Perhaps the thing was just waiting there for him, licking its lips with anticipation.

But there was nothing in the car. Just himself and Tommy and the good relaxed atmosphere of their habitual intercourse. They drove away into the country, an appreciably greener country than it had been ten days ago, and the evening sun came out and sent long golden fingers of light across the calm fields.

"How did the Moymore ceremony come off?" he asked. "The bouquet presentation."

"Oh, heavens: that!" Tommy said, making motions as of a man mopping his forehead.

"Didn't he present it?"

"If letting her have it is presenting it, I suppose technically he presented it. He handed it over with a speech he had thought up himself."

"What kind of speech?"

"I think he had been rehearsing a sort of get-out for himself ever since we talked him into it by making Zoë Kentallen a rebel of some kind. Which was Laura's idea, by the way, not mine. Well, when she stooped to take the great bush of carnations from him—she's very tall—he held them out of her reach for a moment and said firmly, 'I'm only giving you this, mind, because you're a fellow-revolutionary.' She took it without batting an eyelid. She said: 'Yes, of course. How very kind of you,' although she hadn't an idea what he was talking about. She bowled him over, by the way."

"How?"

"In the good old female way. Pat is in the throes of his first infatuation."

Grant looked forward to seeing this phenomenon.

Clune lay very peaceful in its green hollow, and Grant looked at it as one coming home victorious from battle.

The last time he had driven up that sandy road he had been a slave; now he was a free man. He had gone out to look for B Seven and had found himself.

Laura came out to meet him at the doorstep and said, "Alan, have you taken to a tipster's business on the side?"

"No. Why?"

"Or one of those Lonely Hearts columns, or something?"

"No."

"Because Mrs. Mair says there is a whole sackful of mail waiting for you at the post-office."

"Oh. How did Mrs. Mair know that the letters were for me?"

"She said you were the only A. Grant in the district. I take it you haven't advertised for a wife?"

"No, just for a bit of information," he said, going with her into the sitting-room.

The room in the early dusk was full of firelight and wavering shadows. He thought it was empty until he noticed that someone was sitting in the big wing-chair by the hearth. A woman, so long and slender that she seemed as fluid as the shadows and he had to look a second time to be sure that she was not in truth a shadow.

"Lady Kentallen," said Laura's voice behind him, in an introducing tone. "Zoë has come back to Clune for a few days fishing."

The woman leant forward to shake hands with him and he saw that she was a girl.

"Mr. Grant," she said, greeting him. "Laura says that you like to be called Mr."

"Yes. Yes, I do. 'Inspector' has a grim sound in private life."

"And a little unreal, too," she said in her gentle voice. "Like something out of a detective story."

"Yes; people expect you to say, 'Where were you on the evening of the umpteenth inst?'" How could this virginal creature be the mother of three sons, one of them nearly old enough to leave school? "Have you been having any luck on the river?"

"I had a nice grilse this morning. You are going to have it for supper."

She had the kind of beauty that allows a woman to part her hair in the middle and wear it smooth to her head. A dark small head on a long graceful neck.

He remembered suddenly about the newly decorated

bedroom. So the fresh paint had been for Zoë Kentallen, and not for Laura's latest candidate for his interest. That was an enormous relief. It had been bad enough to have Laura's selections put under his nose, but to have had the latest one actually under the same roof would have been, to put it mildly, tiresome.

"The Oban train must have been in time for once," Laura said, remarking on his early arrival.

"Oh, he flew back," Tommy said, throwing another log on the fire. He said it casually, unaware that the fact had any importance.

Grant looked over at Laura and saw her face light with happiness. She turned her head to find him among the shadows and saw that he was looking at her, and smiled. Had it mattered so much to her then? Dear Lalla. Dear kind understanding Lalla.

They began to talk about the Islands. Tommy had a fine tale of a man whose hat blew off as he was boarding a boat in Barra and who found it waiting for him on the pier at Mallaig. Laura was funny about the impossibility of carrying on a conversation in a language that has no words for anything less than two hundred years old and supplied an imaginary account of a road accident. ("Blah-blah bicycle blah-blah S-bend blah-blah brakes blah-blah traction-engine blah-blah ambulance blah-blah stretcher blah-blah anaesthetic blah-blah private ward blah-blah temperature chart blah-blah chrysanthemums freezias ranunculus narcissus carnations . . .") Zoë had stayed in the Islands as a child and was very knowledgeable about poaching salmon, an art she had been taught by local talent under the very nose of her host's game-keeper.

Grant was pleased to find that the family atmosphere of Clune had been in no way disturbed by the presence of this guest. She seemed unaware of her beauty, and unexpectant of attention. He was not surprised that Pat had been "bowled over."

It was only when his bedroom door finally closed on him and he was alone that his mind went to the waiting sack of letters in the post-office at Moymore. A sack of them! Well, that was not unbearably surprising, after all. A life in the C.I.D. conditioned one to the existence of the letter-writer. There were people whose only interest in life was writing letters. To the newspapers, to authors, to strangers, to City Councils, to the police. It did not much matter to whom; the satisfaction of writing seemed to be all. Seven-eighths of that pile of letters would be the product of those whose hobby was writing letters.

But there was still the odd eighth.

What would the odd eighth have to say?

In the morning he watched the guest getting her tackle ready for the river and wished that he was going with her, but still more he wanted to go to the post-office at Moymore. She set off without fuss, self-sufficient and unobtrusive, and Grant, watching her walk down the path, thought that she was more like an adolescent boy than a prospective dowager. She was wearing very elegant trousers and a disreputable old lumber jacket, and he remarked to Tommy that she was one of the few women who looked really well in trousers.

"She's the only woman in the *world*," Tommy said, "who looks beautiful in waders."

So Grant went away to interview Mrs. Mair at Moymore. Mrs. Mair hoped that he had a secretary, and presented him with a paper-knife. It was a thin silver affair, very tarnished, with a thistle head made of amethyst. When he pointed out that the thing was hallmarked and some value nowadays and that he could not accept expensive presents from strange women, she said:

"Mr. Grant, that thing has been in my shop for twenty-five years. It was made for the souvenir trade in the days when people could read. Now they just look and listen. You're the first person I've met in a quarter of a century that *needed* a paper-knife. Indeed, by the time you've slit open all the letters in that sack, you'll need more than a paper-knife, I'm thinking. Anyway it's the first and last time I'll ever have a sack of mail addressed to one person in this office and I'd like to mark the occasion. So you take the wee knife!"

He took it gratefully, hoisted the sack into the car, and went back to Clune.

"The bag's post-office property," she said after him, "so see you bring it back!"

He took the sack to his own room, polished the little knife until it shone with a pleased and grateful air as if glad to be noticed after all those years, emptied the bag on to the floor, and slipped the knife into the first letter to come to hand. The first letter asked him how he dared expose to the public gaze the words the writer had written, with such pain and heart-searching, in the spring of 1911, under the orders of her spirit guide Azul. It was like being publicly exhibited without clothes, to see her own precious lines so wantonly laid bare.

Thirteen other correspondents claimed to have written the lines (without spirit guidance) and asked what was in it for them. Five sent the completed poem—five different poems—and claimed that they were the author of it. Three accused him of blasphemy, and seven said he was plagiarising from Revelation. One said: "Thank you very much for an evening's entertainment, old boy, and how is the fishing on the Turlie this year?" One directed him to the Apocrypha, one to the Arabian Nights, one to Rider Haggard, one to Theosophy, one to Grand Canyon, and five to various parts of Central and South America. Nine sent him cures for alcoholism, and twenty-two sent him circulars about esoteric cults. Two suggested subscriptions to poetry magazines, and one offered to teach him to write salable verse. One said: "If you are the A. Grant I sat through the Monsoon with at Bishenpus this is my present address." One said: "If you are the A. Grant I spent the night with in a rest hotel in Amalfi this is just to say hullo, and I wish my husband was as good." One sent him particulars of a Clan Grant association. Nine were obscene. Three were illegible.

There were one hundred and seventeen letters.

The one that gave him most pleasure was one that read: "I've fathomed your code, you bloody traitor, and I shall report you to the Special Branch."

Not one of them was of any help at all.

Oh, well. He had not really hoped. It had been a shot in the dark.

He had at least had some amusement out of it. Now he could settle down and fish until the end of his sick-leave. He wondered how long Zoë Kentallen was staying.

The guest had taken sandwiches with her and did not appear for lunch, but in the afternoon Grant took his rod and followed her down to the river. She had probably already fished the whole of the Clune water, but perhaps she did not know it as well as he did. She might be glad of some unobtrusive advice. Not, of course, that he was going down to the river for the sole purpose of talking to her. He was going to fish. But he would have to find out first which part of the water she herself was fishing. And he could hardly, having found her, pass with casual wave of the hand.

He did not pass at all, of course. He sat on the bank

96

watching her drop a Green Highlander above the big one that she had been pursuing with various lures for the last hour. "He just thumbs his nose at me," she said. "It has become a personal affair between us." She used her rod with the ease of someone who had fished since she was a child, almost absent-mindedly, as Laura did. It was very satisfying to watch.

He gaffed the fish for her an hour later, and they sat together on the grass and ate the rest of her sandwiches. She asked about his work, not as if it was a sensational matter, but as she might inquire about it if he had been an architect or an engine-driver; she told him about her three boys and what they were going to be. Her simplicity was indestructible, and her unselfconsciousness child-like in its completeness.

"Nigel will be sick when he hears that I have been fishing the Turlie," she said. She said it as a girl might say it of a schoolboy brother; and he deduced that this described with fair accuracy the relationship between herself and her sons.

There were hours yet of daylight, but neither of them made any move to go back to the river. They sat there looking down on the brown water and talked. Grant, out of his wide acquaintance, tried to think of an equivalent to her, and failed. None of the beautiful women he had seen in his time had had her fairy-princess quality, her air of timeless youth. A stray from Tir nan Og, he thought. It was surprising that she should, soberly considered, be the same age as Laura.

"Did you know Laura well at school?"

"Not bosom-friend well. I was terribly in awe of her, you see."

"In awe? Of Laura?"

"Yes. She was very clever, you know, and good at everything, and I never could add two and two."

Since part of his delight in her was the contrast between her Hans-Andersen-illustration quality and her practicality, he deduced that this was an exaggeration. But it was probably true that she had no—no branches to her, so to speak. No multitude of leaves to breathe the air of the world. The climate of her mind was uncritical. Her utterance had none of Laura's swift interest and dissection.

"We are very lucky, you and Laura and I, to have known the Highlands when we were children," she said, when they were talking of early fishing experiences. "That is what I should wish most for a child. To have a beautiful calf-country. When David—my husband—was killed they wanted me to sell Kentallen. We had never had much money, and the Death Duties took the margin that made the place workable. But I wanted to hang on to it at least until Nigel and Timmy and Charles are grown-up. They will hate losing it, but at least they will have had the years that matter in a beautiful country."

He looked at her, putting her tackle neatly away in its box with the sober care of a tidy child, and thought that the solution of her problem was surely remarriage. The West End that he knew so well was lousy with sleek men in shiny cars who could keep Kentallen with no more effort than they would keep a Japanese garden in one of the rooms that they called lounges. The difficulty was, he supposed, that in Zoë Kentallen's world money was neither an introduction nor an absolution.

The spring sunlight faded. The skies grew luminous. The hills went far away and lay down, as Laura had once said as a child, describing in eight easy words the whole look and atmosphere of an evening of settled weather when tomorrow is going to be a wonderful day.

"We ought to be getting back," Zoë said.

As he picked up their fishing things from the bank he thought that there had been more magic in this one afternoon on the Turlie than in all the much advertised Islands of the West.

"You love your work, don't you?" she said as they walked up the hill to Clune. "Laura told me that you could have retired years ago if you had wanted to."

"Yes," he said, a little surprised. "I suppose that I could have retired. My mother's sister left me a legacy. She married a man who did well in Australia and she had no children."

"What would you do if you retired?"

"I don't know. I have never even considered it."

9

But that night, going to sleep, he did consider it. Not as a prospect, but with speculation. What would it be like to retire? To retire while he was still young enough to begin something else? If he began something else what would it be? A sheep-farm like Tommy's? That would be a good life. But could he make a success of an entirely country existence. He doubted it. And if not, then what else could he do?

He played with this nice new toy until he fell asleep, and he took it to the river with him next morning. One of the really charming facets of the game was the thought of Bryce's face when he read his resignation. Bryce would not merely be short of staff for a week or two; he would find himself deprived for good and all of his most valued subordinate. It was a delicious thought.

He fished his favourite pool, below the swing bridge, and conducted delightful conversations with Bryce. Because, of course, there would be a conversation. He would give himself the ineffable delight of laying that written resignation on the desk in front of Bryce's nose; laying it there himself, in person. Then there would be some really satisfying chat, and he would walk out into the street a free man.

Free to do what?

To be himself, at the beck and call of nobody.

To do things he had always wanted to do and had had no time for. To mess about in small boats, for instance.

To get married, perhaps.

Yes, to get married. With leisure there would be time to share his life. Time to love and be loved.

This lasted him very happily for another hour.

About noon he became aware that he was not alone. He looked up and saw that a man was standing on the bridge watching him. He was standing only a few yards from the bank, and since the bridge was motionless he must have been there for some time. The bridge was the usual trough of wire floored with wooden slats, a structure so light that even the wind was capable of moving it. He was grateful to the stranger for not walking into the middle of the thing and swaying about there so that he distracted every fish in the neighbourhood.

He nodded to the man by way of expressing his approval.

"Your name Grant?" asked the man.

After the circumlocutions of a people so devious-minded that they had no word for No, it was pleasant to be asked a straight question in simple English.

"Yes," he said, and wondered a little. The man sounded as if he might be an American.

"You the guy who put that advertisement in the paper?"

There was no doubt about the nationality this time.

"Yes."

The man tipped his hat further back on his head and said in a resigned way, "Oh, well, I'm crazy too, I guess, or I wouldn't be here."

Grant began to reel in.

"Won't you come down, Mr.—"

The man moved off the bridge and came down the bank to him.

He was youngish, well-dressed, and pleasant-looking.

"My name is Cullen," he said. "Tad Cullen. I'm a flyer. I fly freight for OCAL. You know: Oriental Commercial Airlines Ltd."

It was said that all you needed to fly for OCAL was a certificate and no sign of leprosy. But that was an exaggeration. Indeed, it was a perversion. You had to be good

100

to fly for OCAL. In the big shiny passenger lines, if you made a mistake you were on the carpet. In OCAL, if you made a mistake you were out on your ear. OCAL had an unlimited supply of personnel to draw upon. OCAL cared nothing for your grammar, your colour, your antecedents, your manners, your nationality, or your looks, as long as you could fly. You had to be able to fly. Grant looked at Mr. Cullen with a double interest.

"Look, Mr. Grant, I know that that thing, those words in the paper, I know they were just some kind of quotation that you wanted identified, or something like that. And of course I can't identify them. I was never any good at books. I haven't come here to be any use to you. Quite the opposite, I guess. But I've been very worried, and I thought even a long shot like this might be worth trying. You see, Bill used words like that one night when he was a bit high—Bill's my buddy—and I thought, maybe, it might be a place. I mean the description might be a place. Even if it is a quotation. I'm afraid I'm not making myself very clear."

Grant smiled a little and said No, not so far, but suppose they both sat down and straightened it out. "Am I to understand that you have come here looking for me?"

"Yes, I actually came last night. But the post-office place was shut, so I got a bed at the inn. Moymore, they call it. And then I went to the post-office this morning and asked them where I could find the A. Grant who had a lot of letters. I was sure you'd have had a lot, you see, after that advertisement. And they said Oh, yes, if it was Mr. Grant I wanted I would find him on the river somewhere. Well, I came down to look, and the only other person on the river was a lady, so I guessed you must be it. You see, it wasn't any good writing to you because I really hadn't anything that seemed worth putting on paper. I mean, it was just a daffy kind of hope. And you mightn't have bothered answering it anyway—when it had nothing to do with you, I mean." He paused a moment, and added in a half-hopeful, half-hoping-for-nothing tone, "It isn't a night-club, is it?"

"What isn't?" Grant asked, surprised.

"That place with talking beasts at the door. And the odd scenery. It sounded like a fun-fair place. You know: the kind of place where you go in a boat through tunnels in the dark and see ridiculous and frightening things unexpectedly. But Bill wouldn't be interested in a place like

101

that. So I thought of a night-club. You know, one of those got up with oddities to impress the customers. That would be much more Bill's mixture. Especially in Paris. And it was in Paris that I was to meet him."

For the first time a gleam of light appeared.

"You mean that you were due to meet this Bill? And he didn't keep the appointment?"

"He didn't show up at all. And that's very unlike Bill. If Bill says he'll do a thing, or be in a place, or remember a thing, believe you me he'll deliver. That's why I'm so worried. And not a word of explanation. Not a message left at the hotel or anything. Of course, they may have forgotten to put down the message, hotels being what they are. But even if they did forget, there would have been some follow-up. I mean, when I didn't react, Bill would have telephoned again saying: What are you up to, you old so-and-so? Didn't you get my message? But there wasn't anything like that. It's funny, isn't it, that he would book a room and then not turn up to occupy it and not send a word in explanation?"

"Very strange indeed. Especially since you say your friend was a dependable type. But why were you interested in my advertisement? I mean, in connection with Bill? Bill—what, by the way?"

"Bill Kenrick. He's a flyer like me. With OCAL. We've been friends for a year or two now. The best friend I ever had, I don't mind saying. Well, it was like this, Mr. Grant. When he didn't turn up, and no one seemed to know anything about him or to have heard from him—and he had no people in England that I could write to—I thought about what other ways there were of communicating with people. Other than telephones and letters and telegrams and whatnot. And so I thought of what you call the Agony Column. You know, in the newspapers. So I got the Paris edition of the *Clarion*—the files, I mean, at their Paris office—and went through them, and there was nothing. And then I tried *The Times,* and there was nothing there either. This was after some time, of course, so I had to go back through the files, but there was nothing. I was going to give it up because I thought that that was all the English papers that had regular Paris editions, but someone said why didn't I try the *Morning News.* Well, I went to the *News,* and there didn't seem to be anything from Bill, but there was this thing of yours that rang a bell. If Bill hadn't been missing I don't suppose I would have thought twice

102

about it, but having heard Bill gabble something along those lines made me notice it and be interested. Are you with me, as Bill says?"

"Entirely. Go on. When was it that Bill talked about the odd landscape?"

"He didn't talk about it at all. He just babbled one night when we were all a little drunk. Bill doesn't drink, Mr. Grant. I don't want you to get the wrong idea. I mean, drink as a habit. A few of the boys in our lot do, I admit, but they don't last long in OCAL. They don't last long anyway. That's why OCAL heaves them out. They don't mind them killing themselves, but it gets expensive in crates. But now and then we have a night out like other people. And it was on one of those nights out that Bill got going. We were all a little high so I don't remember anything in detail. I know we were drinking toasts and we were running out of subjects by that time. And we were taking it in turn to think up unlikely things to toast. You know, like 'The third daughter of the Lord Mayor of Bagdad,' or 'June Kaye's left little toe.' And Bill said, 'To Paradise!' and then gabbled a piece about talking beasts and singing sands and what not."

"Didn't anyone ask about this Paradise of his?"

"No. The next fellow was just waiting to get his word in. No one was paying any attention to anything. They'd just think Bill's toast pretty dull. I wouldn't have remembered it myself if I hadn't come across the words in the paper when my mind was full of Bill."

"And he never mentioned it again? Never talked about anything like that in his sober moments?"

"No. He isn't much of a talker at the best of times."

"You think, perhaps, if he was greatly interested in something he would keep it to himself?"

"Oh, yes, he does that; he does that. He's not close, you know; just a bit cagey. In most ways he's the most open guy you could imagine. Generous with his roll, and careless with his things, and willing to do anything for anyone. But in the things that—in personal things, if you know what I mean, he sort of shuts the door on you."

"Did he have a girl?"

"Not more than any of us can be said to have one. But that's a very good sample of what I mean. When the rest of us are out for an evening, we take what's going. But Bill will go off by himself to some other quarter of the town where he has picked something more to his fancy."

"What town?"

"Any town we happen to be in. Kuwait, Masquat, Quatif, Mukalla. Anything from Aden to Karachi, if it comes to that. Most of us fly scheduled routes, but some fly tramps. Take anything anywhere."

"What did—does Bill fly?"

"He's flown all sorts. But lately he's been flying between the Gulf and the South Coast."

"Arabia, you mean."

"Yes. It's a damned dreary route but Bill seemed to like it. Me, I think he was too long on it. If you're too long on one route, you get stale."

"Why do you think he was too long on it? Had he changed at all?"

Mr. Cullen hesitated. "Not exactly. He was just the old Bill, easy-going and nice. But he got so that he couldn't leave it behind him."

"Leave his work behind, you mean?"

"Yes. Most of us—all of us, in fact—drop work when we turn the bus over to the ground staff. We don't remember it until we say hello to the mechanic in charge next morning. But Bill got so, that he would pore over maps of the route as if he had never flown the hop before."

"Why this interest in the route, do you think?"

"Well, I did think maybe he was figuring out a way to avoid the bad weather areas. It did begin—the interest in maps, I mean—one time when he came in very late after being blown out of his way by one of those terrific hurricanes that come out of nowhere in that country. We had nearly given him up that time."

"Don't you fly above the weather?"

"On a long hop, of course. But when you're flying freight you have to come down at the oddest places. So you're always more or less at the mercy of the weather."

"I see. And you think Bill changed after that experience?"

"Well, I think it left a mark on him. I was there when he came in. In the plane, I mean. I was waiting for him, on the field. And he seemed to me a bit—concussed, if you get me."

"Suffering from shock."

"Yes. Still back there, if you know what I mean. Not really listening to what you said to him."

"And after that he began to study maps. To plan his route, you think."

"Yes. From then on it was in the forefront of his mind instead of being something that you drop with your working clothes. He even began to come in late as a habit. As if he went out of his way to look for an easier route." He paused a moment, and then added in a quick warning tone, "Please understand, Mr. Grant, I'm not saying Bill has lost his nerve."

"No, of course not."

"Lost nerves don't take you that way at all, believe me. You get quite the opposite. You don't want to think of flying at all. You get short in the temper, and you drink too much and too early in the day, and you try to wangle short hops, and you go sick when there's nothing wrong with you. There's no mystery about lost nerve, Mr. Grant. It announces itself like a name on a marquee. There was nothing like that about Bill—and I don't think there ever will be. It was just that he couldn't leave the thing behind."

"It became an obsession with him."

"That's about it, I suppose."

"Did he have other interests?"

"He read books," Mr. Cullen said, in an apologetic way, as one confessing a peculiarity in a friend. "Even in that, it showed."

"How: showed?"

"I mean, instead of the books being the usual story affairs they'd as likely as not be about Arabia."

"Yes?" Grant said thoughtfully. Ever since this stranger had first mentioned Arabia, Grant had been altogether "with him." Arabia, to all the world meant one thing: sand. And what was more, he realised that when he had had the feeling, that morning in the Scoone hotel, that "singing sands" did actually exist somewhere, it was with Arabia that he should have connected them. Somewhere in Arabia there were in fact sands that were alleged to sing.

"So I was glad when he took his leave earlier than he meant to," Mr. Cullen was saying. "We had planned to go together, and spend our leave in Paris. But he changed his mind and said he wanted a week or two in London first. He's English, you now. So we arranged to meet at the Hotel St. Jacques in Paris. He was to meet me there on the 4th of March."

"*When*?" said Grant, and was suddenly still. Mind and body still, like a pointer with the bird in sight; like a man with the target in his sights.

"The 4th of March. Why?"

Singing sands were anyone's interest. Men who fly for OCAL were two a penny. But the wide, vague, indefinite affair of Bill Kenrick who was obsessed with Southern Arabia and did not turn up to his appointments in Paris narrowed suddenly to one small focused point. To a date.

On the 4th of March, when Bill Kenrick should have turned up in Paris, the London mail had come into Scoone bearing the dead body of a young man who was interested in singing sands. A young man with reckless eyebrows. A young man who, on looks, would have made a very likely flyer. Grant remembered that he had tried him, in imagination, on the bridge of a small ship; a fast small ship, hell in any kind of sea. He had looked well there. But he would look just as well at the controls of a plane.

"Why did Bill choose Paris?"

"Why does anyone choose Paris!"

"It wasn't because he was French?"

"Bill? No, Bill's English. Very English."

"Did you ever see his passport?"

"Not that I can remember. Why?"

"You don't think that he might have been French by birth?"

It wouldn't work out, anyway. The Frenchman was called Martin. Unless his English upbringing had made him want to adopt an English name?

"You don't happen to have a photograph of your friend, do you?"

But Mr. Cullen's attention was on something else. Grant turned to look, and found Zoë was approaching them along the river bank. He looked at his watch.

"Hell!" he said. "And I promised to have the stove going!" He turned to his bag and fished the primus from it.

"Your wife?" asked Mr. Cullen, with that refreshing frankness. In the Islands it would have taken five minutes' conversation to have elicited that information from him.

"No. That's Lady Kentallen."

"Lady? A title?"

"Yes," Grant said, busy with the stove. "She is Viscountess Kentallen."

Mr. Cullen considered this in silence for a little.

"I suppose that's a sort of marked-down Countess."

"No. On the contrary. A very superior kind. Practically a Marchioness. Look, Mr. Cullen, let's postpone this matter of your friend for a little. It's a matter that interests me more than I can say, but—"

"Yes, of course. I'll go. When can I talk to you again about it?"

"Of course you will not go! You'll stay and have some food with us."

"You mean you want me to meet this Marchioness, this —what-you-may-call-it, Viscountess?"

"Why not? She is a very nice person to meet. One of the nicest persons I know."

"Yes?" Mr. Cullen looked with interest at the approaching Zoë. "She's certainly very nice to look at. I didn't know they come like that. Somehow I imagined all aristocrats had beaky noses."

"Specially provided for looking down, I take it."

"Something like that."

"I don't know how far back in English history one would have to go to find an aristocratic nose that was looked down. I doubt if you'd find one at all. The only place to find a looked-down nose is in the suburbs. In what is known as lower-middle-class circles."

Mr. Cullen looked puzzled. "But the aristocrats keep themselves to themselves and look down on the rest, don't they?"

"It has never been possible in England for any class to keep themselves to themselves, as you call it. They have been intermarrying at all levels for two thousand years. There never have been separate and distinct classes—or an aristocratic class at all in the sense that you mean it."

"I suppose nowadays things are evening up," Mr. Cullen suggested, faintly unbelieving.

"Oh, no. It has always been a fluid thing. Even our Royalty. Elizabeth the First was the grand-daughter of a Lord Mayor. And you'll find that Royalty's personal friends have no titles at all: I mean the people who are on calling-terms at Buckingham Palace. Whereas the bold bad baron who sits next you in an expensive restaurant probably started life as a platelayer on the railway. There *is* no keeping oneself to oneself in England, as far as class goes. It can't be done. It can only be done by Mrs. Jones who sniffs at her neighbour Mrs. Smith because Mr. Jones makes two pounds a week more than Mr. Smith."

He turned from the puzzled American to greet Zoë.

"I'm truly sorry about the stove. I'm afraid I got it going too late to be ready. We were having a very interesting

107

conversation. This is Mr. Cullen, who flies freight for Oriental Commercial Airlines."

Zoë shook hands, and asked him what kind of plane he flew.

From the tone of his voice when he told her, Grant deduced that Mr. Cullen thought that Zoë was merely taking a condescending interest. Condescension was what he would expect from an "aristocrat."

"They're very heavy in hand, aren't they?" Zoë remarked sympathetically. "My brother used to fly one when he was on the Australia run. He was always cursing it." She began to open the packets of food. "But now that he works in an office in Sydney he has a little runabout of his own. A Beamish Eight. A lovely thing. I used to fly it when he first bought it, before he took it to Australia. David—my husband—and I used to dream of having one too, but we could never afford it."

"But a Beamish Eight costs only four hundred," Mr. Cullen blurted.

Zoë licked her fingers, sticky from a leaking apple tart, and said, "Yes, I know, but we never had four hundred to spare."

Mr. Cullen, feeling himself being washed out to sea, sought some terra firma.

"I oughtn't to be eating your food this way," he said. "They'll have plenty for me back at the hotel. I really ought to go back."

"Oh, don't go," Zoë said with a simplicity so genuine that it penetrated even Mr. Cullen's defences. "There is enough for a platoon."

So to Grant's pleasure in more ways than one, Mr. Cullen stayed. And Zoë, unaware that she was providing the United States with a revised view of the genus English Aristocrat, ate like a hungry schoolboy and talked in her gentle voice to the stranger as if she had known him all her life. By the apple-tart stage, Mr. Cullen had ceased to be on his guard. By the time that they were handing round the chocolates that Laura had included, he had surrendered unconditionally.

They sat together in the spring sunshine, full-fed and content. Zoë lying back against the grassy bank with her feet crossed and her hands behind her head, her eyes closed against the sun; Grant with his mind busy with B Seven, and the material that Tad Cullen had brought him; Mr. Cullen himself perched on a rock looking down the river to the green civilised strath where the moors ended and the fields began.

"It's a fine little country, this," he said. "I like it. If you ever decide to fight for your freedom, count me in."

"Freedom?" said Zoë, opening her eyes. "Freedom from whom or what?"

"From England, of course."

Zoë looked helpless, but Grant began to laugh. "I think you must have been talking to a little black man in a kilt," he said.

"He had a kilt, yes, but he wasn't coloured," Mr. Cullen said.

"No, I meant black-haired. You've been talking to Archie Brown."

"Who is Archie Brown?" asked Zoë.

"He is the self-appointed saviour of Gaeldom, and our future Sovereign, Commissar, President, or what have you, when Scotland has freed herself from the murderous burden of the English yoke."

"Oh, yes, that man," Zoë, said mildly, identifying Archie in her mind. "He is a little off his head, isn't he? Does he live around here?"

"He is staying at the hotel at Moymore, I understand. He has been doing missionary work on Mr. Cullen, it seems."

"Well," Mr. Cullen grinned a little sheepishly, "I did just wonder if he wasn't over-stating things a bit. I've met some Scots in my time and they didn't seem to me to be the kind of people to put up with the treatment Mr. Brown was describing. Indeed, if you'll forgive me, Mr. Grant, they always seemed to me the kind of people to get the best of whatever bargain was going."

"Did you ever hear the Union better described?" Grant said to Zoë.

"I never knew anything about the Union," Zoë said comfortably, "except that it took place in 1707."

"Was there a battle, then?" Mr. Cullen asked.

"No," Grant said. "Scotland stepped thankfully on to England's band-wagon, and fell heir to all the benefits. Colonies, Shakespeare, soap, solvency, and so forth."

"I hope Mr. Brown doesn't go lecture-touring in the States," Zoë said, half asleep.

"He will," Grant said. "He will. All vociferous minorities go lecture-touring in the States."

"It will give them very wrong ideas, won't it?" Zoë said

mildly. Grant thought with what a blistering phrase Laura would have expressed the same idea. "They have the oddest ideas. When David and I were there, the year before he was killed, we were always being asked why we didn't stop taxing Canada. When we said we had never taxed Canada they just looked at us as if we were telling lies. Not very good lies, either."

From Mr. Cullen's expression Grant deduced that he too had had "odd" ideas about Canadian taxation, but Zoë's eyes were closed. Grant wondered if Mr. Cullen realised that Zoë was quite unaware that he was an American; that it had not occurred to her to consider his accent, his nationality, his clothes or any personal thing about him. She had accepted him as he stood, as a person. He was just a flyer, like her brother; someone who had turned up in time to share their picnic and who was pleasant and interesting to talk to. It would not occur to her to pigeon-hole him, to put him in any special category. If she was conscious at all of his narrow *as* she no doubt took him for a North-countryman.

He looked at her, half asleep there in the sun, and thought how beautiful she was. He looked across at Mr. Cullen and saw that he too was looking at Zoë Kentallen and thinking how beautiful she was. Their glances met and ran away from each other.

Bu Grant, who last night could imagine no greater felicity than to sit and look at Zoë Kentallen, was conscious now of a faint impatience with her, and this so shocked him that he took it out, in his self-analytical way, to examine it. What flaw could there be in this divinity? What imperfection in this princess from a fairytale?

"You know very well what's wrong," said that irreverent voice in him. "You want her to get the hell out of here so that you can find out about B Seven."

And for once he did not try to contradict the voice. He did in brutal fact wish that Zoë would "get the hell out of here." The Zoë whose very presence had made magic of yesterday afternoon was now an encumbrance. Tiny prickles of boredom chased each other up and down his spine. Lovely, simple, heavenly Zoë, do get a move on. Creature of delight and princess of my dreams, go away.

He was rehearsing phrases for taking his own departure, when she gave the abrupt half-sigh half-yawn of a child and said, "Well, there is a seven-pounder in the Cuddy Pool that must be finding life dull without me." And with her usual lack of fuss or chat she took her things and departed into the spring afternoon.

Mr. Cullen looked after her approvingly, and Grant waited for comment. But it seemed that Mr. Cullen too had been waiting for the departure of his "marked-down Countess." He watched her out of earshot and then said immediately:

"Mr. Grant, why did you ask me if I had a photograph of Bill? Does that mean that you think you know him?"

"No. No. But it would eliminate people who could not be Bill."

"Oh. Yes. Well, I haven't one in my pocket but I have one in my grip at the hotel. It isn't a very good one, but it would give you the general idea. Could I bring it to you some time?"

"No. I'll walk down to Moymore with you now."

"You will? You're certainly very kind, Mr. Grant. You think you've got a line on this thing? You haven't told me what those words were. That quotation or whatever it was. That's really what I came to ask you. What the talking-beasts thing was all about. If it was a place he was interested in, you see, he might have gone there, and I could go there too and cross his trail that way."

"You're very fond of this Bill, aren't you?"

"Well, we've been together quite a time, and though we're opposites in most ways we get along fine. Just fine. I wouldn't like anything to happen to Bill."

Grant changed the conversation and asked about Tad Cullen's own life. And while they walked down the glen to Moymore, he heard about the clean small town back in the States, and what a dull place it seemed to a boy who could fly, and how wonderful the East had seemed in the distance and how unexciting close up.

"Just Main Street with smells," Mr. Cullen said.

"What did you do in Paris during your long wait for Bill to turn up?"

"Oh, I helled around some. It wasn't much fun without Bill. I met a couple of fellows I'd known in India, and we went places together, but I was impatient all the time for Bill to be there. I let them go, after a bit, and went to look at some of the places in the tourist folders. Some of those old places are pretty nice. There was one place built right over the water—a castle, I mean—on stone arches, so that the river flowed underneath. That was fine. It would have done very well for the Countess. Is that the kind of place she lives in?"

"No," Grant said, thinking of the difference between Chenonceaux and Kentallen. "She lives in a grim flat grey house with tiny windows and poky rooms and narrow stairs and a front door as welcoming as the exit of a laundry chute. It has two little turrets on the fourth-storey level, next the roof, and in Scotland that makes it a castle."

"Sounds like a prison. Why does she stay?"

"A prison! No prison committee would consider it for a moment; questions would be asked in the House immediately about its lack of light, heating, sanitary conveniences, colour, beauty, space, and what not. She stays because she loves the place. I doubt if she can stay much longer, however. Death duties have been so heavy that she will have to sell."

"But will anyone buy it?"

"Not to live in. But some speculator will buy it, and cut down the woods. The lead on the roof would probably fetch something; and they'd have to take the roof off anyhow to avoid paying tax on the house."

"Hah! Dust-bowl stuff," remarked Mr. Cullen. "It hasn't a moat, by any chance?"

"No. Why?"

"I must see a moat before I go back to OCAL." And then, after a pause, "I'm really very woried about Bill, Mr. Grant."

"Yes, it is certainly very odd."

"That was nice of you." Mr. Cullen said unexpectedly.

"What was?"

"Not to say, 'Don't you worry, he'll turn up all right!' I can hardly keep my hands off people who say, 'Don't you worry, he'll turn up.' I could strangle them."

Moymore Hotel was a tiny version of Kentallen, without the turrets. But it was whitewashed and cheerful, and the trees behind it were coming into leaf. In the little flagged entrance-hall Mr. Cullen hesitated.

"In Britain I notice people don't ask you up to their hotel bedroom. Would you like to wait in the sitting-room, perhaps?"

"Oh, no; I'll come up. I don't think we have any feeling about hotel bedrooms. It is probably just that our hotel sitting-rooms are so near our bedrooms that there is no need to go up, and so we don't suggest it. When a public lounge is a day's journey from your own room, it is easier to take a guest with you, I suppose. That way you are at least in the same hemisphere."

Mr. Cullen had a front room, looking across the road to the fields and the river and the hills beyond. With his professional eye Grant noticed the log fire ready-laid in the hearth and the daffodils in the window: Moymore had standards. With his personal mind he was concerned for this Tad Cullen, who had interrupted his leave and come to the wilds of Caledonia to find the friend who meant so much to him. A foreboding that he could not shake off had grown in him with every step of the way to Moymore, and now it filled him to the point of nausea.

The young man took a letter-case from his travelling-bag and opened it on the dressing-table. It contained practically everything but the wherewithal for writing letters. Among the mess of papers, maps, travel folders, and what not, there were two leather articles: an address-book and a pocket-book. From the pocket-book he took some photographs and riffled through the feminine smiles until he found what he was looking for.

"Here it is. I'm afraid it isn't a very good one. It's just a snapshot, you see. It was taken when a crowd of us were at the beach."

Grant took the proffered piece of paper, almost reluctantly.

"That's—" Tad Cullen was beginning, lifting his arm to point.

"No, wait!" Grant said, stopping him. "Let me see if I— if I recognise anyone."

There were perhaps a dozen young men in the photograph, which had been taken on the verandah of some beach-house. They were clustered round the steps and draped over the rickety wooden railing in various stages of *déshabillé*. Grant swept a swift glance over their laughing faces and was conscious of a great relief. There was no one there that he had ever—

And then he saw the man on the bottom step.

He was sitting with his feet pushed away from him into the sand, his eyes screwed up against the sun and his chin tilted back a little as if he had been in the act of turning to say something to the men behind. It was just so that his head had been tilted back against the pillow in Compartment B Seven on the morning of the 4th of March.

"Well?"

"Is that your friend?" Grant said, pointing to the man on the bottom step.

"Yes, that's Bill. How did you know? Have you met him somewhere, then?"

"I—I'm inclined to think that I have. But of course, on that photograph, I could hardly swear to it."

"I don't want you to do any swearing. Just give me a general weather report. Just tell me roughly when and where you saw him and I'll track him down, don't you be in any doubt about it. Do you know where you met him? I mean, do you remember?"

"Oh, yes. I remember. I saw him in a compartment—a sleeping-berth compartment—of the London mail when it was running into Scoone early in the morning of the 4th of March. That was the train I came north on."

"You mean Bill came *here*? To Scotland? What for?"

"I don't know."

"Didn't he tell you? Did you talk to him?"

"No. I couldn't."

Why not?"

Grant put out his hand and pushed his companion gently backwards so that he sat down in the chair that was behind him.

"I couldn't because he was no longer alive."

There was a short silence.

"I'm truly sorry, Cullen. I wish I could pretend to you that it might not be Bill, but short of going into a witness-box on oath I am prepared to back my belief that it is."

After another little silence Cullen said: "Why was he dead? What happened to him?"

"He had had a fair load of whiskey and he fell backwards against the solid procelain wash-basin. It fractured his skull."

"Who said all this?"

"That was the finding of the coroner's court. In London."

"In London? Why in London?"

"Because he had died, according to the post-mortem, very shortly after leaving Euston. And by English law, a sudden death is investigated by a coroner and a jury."

"But all that's just—just supposition," Cullen said, beginning to come alive and be angry. "If he was alone, how can anyone tell what happened to him?"

"Because the English police are the most painstaking creatures as well as the most suspicious."

"Police? There were police in on this thing?"

"Oh, assuredly. The police do the investigating and report in public to the coroner and his jury. In this case there had been the most exhaustive examination and tests. They knew in the end almost to a mouthful how much neat whisky he had drunk, and at what intervals before his—his death."

"And that about his falling backwards—how could they know that?"

"They went prowling with microscopes. The oil and broken hair were still evident on the edge of the basin. And the skull injury was consistent with a backwards fall against just such an object."

Cullen calmed down at this, but he looked disorientated.

"How do you know all this?" he asked, vaguely; and then with growing suspicion, "How did you come to see him anyway?"

"When I was on my way out, I came across the sleeping-car attendant trying to rouse him. The man thought he was just sleeping it off, because the whisky bottle had rolled all over the floor, and the compartment smelt as if he had been making a night of it."

This did not satisfy Cullen. "You mean that was the only time you saw him? Just for a moment, lying—lying dead there, and you could recognise him from a snapshot —a not very good snapshot—weeks later?"

"Yes. I was impressed by his face. Faces are my business, and in a way my hobby. I was interested in the way the slant of the eyebrows gave the face a reckless expression, even—even as it was, without any real expression whatever. And the interest was intensified in a way that was quite accidental."

"What was that?" Cullen was not giving an inch.

"When I was having breakfast, in the Station Hotel at Scoone, I found that I had picked up by accident a newspaper that had been tumbled off the berth when the Press —the blank space, you know—someone had been pencilling some lines of verse. 'The beasts that talk, the streams that stand, the stones that walk, the singing sand—' then two blank lines, and then, 'that guard the way to Paradise.' "

"That was what you advertised about," Cullen said, his face growing momentarily blacker. "What was it to you that you went to the trouble of advertising about it?"

"I wanted to know where the lines came from if they

were lines from some book. If they were lines in the process of being made into a poem, then I wanted to know what the subject was."

"Why? What should you care?"

"I had no choice in the matter. The thing ran round and round in my head. Do you know ányone called Charles Martin?"

"No, I don't. And don't change the subject."

"I'm not changing the subject, oddly enough. Do me the kindness to think of it seriously for a moment. Have you ever, at any time, heard of or known a Charles Martin?"

"I've told you, no! I don't have to think. And *of course* you're changing the subject! What has Charles Martin got to do with this?"

According to the police, the man who was found dead in Compartment B Seven was a French mechanic called Charles Martin."

After a moment Cullen said: "Look, Mr. Grant, maybe I'm not very bright, but you're not making sense. What you're saying is that you saw Bill Kenrick lying dead in a compartment of a train, but he wasn't Bill Kenrick at all; he was a man called Martin."

"No, what I'm saying is that the police believe him to be a man called Martin."

"Well, I take it they have good grounds for their belief."

"Excellent grounds. He had letters, and identity papers. Even better, his people have identified him."

"They did! Then what have you been stringing me along for! There isn't any suggestion that that man was Bill! If the police are satisfied that the man was a Frenchman called Martin, why in thunder should you decide that he wasn't Martin at all but Bill Kenrick!"

"Because I'm the only person in the world who has seen both the man in B Seven and that snapshot." Grant nodded at the photograph where it lay on the dressing-table.

This gave Cullen pause. Then he said: "But that's a poor photograph. It can't convey much to someone who has never seen Bill."

"It may be a poor photograph in the sense that it is a mere snapshot, but it is a very good likeness indeed."

"Yes," Cullen said slowly, "it is."

"Consider three things, three facts. One: Charles Martin's people had not seen him for years, and then they saw only a dead face; if you are told that your son has died, and no one suggests that there is any doubt as to identity, you see the face you expected to see. Two: the man known as Charles Martin was found dead on a train on the same day as Bill Kenrick was due to join you in Paris. Three: in his compartment there was a pencilled jingle about talking beasts and singing sands, a subject that on your own showing had interested Bill Kenrick."

"Did you tell the police about the paper?"

"I tried to. They weren't interested. There was no mystery, you see. They knew who the man was, and how he died, and that was all that concerned them."

"It might have interested them that he was writing verse in English."

"Oh, no. There is no evidence that he wrote anything, or that the paper belonged to him at all. He may have picked it up somewhere."

"The whole thing's crazy," Cullen said, angry and bewildered.

"It's fantastic. But at the heart of all the whirling absurdity there is a small core of stillness."

"Yes?"

"Yes. There is one small clear space on which one can stand while taking one's bearings."

"What is that?"

"Your friend Bill Kenrick is missing. And out of a crowd of strange faces, I pick Bill Kenrick as a man I saw dead in a sleeping-compartment at Scoone on the morning of the 4th of March."

Cullen thought this over. "Yes," he said drearily, "I suppose that makes sense. I suppose it must be Bill. I suppose I knew all the time that something—something awful had happened. He would never have left me without word. He would have written or telephoned or something to say why he hadn't turned up on time. But what was he doing on a train to Scotland? What was he doing on a train anyhow?"

"How: anyhow?"

"If Bill wanted to go somewhere, he would fly. He wouldn't take a train."

"Lots of people take a night train because it saves time. You sleep and travel at the same time. The question is: why as Charles Martin?"

"I think it's a case for Scotland Yard."

"I don't think the Yard would thank us."

"I'm not asking for their thanks," Cullen said tartly.

"I'm instructing them to find out what happened to my buddy."

"I still don't think they would be interested."

"They'd better be!"

"You have no evidence at all that Bill Kenrick didn't duck of his own accord; that he isn't having a goodtime on his own until it is time to go back to OCAL."

"But he was found dead in a railway compartment!" Cullen said in a voice that was nearly a howl.

"Oh, no. That was Charles Martin. About whom there is no mystery whatever."

"But you can identify Martin as Kenrick!"

"I can say, of course, that in my opinion that face in the snapshot is the face I saw in Compartment B Seven on the morning of March the 4th. Scotland Yard will say that I am entitled to my opinion, but that I am without doubt misled by a resemblance, since the man in Compartment B Seven is one Charles Martin, a mechanic, and a native of Marseilles, in the suburbs of which his parents still live."

"You're very smooth in the part of Scotland Yard, aren't you? All the same—"

"I ought to be. I've worked there for more years than I care to think about. I shall be going back there a week Monday, as soon as my holiday is over."

"You mean that *you* are Scotland Yard?"

"Not the whole of it. One of its minor props. Props in the support sense. I don't carry cards in my fishing clothes, but if you come up to my host's house with me he will vouch for my genuineness."

"Oh. No. No, of course I believe you, Mr.—er—"

"Inspector. But we'll stick to Mr., since I'm off duty."

"I'm sorry if I was fresh. It just didn't occur to me— You see, you don't expect to meet Scotland Yard in real life. It's just something you read about. You don't expect them to—to—"

"To go fishing."

"No, I guess you don't, at that. Only in books."

"Well, now that you have accepted me as genuine, and you know that my version of Scotland Yard's reaction is not only accurate but straight from the horse's mouth, what are we going to do?"

10

When Laura heard next morning that Grant intended to go in to Scoone instead of spending the day on the river, she was indignant.

"But I've just made up a wonderful luncheon for you and Zoë," she said. He was left with the impression that her dismay was rooted in some cause more valid than a miscalculated meal, but his mind was too busy with more important matters to analyse trivialities.

"There's a young American staying at Moymore who has come to ask my help about something. I thought that he might take my place on the river, if no one has any objection. He has fished quite a bit, he tells me. Perhaps Pat would like to show him the ropes."

Pat had come to breakfast in a state so radiant that the glow of it could be felt clear across the table. It was the first day of the Easter holidays. He looked with interest when he heard his cousin's suggestion. There were few things in life that he enjoyed so much as showing someone something.

"What's his name?" he asked.

"Tad Cullen."

"What's 'Tad'?"

"I don't know. Short for Theodore, perhaps."

"M-m-m," said Pat doubtfully.

"He's a flyer."

"Oh," said Pat, his brow clearing. "I thought maybe with a name like that he was a professor."

"No. He flies to and fro across Arabia."

"Arabia!" said Pat, rolling the *r* so that the mundane Scots breakfast table scintillated with reflections of the jewelled East. Between modern transport and ancient Bagdad, Tad Cullen seemed to have satisfactory credentials. Pat would "show him" with pleasure.

"Of course Zoë gets first choice of places to fish," Pat said.

If Grant had imagined that Pat's infatuation would take the form of blushing silences and a mooning adoration, he was wrong. Pat's only sign of surrender was the constant interjection of "me and Zoë" into his conversation; and it was to be observed that the personal pronoun still came first.

Grant borrowed the car after breakfast and went down to Moymore to tell Tad Cullen that a small boy with red hair and a green kilt would be waiting for him, with all appliances and means to boot, by the swing bridge across the Turlie. He himself would be back from Scoone in time to join them on the river some time in the afternoon, he hoped.

"I'd like to come with you, Mr. Grant," Cullen said. "Have you got a line on this thing? Is that why you're going in to Scoone this morning?"

"No. It's to look for a line that I'm going in. There's not a thing you can do just now, so you might as well have a day on the river."

"All right, Mr. Grant. You're the boss. What's your young friend's name?"

"Pat Rankin," Grant said, and drove away to Scoone.

He had spent most of last night lying awake with his eyes on the ceiling, letting the patterns in his mind slip and fade into each other like trick camera work in a film. Constantly the patterns materialised and broke and dissolved, never the same for two moments together. He lay supine and let them dance their endless slow interlacing; taking no part in their gyrations, as detached as if they were a display of Northern Lights.

It was that way his mind worked best. It would also work the other way, of course. Work very well. In problems involving a time-place sequence, for instance. In matters where A was at a spot X at 5:30 P.M. on the umpteenth inst., Grant's mind worked with the tidiness of a calculating machine. But in an affair where motive was all, he sat back and let his mind loose on the problem. Presently, if he left it alone, it would throw up the pattern that he needed.

He still had no idea why Bill Kenrick had journeyed to the north of Scotland when he should have been travelling to Paris to meet his friend, still less had he any idea why he should have been travelling with another man's papers. But he was beginning to have an idea as to why Bill Kenrick developed his sudden interest in Arabia. Cullen, looking at the world from his limited, flyer's point of view, had thought of that interest in terms of flying routes. But Grant was sure that the interest had other origins. On Cullen's own showing, Kenrick had exhibited none of the usual signs of "nerves." It was unlikely that his obsession with the route he flew had anything to do with weather in any of its forms. Somewhere, some time, on one of those flights over that "damned dreary" route, Kenrick had found something that interested him. And that interest had begun on an occasion when he had been blown far off his course by one of the dust-storms that haunted the interior of Arabia. He had come back from that experience "concussed," "not listening to what was said to him," "still back there."

So this morning Grant was going in to Scoone to find out what might possibly have interested Bill Kenrick in the interior of that bleak and stony immensity, in the desert and forbidding half-continent that was Arabia. And for that, of course, he was going to Mr. Tallisker. Whether it was the rateable value of a cottage or the composition of lava that one wanted to be enlightened about, one went to Mr. Tallisker.

The public library in Scoone was deserted at that hour of the morning, and he found Mr. Tallisker having a doughnut and a cup of coffee. Grant thought the doughnut an endearingly childish and robust choice for a man who looked as though he lived on gaufrettes and China tea with lemon. Mr. Tallisker was delighted to see Grant, asked how his study of the Islands was progressing, listened with interest to Grant's heretic account of that Paradise, and was helpful about his new search. Arabia? Oh, yes, they had a whole shelf of books about the country. Almost as

121

many people wrote books about Arabia as about the Hebrides. There was, too, if Mr. Tallisker might be permitted to say so, the same tendency to idealise the subject in its devotees.

"You think that, boiled down to plain fact, they are both just windy deserts."

Oh, no; not entirely. That was being a little—wholesale. Mr. Tallisker had had much happiness and beauty from the Islands. But the tendency to idealise a primitive people was perhaps the same in each case. And here was the shelf of books on the subject, and he would leave Mr. Grant to study them at his leisure.

The books were in a reference room, and there was no other reader there. The door closed on the silence and he was left with his search. He went through the row of books very much as he had gone through the row about the Hebrides in the sitting-room at Clune, gutting each book with a swift, practised eye. The range was much the same as it had been in the earlier case: all the way from the sentimentalists to the scientists. The only difference was that in this case some of the books were classics, as befitted a classic subject.

If Grant had had any last lingering doubt that the man in B Seven was Bill Kenrick, it went when he found that the desert part of south-eastern Arabia, the Empty Quarter, was called the Rub'al-Khali.

So that was what "robbing the Caley" had been!

After that he devoted his interest to the Empty Quarter, picking each book from the shelf, flipping through the pages on this one region, and putting it back again to go on to the next. And presently a phrase caught his eye: "Inhabited by monkeys." Monkeys, said his mind. Talking beasts. He turned the page back to see what the paragraph had been talking about.

It was talking about Wabar.

Wabar, it seemed, was the Atlantis of Arabia. The fabled city of Ad ibn Kin'ad. Somewhere in the time between legend and history it had been destroyed by fire for its sins. For it had been rich and sinful beyond the power of words to express. Its palaces had housed the most beautiful concubines and its stables the most perfect horses in the world, the one no less finely decked than the other. It stood in country so fertile that one had only to reach out a hand to pluck the fruits of the soil. There was infinite

122

leisure to sin old sins and devise new ones. So destruction had come on the city. It had come in a night, with cleansing fire. And now Wabar, the fabled city, was a cluster of ruins guarded by the shifting sands, by cliffs of stone that forever changed place and form; and inhabited by a monkey race and by evil jinns. No one could approach the place because the jinns blew dust-storms in the faces of those who sought it.

That was Wabar.

And no one, it seemed, had ever found the ruins, although every Arabian explorer had looked for them, openly or secretly. Indeed, no two explorers agreed as to which part of Arabia the legend referred to. Grant went back through the various volumes, using the magic key, the word Wabar, and found that each authority had his own pet theory, and that the argued sites lay as far apart as Oman and the Yemen. None of the writers, he noticed, attempted to belittle or discount the legend as palliation of their failure; the story was universal in Arabia and constant in its form, and sentimentalist and scientist alike believed that it had its basis in fact. It had been every explorer's dream to be the discoverer of Wabar, but the sands and the jinns and the mirages had guarded it well.

"It is probable," wrote one of the greatest, "that when the fabled city is at last found it will be by no striving or calculation but by accident."

By accident.

By a flyer blown off his course by a dust-storm?

Was that what Bill Kenrick had seen when he came out of the solid brown cloud of sand that had blinded and buffeted him? Empty palaces in the sand? Was that what he had gone out of his way to look for—perhaps to look at— when he "began to come in late as a habit?"

He had said nothing after that first experience. And that, if what he had seen was a city in the sand, was understandable. He would have been teased about it: teased about mirages, and one over the eight, and what not. Even if any of the OCAL boys had ever heard the legend—and in so shifting, so easy-come a crowd it was unlikely—they would still have teased him about wish-fathered ideas. So Bill, who wrote those tight-closed *ms* and *ns* and was "just a bit cagey," said nothing and went back to have another look. Went back again and again. Either because he wanted to find the place he had seen, or to look at a place he had already pin-pointed.

He studied maps. He read books about Arabia. And then—

Then he decided to come to England.

He had arranged to go to Paris with Tad Cullen. But instead he wanted to little time by himself in England. He had no people in England. He had not been in England for years, and according to Cullen had never seemed homesick for the place nor written to anyone there in any kind of regular correspondence. He had been brought up by an aunt when his parents were killed, and she too was now dead. He had never until then had any desire to go back to England.

Grant sat back and let the stillness fall round him. He could almost hear the dust coming to rest. Year after year the dust falling in the quiet. Like Wabar.

Bill Kenrick came to England. And about three weeks later, when he is due to meet his friend in Paris, he turns up in Scotland as Charles Martin.

Grant could imagine why he wanted to come to England, but why the masquerade? Why the flying visit to the North?

Whom was he going to visit as Charles Martin?

He could have paid that flying visit and still have met his friend in Paris on the appointed date if it had not been for the accident of his tipsy fall. He could have interviewed someone in the Highlands and then flown from Scoone to meet his friend at the Hotel St. Jacques for dinner.

But why as Charles Martin?

Grant put the books back on their shelf with an approving pat that he had never wasted on the Hebrides selection, and went to call on Mr. Tallisker in his little office. He had at least got his line on Kenrick. He knew how to cross his trail.

"Who would you say was the greatest authority on Arabia in England today?" he asked Mr. Tallisker.

Mr. Tallisker waved his beribboned pince-nez and smiled in a deprecating way. There were what might be termed a swarm of successors to Thomas and Philby and the other great names, he said, but he supposed that only Heron Lloyd ranked as a really great authority. It was possible that he, Mr. Tallisker, was prejudiced in Lloyd's favour because he was the only one of the crowd who wrote English that was literature, but it was true that apart from his gifts as a writer he had stature and integrity and

124

a great reputation. He had done some spectacular journeys in the course of his various explorations, and had considerable standing among the Arabs.

Grant thanked Mr. Tallisker and went away to look up *Who's Who*. He wanted Heron Lloyd's address.

Then he went to have a meal; and instead of going to the Caledonian, which was convenient and sufficiently bestarred, he obeyed an obscure impulse and walked to the other side of the town so that he could eat where he had eaten breakfast with the shade of B Seven on that dark morning only a few weeks ago.

There was no half-lit gloom in the dining-room today; the place was starched and shining, silver, glass, and linen. There was even a shirt-front where a head waiter hovered. But there was also Mary, calm and comfortable and plump as she had been that morning. He remembered how in need of soothing and reassurance he had been, and could hardly believe that that tortured and exhausted creature could have been himself.

He sat down at the same table, near the screens in front of the service door, and Mary came to take his order and to ask how the fishing on the Turlie was these days.

"How did you know I was fishing the Turlie?"

"You were with Mr. Rankin when you came in for breakfast, off the train."

Off the train. He had come off the train after that night of conflict and suffering; that loathsome night. He had come off the train, leaving B Seven dead there with a casual glance and a passing moment of regret. But B Seven had paid back a hundred-fold that moment of easy compassion. B Seven had come with him and in the end had saved him. It was B Seven who had sent him to the Islands, on that mad, cold, blown search for nothing. In that strange absurd limbo he had done all those things that he could never have done elsewhere; he had laughed till the tears ran, he had danced, he had let himself be flung about like a leaf from one empty horizon to the next, he had sung, he had sat still and looked. And he had come back a whole man. He owed B Seven more than he could ever repay.

He thought about Bill Kenrick while he had his luncheon; the young man who had had no roots. Had he been lonely in his unattached life, or just free? And if free, was it a swallow's freedom, or an eagle's? A sun-seeking skimming, or a soaring lordliness?

At least he had had a trait that in all climes and ages had been both rare and endearing: he was the man of action who was also by instinct a poet. It was what distinguished him from the light-come crowds of OCAL employees who spun their airy patterns across the continents as unthinking as mosquitoes. It was what distinguished him from the milling five-o'clock crowds in a London railway station to whom adventure was half-a-crown each way. If the dead boy in B Seven had been neither a Sidney nor a Grenfell, he had at least been of their kind.

And for that Grant loved him.

He over-tipped Mary and went away to book two seats on the morning plane to London. He had still more than a week of holiday to come, and the Turlie still swarmed with fish, beautiful silver clean-run fighting fish, but he had other business. Since yesterday afternoon he had only one business: Bill Kenrick.

He had qualms about the air journey to London, but not very serious qualms. He could hardly recognise, when he looked back at him, the demon-ridden frightened creature who had stepped down on to Scoone platform from the London mail less than a month ago. All that was left of that deplorable object was a slight fear of being afraid.

The terror itself was no longer there.

He bought enough sweets for Patrick to keep him sick for three months on end, and drove back to the hills. He was afraid that the sweets were a little too elegant to please Patrick entirely—a little too "jessie-like" perhaps —since Pat's avowed favourites were something in Mr. Mair's window labelled Ogo-Pogo Eyes. But Laura would no doubt dole out the Scoone ones in driblets anyway.

He halted the car above the river, half-way between Moymore and Scoone, and went down across the moor to look for Tad Cullen. It was still early afternoon, and he would not yet have finished his after-luncheon spell on the river.

He had not yet begun it. As Grant came to the edge of the moor and looked down at the river's immediate hollow, he saw below him in the mid-distance a small group of three persons, idle and relaxed on the bank. Zoë was propped in her favourite position against a rock, and on either side of her, on a level with her crossed feet and a gazing at her with an unwavering attention, were her two followers: Pat Rankin and Tad Cullen. Looking at them, amused and indulgent, Grant became aware that Bill Kenrick had done him a final service for which he had not yet had credit. Bill Kenrick had saved him from falling in love with Zoë Kentallen.

A few more hours would have done it. A few more hours in her uninterrupted company, and he would have been involved past recovery. Bill Kenrick had intervened just in time.

It was Pat who saw him first and came to meet him and bring him back to the company as children and dogs do to those of whom they approve. Zoë tilted her head back to watch him come and said: "You haven't missed anything, Mr. Grant. No one has had a nibble all day. Would you like to take my rod for a little? Perhaps a change of rhythm will fetch them."

Grant said that he would like that very much, since his time for fishing was running out.

"You have still a week to catch everything in the river," she said.

Grant wondered how she had known that. "No," he said, "I am going back to London tomorrow morning," and for the first time saw Zoë react to a stimulus as an adult would. The instant regret on her face was as vivid as that on Pat's, but unlike Pat she controlled and removed it. She said in her polite gentle voice how sorry she was, but her face no longer showed any emotion. It was her fairy-tale face again, the Hans Andersen illustration.

Before he could consider the phenomenon, Tad Cullen said: "Can I come back with you, Mr. Grant? To London."

"I meant you to. I've booked two seats on the morning plane."

In the end Grant took the rod that Tad Cullen was using —a spare one from Clune—so that they could go downriver together and talk. But Zoë made no motion to continue her fishing.

"I've had enough," she said, unjointing her rod. "I think I shall go back to Clune and write some letters."

Pat stood irresolute, still like a friendly dog between two allegiances, and then said, "I'm going back with Zoe."

He said it, Grant thought, almost as if he were championing her instead of merely accompanying her; as if he had joined an Unfair-to-Zoë movement. But since no one could ever think of being unfair to Zoë, his attitude was surely unnecessary.

From the rock where he sat with Tad Cullen to give him the news, he watched the two figures grow small across the moor, and wondered a little at that sudden withdrawal, at the dispirited air that hung about her progress. She looked like a discouraged child, tired and trailing homeward unexpectant. Perhaps the thought of David, her husband, had suddenly drowned her. That was the way with grief: it left you alone for months together until you thought that you were cured, and then without warning it blotted out the sunlight.

"But that wouldn't be much to get excited about, would it?" Tad Cullen was saying.

"What wouldn't?"

"This ancient city you're talking about. Would anyone get all that excited about it? I mean, about a few ruins. Ruins are two a nickel in the world nowadays."

"Not these, they aren't," Grant said, forgetting Zoë. "The man who found Wabar would make history."

"I thought when you said he had found something important, you were going to say munition works in the desert or something like that."

"Now that really *is* something that is two for a nickel!"

"What?"

"Secret munition plants. No one who found one of those would be a celebrity."

Tad's ears pricked. "A celebrity? You mean the man who found this place would be a celebrity?"

"I've already said so."

"No. You just said he would make history."

"True. Too true." Grant said. "The terms are not synonymous any more. Yes, he would be a celebrity. Tutankhamen's tomb would be nothing to it."

"And you think Bill will have gone to see this fellow, this Lloyd guy?"

"If not to him, then to someone else in the line. He wanted to talk to someone who would take what he had to tell as a serious matter; I mean, who would not just tease him about seeing things. And he wanted to meet someone who would be personally interested and excited by his news. Well, he would do just what I did. He would go to a museum, or a library, or perhaps even to one of the Information Departments, and find out who the best-known English explorer of Arabia happened to be. He would probably be given a choice, since librarians and curators are pedantic people and Information Departments subject to the law of libel, but Lloyd is head and shoulders above the others because he writes almost as well as he explores. He is the household word of the bunch, so to speak. So the chances are twenty to one that Bill would choose Lloyd."

"So we find out when and where he saw Lloyd and pick up his trail from there."

"Yes. We also find out whether he went to see Lloyd as Charles Martin or under his own name."

"Why would he go as Charles Martin?"

"Who knows? You said that he was a little cagey. He may have wanted to keep back his connection with OCAL. Are OCAL strict about their routes and schedules? It may be as simple as that."

Cullen sat in silence for a little, making a pattern in the turf with the butt of the fishing-rod. Then he said:

"Mr. Grant, don't think I'm being dramatic or—or sensational or silly, but you don't think, do you, that Bill could have been bumped off?"

"He could have been, of course. Murder does happen. Even clever murders. But the chances against it are very long."

"Why?"

"Well, for one thing it has passed a police investigation. In spite of all the detective stories to the contrary, the Criminal Investigation Department really is a highly efficent organisation. By far the most efficient organisation, if you'll accept a slightly prejudiced opinion, that exists in this country today—or in any other country, in any period."

"But the police have already been wrong about one thing."

"About his identity, you mean. Yes, but they can hardly be blamed for that."

"You mean, because the set-up was perfect. Well, what's to hinder the other set-up being as perfect as the Charles Martin one?"

"Nothing, of course. Clever murders, as I say, do happen. But it is much easier to forge an identity than to get away with murder. How do you think it was done? Someone came in and slugged him after the train left Euston, and arranged it to look like a fall?"

"Yes."

"But no one visited B Seven after the train left Euston. B Eight heard him come back shortly after the attendant

129

had done his round, and close his door. After that there was no conversation."

"It doesn't need conversation to slug a man on the back of the head."

"No, but it does need opportunity. The chances against opening that door and finding the occupant in the right position for slugging him are astronomical. A sleeping-compartment is not an easy place to take a swing at anyone, even choosing your own time. Anyone with lethal intentions would have to come into the compartment: it couldn't be done from the corridor. It couldn't be done when the victim was in bed. And it couldn't be done with the victim facing you; and he would face round as soon as he was aware that there was someone in the compartment. Therefore it could only be done after preliminary conversation. And B Eight says there was no conversation or visiting. B Eight is the kind of woman who 'can't sleep on a train.' She makes up her mind about that beforehand, and every little sound and squeak and rattle is welcomed as a sign of her suffering. She is usually dead asleep and snoring by about half-past two; but long before that time Bill Kenrick was dead."

"Did she hear him fall?"

"She heard a 'thump,' it seems, and thought that he was taking down a suitcase. He had no suitcase, of course, that would make a thump in being handled. Did Bill speak French, by the way?"

"Well enough to get by."

"*Avec moi.*"

"Yes. About that. Why?"

"I just wondered. It looks as if he planned to spend a night somewhere."

"In Scotland, you mean?"

"Yes. The Testament and the French novel. And yet he didn't speak French."

"Perhaps the Scotch party didn't either."

"No. Scotch parties usually don't. But if he planned to spend a night somewhere, he couldn't meet you that day in Paris."

"Oh, being a day late wouldn't worry Bill. He could have sent me a wire on the 4th."

"Yes . . . I wish I could think of his reason for blacking himself all over."

"Blacking himself?"

"Yes. Dressing the part so completely. Why did he want someone to think that he was French?"

"I can't think why anyone would want anyone to think they were French," Mr. Cullen said. "What are you hoping from this Lloyd guy?"

"I'm hoping that it was Lloyd who saw him away at Euston. They were talking about the Rub'al-Khali, remember. What sounded to Old Yoghourt's ear—quite typically—as 'rob the Calley.' "

"Does this Lloyd live in London?"

"Yes. In Chelsea."

"I hope he's home."

"I hope so indeed. Now I am going to have a last hour with the Turlie, and if you can bear just to sit and think the problem over for a little then perhaps you would come back to supper at Clune and meet the Rankin family?"

"That would be fine," Tad said. "I haven't said good-bye to the Countess. I'm a convert to Countesses. Would you say that the Countess is typical of your aristocracy, Mr. Grant?"

"In the sense of having all the qualities of the type, she is indeed typical," Grant said, picking his way down the bank to the water.

He fished until the level light warned him that it was evening, but he caught nothing. This was a result that neither surprised nor disappointed him. His thoughts were elsewhere. He no longer saw Bill Kenrick's dead face in the swirling water, but Bill Kenrick's personality was all round him. Bill Kenrick possessed his mind.

He reeled in for the last time with a sigh, not for his empty bag or his farewell to the Turlie, but because he was no nearer to finding a reason why Bill Kenrick should have blacked himself all over.

"I'm glad I had this chance of seeing this island," Tad said as they walked up to Clune. "It's not a bit the way I imagined it."

From his tone Grant deduced that he had imagined it as a sort of Wabar, inhabited by monkeys and jinns.

"I wish it had been a happier way of seeing it," he said. "You must come back some day and fish in peace."

Tad grinned a little shamefacedly and rubbed his tumbled hair. "Oh, I guess it will always be Paris for me. Or Vienna, maybe. When you spend your days in God-forsaken little towns, you look forward to the bright lights."

"Well, we do have bright lights in London."

"Yes. Maybe I'll have another smack at London. London's all right."

Laura came to the door as they arrived and said, "Alan, what's this I hear about—" and then noticed his companion. "Oh. You must be Tad. Pat says you don't believe that there *are* any fish in the Turlie. How d'you do. I'm so glad you've come up. Go in and Pat will show you where to wash, and then come and join us in a drink before supper." She summoned Pat, who was hovering, and passed the visitor into his charge, blocking the way firmly on any advance by her cousin. When she had got rid of Mr. Cullen, she turned again to her charge. "Alan, you're *not* going back to town tomorrow?"

"But I'm cured, Lalla," he said, thinking that that was what disturbed her.

"Well, what if you are? There is still more than a week of your leave, and the Turlie better than it has been for seasons. You can't give up all that just to get some young man out of some hole that he's got himself into."

"Tad Cullen's not in any hole. I'm not being quixotic, if that is what you're thinking. I'm going away tomorrow because that is the thing I want to do." He was going to add, "I just can't wait to get away," but even with an intimate like Laura that might lead to misunderstanding.

"But we are all so happy, and things were—" She broke off. "Oh, well. Nothing I can say will make you change your mind. I ought to know that. Nothing has ever made you deviate by a hair's breadth from any line that you once set your mind on. You've always been a damned Juggernaut."

"A damned horrible metaphor," he said. "Couldn't you make it a bullet or a bee-line or something equally undeviating but less destructive?"

She put her arm through his, friendly and a little amused. "But you are destructive, darling." And as he began to protest: "All in the very kindest and most lethal way imaginable. Come and have a drink. You look as if you could do with one."

11

Even the undeviating Grant, of course, had his unsure moments.

"You fool!" said that inner voice, as he was climbing into the London plane at Scoone. "Giving up even a day of your precious leave to hunt will-o'-the-wisps."

"I'm not hunting any will-o'-wisps. I just want to know what happened to Bill Kenrick."

"And what is Bill Kenrick to you that you should give up even an hour of your free time for him?"

"I'm interested in him. If you want to know, I like him."

"You don't know a thing about him. You have made a god in your own image, and are busy worshipping it."

"I know quite a lot about him. I've listened to Tad Cullen."

"A prejudiced witness."

"A nice boy, which is more important. The Cullen boy had a wide choice of friends in an organisation like OCAL, and he chose Bill Kenrick."

"Lots of nice boys have chosen criminal friends."

"Come to that, I've known some nice criminals."

"Yeah? How many? And how many minutes of your leave would you give up to a criminal type?"

"Not thirty seconds. But the Kenrick boy is no criminal."

"A complete set of another man's papers isn't a particularly law-abiding thing to be carrying round, is it?"

"I'll find out about that presently. Meanwhile shut up and leave me alone."

"Huh! Stumped, aren't you!"

"Go away."

"Sticking your neck out for an unknown boy at your age!"

"Who's sticking his neck out?"

"You didn't have to do this plane journey at all. You could have gone back by train or by road. But no, you had to arrange to have yourself shut into a box. A box without a window or a door that will open. A box you can't escape from. A tight, silent, enclosed, sealed—"

"Shut up!"

"Huh! You're breathing short already! In about ten minutes the thing will hit you for six. You ought to have your head examined, Grant; you certainly ought to have you head examined."

"There is one part of my cranial equipment that is still in admirable working order."

"What is that?"

"My teeth."

"You planning to chew something? That's no cure."

"No. I plan to grit them."

And whether it was because he had thumbed his nose at the devil or whether it was that Bill Kenrick stood beside him all the way, Grant made the journey in peace. Tad Cullen slumped into the seat beside him and fell instantly asleep. Grant closed his eyes and let the patterns form in his mind and dissolve and fade and form anew.

Why had Bill Kenrick blacked himself all over?

Whom was he trying to fool?

Why had it been necessary to fool anyone?

As they were circling to land, Tad woke up and without looking out of the window began to pull up his tie and smooth his hair. Apparently some sixth sense in a flyer's brain kept tally of speed, distance, and angle, even when he was unconscious.

"Well," said Tad, "back to the lights of London and the old Westmorland."

"You don't have to go back to your hotel," Grant said. "I can give you a bed."

"That's very kind of you, Mr. Grant, and I appreciate it. But I don't have to put your wife—or—or whoever it is—"

"My housekeeper."

"I don't have to put your housekeeper out." He slapped his pocket. "I'm loaded."

"Even after—what was it?—a fortnight in Paris? I congratulate you."

"Oh, well. I don't think Paris is what it used to be. Or perhaps it was just that I missed Bill. Anyhow, I don't need to fuss anyone making beds for me, thanks all the same. And if you're going to be busy, you don't want me around. But you'll not shut me out of this thing, will you? You'll keep me 'with you,' as Bill says. Said, I mean."

"I will indeed, Tad; I will indeed. I put a fly on a line in a hotel in Oban and fished you out of the white population of the world. I'm certainly not going to throw you back now."

Tad grinned. "I suppose you know what you're talking about. When are you going to see this Lloyd guy?"

"This evening if he is at home. The worst of explorers is that if they are not exploring they are lecturing; so he may be anywhere between China and Peru. What startled you?"

"How did you know I was startled?"

"My dear Tad, your fresh and open countenance was never made for either poker or diplomacy."

"No, it was just that you chose two places that Bill always chose. He used to say that, 'From China to Peru.'"

"He did? He seems to have known his Johnson."

"Johnson?"

"Yes. Samuel Johnson. It's a quotation."

"Oh. Oh, I see." Tad looked faintly abashed.

"If you're still doubtful about me, Tad Cullen, you had better come along the Embankment with me now and let some of my colleagues vouch for me."

Mr. Cullen's fair skin went a deep red. "I'm sorry. Just for a moment there I— It did sound as if you had known Bill. You'll have to forgive me being suspicious, Mr. Grant. I'm all at sea, you know. I don't know a soul in this country. I just have to take people as they come. On face value, I mean. Of *course* I'm not doubtful about you. I'm too grateful to you to be able to find words to describe how grateful I am. You have to believe that."

"Of course I believe it. I was only teasing you, and I had no right to. It would be unintelligent of you not to be suspicious. Here is my address and telephone number. I'll telephone you as soon as I've seen Lloyd."

"You don't think I should come with you, perhaps?"

"No. I think a deputation of two would be a little excessive for so slight an occasion. What time will you be at the Westmorland tonight to take a phone call?"

"Mr. Grant, I'll be sitting with my hand on that thing until you call."

"Better eat some time. I'll call you at half-past eight."

"Okay. Half-past eight."

London was a misty grey with scarlet trimmings, and Grant looked at it with affection. Army nurses used to have that rig-out, that grey and scarlet. And in some ways London gave one the same sense of grace and power that went with that Sister's uniform. The dignity, the underlying kindness beneath the surface indifference, the respect-worthiness that compensated for the lack of pretty frills. He watched the red buses making the grey day beautiful, and blessed them. What a happy thing it was that London buses should be scarlet. In Scotland the buses were painted that most miserable of all colours: blue. A colour so miserable that it was a synonym for depression. But the English, God bless them, had had gayer ideas.

He found Mrs. Tinker turning out the spare bedroom. There was not the slightest need for anyone to turn out the spare bedroom, but Mrs. Tinker obtained the same pleasure from turning out a room that other people get from writing a symphony, or winning a cup at golf, or swimming the Channel. She belonged to that numerous species once succinctly described by Laura as "the kind of woman who washes her front doorstep every day and her hair every six weeks."

She came to the door of the spare bedroom when she heard the key in the lock, and said: "Well, now! And not a bite in the house! Why didn't you let me know you was comin' back from foreign parts before your time?"

"It's all right, Tink. I don't want a meal anyhow. I've just looked in to leave my luggage. Get in something for me to eat tonight."

Mrs. Tinker went home every night, partly because she had to see to the evening meal of someone she referred to as "Tinker," and partly because Grant had always liked to have the flat to himself in the evenings. Grant had never seen Tinker, and Mrs. Tinker's only connection with him seemed to consist of this matter of an evening meal and some marriage lines. Her real life and interest was in 19 Tenby Cort, S.W.1.

"Any telephones?" Grant asked, thumbing through the telephone pad.

"Miss Hallard telephoned to say ring her up and dine with her as soon as you were back."

"Oh. Did the new play go well? What were the notices like?"

"Stinkers."

"All of them?"

"Every one I seen, anyway."

In the days of her freedom, before Tinker, Mrs. Tinker had been a theatre dresser. Indeed, if it had not been for the ritual of the evening meal it was likely that she would still be dressing someone each evening in W.1 or W.C.2 instead of turning out spare bedrooms in S.W.1. Her interest in theatre matters was therefore that of an initiate.

"Have you seen the play?"

"Not me. It's one of them plays what means something else. You know. She keeps a china dog on the mantelpiece, but it isn't a china dog at all, it's 'er ex-husband; and 'e breaks the dog, the new boy-friend does, and she goes mad. Not *gets* mad, you know; *goes* mad. 'Ighbrow. But I suppose if you want to be a Dame you got to act 'ighbrow plays. What was you thinkin' of 'avin' for your supper?"

"I wasn't thinking."

"I could leave a nice bit of fish poachin' over some hot water for you."

"Not fish, if you love me. I've eaten enough fish in the last month to last me a lifetime. As long as it isn't fish or mutton, I don't mind what it is."

"Well, it's too late now to get any kidneys out of Mr. Bridges, but I'll see what I can do. You 'ad a good 'oliday?"

"A wonderful, wonderful holiday."

"That's good. You bin and put on a little weight, I'm glad to see. And you needn't slap you stomach in that doubtful way neither. A little bit of weight never 'urt no one. It don't do to be as thin as a rail. You don't 'ave no reserves."

She hung around while Grant changed into his best town suit, doling out bits of gossip as they happened to occur to her. Then he shooed her back to her piece of self-indulgence with the spare bedroom, dealt with the small businesses that had piled up in his absence, and went out into the calm of the early April evening. He went round to the garage, answered questions about his fishing, listened to three fishing stories that he had listened to before he set out for the Highlands a month ago, and reclaimed the little two-seater that he used when on his own business.

Number 5 Britt Lane took some finding. In the huddle of old houses all kinds of adaptation and conditioning had taken place. Stables had become cottages, kitchen wings had become houses, odd storeys had become maisonettes. Number 5 Britt Lane seemed to be just a number on a gate. The gate was in a brick wall, and its iron-studded oak seemed to Grant a little affected in so unpretentious a stretch of ordinary London brick. However, it was solid and in itself unexceptional, and it opened easily when asked to. It opened on to what had been a kitchen yard when Number 5 had been merely the back wing of a house in another street altogether. Now the yard was a small paved court with a fountain playing in the middle of it, and the one-time wing was a small flat stucco house of three storeys, painted cream with green window-sashes. As Grant crossed the little court to the doorway, he noticed that the paving was of tiles, some of them old and many of them beautiful. The fountain too was beautiful. He mentally applauded Heron Lloyd for not having replaced the plain London electric bell-push by some more aesthetic piece of fancy-work; it augured a good taste that the inappropriate gate had left open to question.

The interior of the house, too, had the Arab bareness and space without any suggestion that a piece of the East had been transported to London. Beyond the figure of the manservant who answered his ring, he could see the clean walls and the rich carpet; an idiom adapted, not a décor transposed. His respect for Heron Lloyd mounted.

The manservant appeared to be Arab, an Arab of the towns, plumpish, lively-eyed, and good-mannered. He listened to Grant's inquiry and asked in a gentle, too correct English if he had an appointment. Grant said no, but that he would not detain Mr. Lloyd more than a moment. Mr. Lloyd could be of some help in giving information connected with Arabia.

"If you will come in, please, and wait for a moment, I will ask."

He ushered Grant into a tiny room just inside the front door, which judging from its limited space and scanty furnishing, was used for the purpose of waiting. He supposed that someone like Heron Lloyd must be used to strangers appearing on his doorstep to claim his interest or help. Even perhaps just to ask for his autograph. A realisation that made his own intrusion less deplorable.

Mr. Lloyd had not debated his desirability very long, it seemed, for the man was back in a few moments.

"Will you come, please? Mr. Lloyd will be very happy to see you."

A formula, but such a pleasant formula. How good manners did cushion life, he thought as he followed the man up the narrow stairs and into the big room that occupied the whole of the first floor.

"Mr. Grant, *hadji*," said the man, standing aside to let him come. Grant caught the word and thought: That is the first piece of chi-chi. Englishmen don't make the pilgrimage to Mecca, surely.

Watching Heron Lloyd as he was made welcome, Grant wondered whether he had first thought of going to desert Arabia because he looked like a desert Arab, or whether he had come to look like a desert Arab after years in desert Arabia. Lloyd was the Arab of the desert idealised to the *nth*. He was, Grant thought with amusement, the Arab of the circulating libraries. It was across the saddle of Arabs like Heron Lloyd that blameless matrons in the Crescents and Drives and Avenues had been carried off to a fate worse than death. The black eyes, the lean brown face, the white teeth, the whip-lash body, the delicate hands, the graceful movements: it was all there, straight out of Page Seventeen of Miss Tilly Tally's latest (two hundred and fifty-four thousand, new printing next week). Grant had to remind himself forcibly that he must not judge on looks.

For this man had done journeys that had made history in the world of exploration, and had written about them in English which, even if a little lush (Grant had bought a copy of his latest in Scoone yesterday afternoon) was nevertheless recognisable as literature. Heron Lloyd was no parlour sheik.

Lloyd was wearing orthodox London clothes and a manner to match. If one had never heard of him, one would accept him as a Londoner of the well-to-do professional classes. One of the slightly more flamboyant classes, perhaps; an actor, or conceivably a Harley street consultant or a society photographer; but a Londoner of the orthodox professions, when all was considered.

"Mr. Grant," he said, shaking hands. "Mahmoud says that I can be of service to you."

His voice surprised Grant. It had no body and a faintly querulous tone that had nothing to do with the sense of the words or their mood. He took a box of cigarettes from the low coffee table and offered them. He did not smoke himself, he said, because the had adopted Mohammedan customs during his long life in the East, but he could recommend the cigarettes if Grant cared to try something that tasted a little out of the ordinary.

Grant took the cigarette, as he took every new experience and sensation, with interest, and apologised for his intrusion. He wanted to know whether a young man called Charles Martin had applied to him at any time within the last year or so for information about Arabia.

"Charles Martin? No. No, I don't think so. Many people do come, of course, to see me about one thing and another. And I cannot always remember their names afterwards. But I think I should remember anyone with that simple name. You like that tobacco? I know the very half-acre where it is grown. A beautiful place that has not changed since Alexander the Macedonian passed that way." He smiled a little and added: "Except, of course, that they have learned how to grow this weed. The weed, I understand, goes very well with a not too dry sherry. Another of the grosser indulgences that I avoid; but I shall have a fruit drink to keep you company."

Grant thought that the desert tradition of hospitality to the stranger must come a little expensive in a London where you were a celebrity and all and sundry were free to drop in. He noticed that the label on the bottle that Lloyd had picked up was a guarantee as well as an announcement. It seemed that Lloyd was neither a pauper nor a piker.

140

"Charles Martin was also known as Bill Kenrick," he said.

Lloyd lowered the glass which he was about to fill, and said:

"Kenrick! But he was here only the other day. Or rather, when I say only the other day, I mean a week or two ago. Quite lately, anyway. Why should he have an alias?"

"I don't know that myself. I am making inquiries about him on behalf of his friend. He was due to meet his friend in Paris at the beginning of March. On the 4th, to be exact. But he didn't turn up. We have discovered that he should have turned up in Paris."

Lloyd put the glass slowly down on to the table.

"So *that* is why he did not come back," he said in that querulous voice that did not mean to be querulous. "Poor boy. Poor boy."

"You had arranged to see him again?"

"Yes. I thought him charming and very intelligent. He was bitten with the desert—but perhaps you know that. He had ideas about exploring. A few young men still have. There are still the adventurers, even in this hedged and garnished world. Of which one must be glad. What happened to Kenrick? A car smash?"

"No. He had a fall on a train and fractured his skull."

"Poor wretch. Poor wretch. A pity. I could have supplied the jealous gods with a dozen more expendable in his place. An atrocious word: expendable. The expression of an idea that would not even have been conceivable a few years ago. So far have we progressed towards our ultimate barbarism. Why did you want to know if the Kenrick boy had come to see me?"

"We wanted to pick up his trail. When he died he was masquerading as Charles Martin, with a complete set of Charles Martin's papers. We want to know at what stage he began to be Charles Martin. We were almost certain that, being bitten by the desert, he would come to see some authority on the subject in London, and since you, sir, are the ultimate authority we began with you."

"I see. Well, it was most certainly as Kenrick, Bill Kenrick I think, that he came to see me. A dark young man, very attractive. Tough, too, in a nice way.

141

I mean, good manners covering unknown possibilities. I found him delightful."

"Had he come to you with any definite plans? I mean, with a specific proposition?"

Lloyd smiled a little. "He came to me with one of the commonest of all the propositions that are habitually put to me. An expedition to the site of Wabar. Do you know about Wabar? It is the fabled city of Arabia. It is Arabia's 'cities of the plain.' How that pattern does repeat itself in legend. The human race feels eternally guilty when it is happy. We cannot even remark on our good health without touching wood or crossing our fingers or otherwise averting the gods' anger at mortal well-being. So Arabia has its Wabar: the city that was destroyed by fire because of its wealth and its sins."

"And Kenrick thought that he had discovered the site."

"He was sure of it. Poor boy, I hope that I was not short-tempered with him."

"You think that he was wrong, then?"

"Mr. Grant, the legend of Wabar exists from the Red Sea clear across Arabia to the Persian Gulf, and for almost every mile of that distance there is a different alleged site for the city."

"And you don't believe that perhaps someone might stumble on it by accident?"

"By accident?"

"Kenrick was a flyer. It is possible that he saw the place when blown off his course, isn't it?"

"Had he talked to his friend about it then?"

"No. He had talked to no one that I know of. That was my own deduction. What is to hinder the discovery being made that way?"

"Nothing, of course, nothing; if the place exists at all. I have said it is a legend almost universal throughout the world. But where stories of ruins have been tracked to their source the 'ruins' have always proved to be something else. Natural rock formation, mirage-cloud formation even. I think what poor Kenrick saw was the crater of a meteor. I have seen the place myself. A predecessor of mine discovered it when he was looking for Wabar. It is unbelievably like a place made with hands. The thrown-up earth makes pinnacles and jagged ruinous-looking heights. I think I have a photograph somewhere. You might like to see it: it is a unique affair." He got up and slid back a panel in the bare painted-woodwall, disclosing shelves of books all the way from floor to ceiling. "It is, perhaps mercifully, not every day a meteor of any size falls on the earth."

He picked a photograph album from one of the lower shelves, and came back across the room looking for the place in the collection. And Grant was seized without warning by a strange sense of familiarity, a feeling of having met Lloyd somewhere before.

He looked at the photograph that Lloyd laid before him. It was certainly an uncanny thing. An almost mocking pastiche of human achievement. But his mind was busy with that odd moment of recognition.

Was it just that he had seen Heron Lloyd's photograph somewhere? But if it had been that, if he had merely seen Lloyd's face as adjunct to some description of his exploits, then the sense of recognition would have come when he had first walked into the room and seen him. It was not so much a recognition as a sense of having known Lloyd somewhere else. In some other surroundings.

"You see?" Lloyd was saying. "Even on the ground, one has to go close up to it before one can be sure that the thing is not a collection of human dwellings. How much more misleading it must be from the air."

"Yes," agreed Grant, and did not believe it. For one very good reason. From the air the crater would have been plainly visible. From the air it would have looked exactly what it was: a circular hollow surrounded by the thrown-up earth. But he was not going to say that to Lloyd. Let Lloyd talk. He was growing very interested in Lloyd.

"That lies very close to the Kenrick boy's route across the desert, as described by himself, and I think that that is what he saw."

"Did he pin-point the place, do you know?"

"I don't know. I didn't ask him. But I should think he would. He struck me as being a very efficient and intelligent young man."

"You didn't ask him for details?"

"If someone told you, Mr. Grant, that he had discovered a holly tree growing in the middle of Piccadilly immediately opposite the In and Out, would you be interested? Or would you just think that you must be patient with him? I know the Empty Quarter as well as you know Piccadilly."

"Yes, of course. Then it was not you who saw him off at the station?"

"Mr. Grant, I never see *anyone* off. A combination of masochism and sadism that I have always deplored. Off where, by the way?"

"To Scoone."

"To the Highlands? I understood that he was longing for some gaiety. Why was he going to the Highlands?"

"We don't know. That is one of the things we are most anxious to find out. He said nothing to you that might provide a clue?"

"No. He did suggest finding other backing. I mean, when I had proved a broken reed. Perhaps he had found a backer, or hoped to find a backer, who lives up there. I can't think of any obvious one off-hand. There is Kinsey-Hewitt, of course. He has Scottish connections. But I think he is in Arabia at the moment."

Well, at least Lloyd had provided the first reasonable explanation of the flying visit north with an overnight case. To talk to a possible backer. He had found a backer at the last moment, when he was almost due to meet Tad Cullen in Paris, and had dashed north to see him. That fitted beautifully. They were getting on. But why as Charles Martin?

As if the thought had been transferred, Lloyd said: "By the way, if the Kenrick boy was traveling as Charles Martin, how has he been identified as Kenrick?"

"I travelled on that train to Scoone. I saw him when he was dead, and grew interested in some verse he had been scribbling."

"Scribbling? On what?"

"On a blank bit of an evening paper," Grant said, wondering why it should matter what Kenrick had been writing on.

"Oh."

"I was on holiday, with nothing else to do, so I amused myself with the clues provided."

"You played detective."

"Yes."

"What is your profession, Mr. Grant?"

"I'm a Civil Servant."

"Ah, I was going to suggest the Army." He smiled

a little and picked up Grant's glass to refill it. "The more rarefied ranks, of course."

"G.S.O. 1?"

"No. An attaché, I think. Or Intelligence."

"I have done a spot of Intelligence during my Army career."

"So that is where you developed your taste for it. May I say, your flair."

"Thank you."

"Or had he Kenrick belongings that made the identification easy?"

"No. He was buried as Charles Martin."

Lloyd paused as he was setting the filled glass down and said: "That is so typical of the careless Scottish way of dealing with sudden death. They are always very smug about their lack of inquests. Myself, I think Scotland must be an ideal place in which to get away with murder. If ever I plan one, I shall lure my victim north of the Border."

"There was an inquest, as it happens. The accident took place shortly after the train left Euston."

"Oh." Lloyd thought this over and then said: "Don't you think that this should be reported to the police? I mean the fact that they have buried someone under a wrong name."

Grant was about to say, "The only proof we have that the dead Charles Martin was Kenrick is my identification of a not very good snapshot," but something stopped him. Instead he said, "We should like first to know why he had Charles Martin's papers."

"Ah, yes. I see. That of course is a sufficiently questionable matter. One doesn't acquire a man's papers without some—preliminaries. Does anyone know who Charles Martin is—or was?"

"Yes. The police were satisfied on that score. There was no mystery."

"The only mystery is how Kenrick came by his papers. I see why you are reluctant to go to official sources. What about this man who saw him off? At Euston. Could he have been Charles Martin?"

"He could, I suppose."

"The papers may merely have been lent. Kenrick somehow did not strike me as a—shall we say, nefarious type?"

"No. On all the evidence, he wasn't."

"It's a very curious business altogether. This accident that you say he had: I suppose there is no doubt that it was an accident? No suggestion of a quarrel?"

"No, it was just one of those things. A fall that might happen to anyone."

"Distressing. As I say, there are too few young men nowadays who have the combination of courage and intelligence. A great many come to me, indeed they travel great distances to see me—"

He went on talking, and Grant sat watching and listening.

Were there, in fact, so many who came? Lloyd seemed very pleased to sit and talk to a stranger. There was no suggestion that he had an engagement for the evening or guests coming to dinner. None of the convenient pauses that a host leaves in the conversation so that a casual guest may take his leave. Lloyd sat talking in that thin, complacent voice and admiring the hands that lay in his lap. He continually changed the position of the hands, not as a gesture to emphasise a phrase, but as one making a new arrangement of some decoration. Grant found this Narcissus-like preoccupation fascinating. He listened to the silence of the little house, shut away from the town and its traffic. In the biography in *Who's Who* there had been no mention of wife or children, possessions that the owners of both are habitually proud to mention; so the household no doubt consisted of Lloyd and his servants. Had he sufficient interests to compensate for that lack of human companionship?

He, Alan Grant, had a household just as bare of human warmth; but his life was so full of people that to come back to his empty flat was a luxury, a spiritual delight. Was Heron Lloyd's life full and satisfying?

Or did your true Narcissus ever need any company other than his own image?

He wondered how old the man was. Older than he seemed, certainly; he was the doyen of Arabian exploration. Fifty-five or more. Probably nearer sixty. He had not given his date of birth in the biography, so the chances were that he was nearly sixty. There could not be many years of hard-living left to him, even given his good physique and condition. What would he do with the remaining years? Spend them admiring his hands?

"The only true democracy in the world today," Lloyd

was saying, "and it is being destroyed by the thing that we call civilisation."

And again Grant had the sense of familiarity, of recognition. Was it that he had met Lloyd before? Or was it that Lloyd reminded him of someone?

If so, of whom?

He must get away and think about it. It was time that he took this leave anyhow.

"Did Kenrick tell you where he was staying?" he asked as he began to take his leave.

"No. We made no definite appointment to meet again, you understand. I asked him to come to see me again before he left London. When he did not come I believed that he was resentful, perhaps angry, at my lack of—sympathy, shall we say?"

"Yes, it must have been a blow to him. Well, I have taken up a great deal of your time, and you have been very forbearing. I am most grateful."

"I am very glad to have been of help. I am afraid it has not been very valuable help. If there is anything else that I can do in the matter, I hope very much that you will not hesitate to call on me."

"Well—there is one thing, but you have already been so kind that I hate to ask you. Especially since it is a little irrelevant."

"What is it?"

"May I perhaps borrow the photograph?"

"The photograph?"

"The photograph of the meteor crater. I notice that the print is slotted into your album, not pasted. I should like very much to show it to Kenrick's friend. I promise faithfully to return it. And in perfect—"

"But of course you may have the photograph. And don't bother to return it. I took the picture myself, and the negative is filed in the proper place. I can replace the print at any time with ease."

He manoeuvred the print from its anchorage in the album, and handed it to Grant. He came downstairs with Grant and saw him to the door, talked a bit about the little courtyard when Grant admired it, and waited courteously until Grant had reached the gate before closing the door on him.

Grant opened the evening paper that was lying on the car cushions and laid the photograph carefully between its folds. Then he drove down to the river and along the Embankment.

The old place looked very much as usual, he thought, as the hideous pile loomed up in the dusk. And so, too, did the fingerprint department once he got there. Cartwright was stubbing out a cigarette in the saucer of a half-drunk cup of cold tea and admiring his latest handiwork: a complete set of left-hand prints.

"Lovely, 'im?" he said, looking up as Grant's shadow fell across him. "These are going to hang Pinky Mason."

"Hadn't Pinky the price of a pair of gloves?"

"Huh! Pinky could have bought up Dent's. He just couldn't believe, clever little man Pinky, that the police would ever get round to thinking it anything but a suicide. Gloves are for small-time trash, burglars, and such, not for master-minds like Pinky. You been away?"

"Yes. I've been fishing in the Highlands. If you're not too busy, could you do something off the cuff for me?"

"Now?"

"Oh, no. Tomorrow would do."

Cartwright looked at the clock. "I've nothing to do till I meet my wife at the theatre. We're going to Marta Hallard's new play. So I can do it now, if you like. Is it a difficult job?"

"No. Dead easy. Just here, in the lower right-hand corner of this photograph, there is a beautiful thumb-print. And at the back I think you'll find a nice set of finger-tips. I want to check them with the files."

"All right. Will you wait?"

"I'm going to the library. I'll come back."

In the library he took down *Who's Who*, and looked up Kinsey-Hewitt. The paragraph on Kinsey-Hewitt was a very modest little affair compared with the half-column on Heron Lloyd. He was a much younger man, it seemed; married, with two children; and his address was a London one. The "Scottish connection" that Lloyd had mentioned seemed to consist in the fact that he was the younger son of some Kinsey-Hewitt who had a place in Fife.

Well, there was always the chance that he was now, or had been lately, in Scotland. Grant went to a telephone and called the London address. A woman with a pleasant voice answered, and said that her husband was not at home. No, he would not be at home for some time; he was in Arabia. He had been in Arabia since November and was not expected back until May at the earliest. Grant thanked her and hung up. It had not been to Kinsey-Hewitt that Bill Kenrick had gone. Tomorrow he would have to go through the various authorities on Arabia, one by one, and ask them the question.

He went back, after some coffee-housing with such friends as he happened to run into at that hour, to Cartwright.

"Got the photograph or am I too early?"

"I've not only got it but looked it up for you. The answer is No."

"No, I didn't really think there would be anything. I was just clearing decks. But thank you, all the same. I'll take the print with me. I thought the new Hallard show got awful notices."

"Did it? I never read 'em. Neither does Beryl. She just likes Marta Hallard. So do I, if it comes to that. Nice long legs. Good night."

"Good night, and thanks again."

12

"You don't seem awfully sweet on this guy," Tad Cullen said, when Grant had finished his story over the telephone.

"Don't I? Oh, well, perhaps it's just that he doesn't happen to be what we call my cup of tea. Look, Tad, you're quite sure that you have no idea, even in the back of your mind, where Bill could have been staying?"

"I haven't got a back to my mind. I have just a small, narrow space in front where I keep all that's useful to me. A few telephone numbers, and a prayer or two."

"Well, tomorrow I'd like you to do the round of the more obvious places, if you would."

"Yes, sure. I'll do anything. Anything you say."

"All right. Have you got a pen? Here's the list."

Grant gave him the names of twenty of the more likely places, going on the assumption that a young man from the wide open spaces and the small towns would look for a caravanserai that was both large and gay and not too expensive. And just for good measure he added a couple of the best-known expensive ones; young men with several months' back-pay were liable to be extravagant.

"I don't think I'd bother with any more than that," he said.

"*Are* there any more?"

"If he didn't stay in one of these, then we're sunk, because if he didn't stay in any of them we'd have to hunt every hotel in London to find him, to say nothing of the boarding-houses."

"Okay. I'll start first thing in the morning. Mr. Grant, I'd like to tell you how much I appreciate what you're doing for me. Giving up your time to something that no one else could do; I mean, something the police wouldn't touch. If it wasn't for you—"

"Listen, Tad. I'm not being benevolent. I'm being self-indulgent and typically nosey and I'm enjoying myself to the top of my bent. If I wasn't, believe me I wouldn't be in London. I'd be going to sleep tonight in Clune. So good night and sleep well. We'll crack this thing between us."

He hung and went to see what Mrs. Tinker had left on the stove. It seemed to be a sort of shepherd's pie. He carried it into the living-room and ate it absent-mindedly, his thoughts still on Lloyd.

What was familiar about Lloyd?

He went back in his mind over the few moments before his first feeling of recognition. What had Lloyd been doing? Pulling open the panel of the book cupboard. Pulling it open with a gesture self-consciously graceful, faintly exhibitionist. What was there in that to provoke a sense of familiarity?

And there was something even more curious.

Why had Lloyd said "On what?" when he had mentioned Kenrick's scribbling?

That, surely, was a most unnatural reaction.

What exactly had he said to Lloyd? He had said that he became interested in Kenrick because of some verses he had been scribbling. The normal come-back to that was surely, "Verses?" The operative word in the sentence was "verses." That he was scribbling was entirely by the way. And that anyone's reaction to the information should be to say "On what?" was inexplicable.

Except that no human reaction was inexplicable.

It was Grant's experience that it was the irrelevant, the unconsidered words in a statement that were important. Quite surprising and gratifying revelations lay in the gap between an assertion and a non-sequitur.

151

Why had Lloyd said "On what?"

He took the problem to bed with him, and fell asleep with it.

In the morning he began his hunt through the authorities on Arabia, and finished it not at all astonished that it had produced no result. People who explored Arabia as a hobby very seldom had money to back anything. They were, on the contrary, usually prospecting for backing themselves. The only chance had been that some one of them had proved interested to the point of being willing to share his backing. But none of them had ever heard of either Charles Martin or Bill Kenrick.

It was lunch-time before he finished, and he stood by the window waiting for Tad's call and wondering whether to go out to luncheon or to let Mrs. Tinker make him an omelette. It was another grey day, but there was a slight breeze and a smell of damp earth that was queerly countrified. A fine fishing day, he noted. He wished for a moment that he was walking down over the moor to the river instead of wrestling with the London telephone system. It wouldn't even have to be the river. He would settle for an afternoon on Lochan Dhu in a leaky boat with Pat for company.

He turned to his desk and began to clear up the mess of the morning's opened mail. He had stooped to throw the torn pages and the empty envelopes into the wastepaper basket, but he stopped with the action half-spent.

It had come to him.

He knew now who it was that Heron Lloyd reminded him of.

It was Wee Archie.

This was so unexpected and so ridiculous that he sat down on the chair by his desk and began to laugh.

What had Wee Archie in common with that elegant and sophisticated creature who was Heron Lloyd?

Frustration? Of a surety not. The fact that he was an Auslander in the country of his devotion? No; too far-fetched. It was something nearer home than that.

For it *was* of Wee Archie that Lloyd had reminded him. He had no doubt of that now. He was experiencing that inimitable relief that comes when one has remembered a name that has eluded one.

Yes, it was Wee Archie.

But why?

What had that incongruous pair in common?

152

Their gestures? No. Their physique? No. Their voices? Was that it?

"Their vanity, you fool!" said the inner voice in him.

Yes; that was it. Their vanity. Their pathological vanity.

He sat very still, considering; he was not amused any longer.

Vanity. The first requisite in wrong-doing. The constant factor in the criminal mind.

Just supposing that—

The telephone at his elbow gave its sudden purr.

It was Tad. He had reached number eighteen, he said, and was now an old old man but the blood of pioneers was in his veins and he was pursuing the search.

"Drop it for a little and come and eat with me somewhere."

"Oh, I've had my lunch. I had a couple of bananas and a milk shake in Leicester Square."

"Merciful Heaven!" said Grant.

"What's the matter with that?"

"Starch; that's what's the matter with it."

"A little starch is fine when you're ironed out. No luck your end?"

"No. If it was a backer he was going North to see, then the backer was merely some amateur who had money; not anyone actively engaged in Arabian exploration."

"Oh. Well. I'll be on my way. When shall I ring you next?"

"As soon as you come to the end of the list. I'll wait here for your call."

Grant decided to have the omelette, and while Mrs. Tinker prepared it he walked about his living-room letting his mind soar into speculation and pulling it down instantly to a common-sense level, so that it behaved like telegraph lines outside a railway compartment, continually soaring and continually caught back.

If only they had a starting point. What if Tad came to the end of the likely hotels and still drew a blank? It was only a matter of days before he would have to go back to work. He stopped speculating on vanity and its possibilities and began to reckon how long it would take Tad to cover the remaining four hotels.

But before his omelette was half finished, Tad arrived in person. He was flushed and triumphant.

153

"I don't know how you ever thought of that dull little dump in connection with Bill," he said, "but you were right. That's where he stayed all right."

"And which is the dull little dump?"

"The Pentland. How did you think of that one?"

"It has an international reputation."

"*That* one has?"

"And English people go on going to it generation after generation."

"That's what it looks like!"

"So that is where Bill Kenrick stayed. I like him more than ever."

"Yeah," Tad said more quietly. And the flush of triumph died away. "I wish you'd known Bill. I sure wish you'd known him. They don't come any better than Bill."

"Sit down and have some coffee to settle your milk shake. Or would you like a drink?"

"No, thanks, I'll have coffee. It actually smells like coffee," he added in a surprised way. "Bill checked out on the 3rd. The 3rd of March."

"Did you ask about his luggage?"

"Sure. They weren't all that interested at first. But eventually they got out a ledger the size of the Judgment Book and said that Mr. Kenrick had left nothing either in the box-room or the safe."

"That means that he took them to a cloak-room—or a left-luggage office, that is—to be ready to his hand when he came back from Scotland. If he meant to fly when he came back, then I suppose he would leave them at Euston to be picked up on his way to the airport. If he meant to go by sea, then he may have taken them to Victoria before going to Euston. Did he like the sea?"

"So-so. He wasn't daffy about it. But he had a mania for ferries."

"Ferries?"

"Yes. Seems it began when he was a kid at a place called Pompey—know where that is?" Grant nodded. "And he spent all his time on a penny ferry."

"A ha'penny one, it used to be."

"Well, anyway."

"So the train-ferry might have had an interest for him, you think. Well, we can but try. But if he was going to be late in meeting you, I should think he would fly over. Would you know the cases if you saw them?"

"Oh, yes. Bill and I shared a Company bungalow. I

helped pack them. In fact one of them's mine, if it comes to that. He just took the two of them. He said if we bought many things we could buy a suitcase to—" Tad's voice died away suddenly, and he buried his face in his coffee cup. It was a great flat bowl of a cup, willow-patterned in pink, which Marta Hallard had brought back from Sweden for Grant because he liked his coffee out of large cups; and it made a very good screen for emotion.

"We have no ticket to recover them with, you see. And I can't use any official means. But I know most of the men on duty at the big terminuses, and can probably wangle our way behind the scenes. It will be up to you to spot the cases. Was Bill a labeller by nature, would you say?"

"I expect he'd label things he was going to leave behind like that. Why, do you think, didn't he have the left-luggage ticket in his wallet?"

"I did think that someone else may have deposited those cases for him. The person who saw him off at Euston, for instance."

"The Martin guy?"

"It might be. If he had borrowed papers for this odd masquerade, he would have to return them. Perhaps Martin was going to meet him at the airport, or at Victoria, or wherever it was that he planned to leave England from, with the cases and collect his own papers."

"Yeah. That makes sense. I suppose we couldn't Agony-advertise for this Martin?"

"I don't think that this Martin would be very willing to answer, having lent his papers for a piece of sharp practice and being now without identity."

"No. Perhaps you're right. He wasn't anyone who was staying at that hotel, anyway."

"How do you know that?" asked Grant, surprised.

"I looked through the book: the register. When I was identifying Bill's signature."

"You're wasted in OCAL, Tad. You should come to us."

But Tad was not listening. "You've got no idea what a queer feeling it was to see Bill's writing suddenly like that, among all those strange names. It sort of stopped my breath."

Grant took Lloyd's picture of the crater "ruins" from

his desk and brought it over to the table. "That is what Heron Lloyd thinks that Bill saw."

Tad looked at it with interest. "It sure is queer, isn't it? Just like ruined sky-scrapers. You know, until I saw Arabia I thought the United States invented sky-scrapers. But some of those old Arab towns are just the Empire State on a smaller scale. But you say it couldn't have been this that Bill saw."

"No. From the air it must be quiet obvious what it is."

"Did you tell Lloyd that?"

"No. I just let him talk."

"Why do you dislike the guy so much?"

"I didn't say that I disliked him."

"You don't have to."

Grant hesitated, analysing, as always just exactly what he did feel.

"I find vanity repellent. As a person I loathe it, and as a policeman I distrust it."

"It's a harmless sort of weakness," Tad said, with a tolerant lift of a shoulder.

"That is just where you are wrong. It is *the* utterly destructive quality. When you say vanity, you are thinking of the kind that admires itself in mirrors and buys things to deck itself out in. But that is merely personal conceit. Real vanity is something quite different. A matter not of person but of personality. Vanity says, 'I must have this because I am me.' It is a frightening thing because it is incurable. You can never convince Vanity that anyone else is of the slightest importance; he just doesn't understand what you are talking about. He will kill a person rather than be put to the inconvenience of doing a six months' stretch."

"But that's being insane."

"Not according to Vanity's reckoning. And certainly not in the medical sense. It is merely Vanity being logical. It is, as I said, a frightening trait, and the basis of all criminal personality. Criminals—true criminals, as opposed to the little man who cooks the accounts in an emergency or the man who kills his wife when he finds her in bed with a stranger—true criminals vary in looks and tastes and intelligence and method as widely as the rest of the world does, but they have one invariable characteristic: their pathological vanity."

Tad looked as though he were only half-listening because he was using this information on some private reference of his own. "Listen, Mr. Grant," he said. "Are you saying that this guy Lloyd isn't to be trusted?"

Grant thought that over.

"I wish I knew," he said at last. "I wish I knew."

"We-e-ll!" said Tad. "That sure puts a different look on things, doesn't it!"

"I've spent quite a long time this morning wondering whether I have seen so much of the vanity in criminals that I have begun to have a 'thing' about it; to distrust it unduly. On the face of it Heron Lloyd is irreproachable. He is more: he is admirable. He has a fine record behind him; he lives simply; he has excellent taste, which means a natural sense of proportion; and he has achieved enough surely to satisfy the most egotistical soul."

"But you think—there's something wrong somewhere."

"Do you remember a little man in the hotel at Moymore who did missionary work on you?"

"Persecuted Scotland! The little man in kilts."

"A kilt," said Grant automatically. "Well, for some reason Lloyd gives me the same feeling as Archie Brown. It's absurd, but it is very strong. They have the same—" He looked for a word.

"Smell," said Tad.

"Yes. That's about it. They have the same smell."

After a long silence Tad said: "Mr. Grant, are you still of the opinion that what happened to Bill was an accident?"

"Yes, because there is no evidence to the contrary. But I'm quite prepared to believe that it wasn't, if I can see any reason for it. Can you clean windows?"

"Can I what?"

"Clean windows."

"I could make a shot at it if really pushed, I suppose," Tad said, staring. "Why?"

"You may have to before this is over. Let us go and collect those suitcases. I'm hoping that all the information we want will be in those cases. I've just remembered that Bill booked that berth to Scoone a week in advance."

"Perhaps his backer in Scotland couldn't see him until the 4th."

"Perhaps. Anyhow, all his papers and personal things will be in one of the cases, and I'm hoping that it will include a diary."

"Bill wouldn't keep a diary!"

"Not that kind. The Meet-Jack-1.15-Call-for-Toots-7:30 kind."

"Oh, yes, that. Yes, I expect he'd have one of those if he was going touting round London for backing. Brother, that may be all we need!"

"That *will* be all we need. If it is there."

But nothing was there.

Nothing at all.

They began light-heartedly with the obvious places: Euston, the airport, Victoria; pleased with the formula that worked so well.

"Hullo, Inspector. What can I do for you today?"

"Well, you might be able to help my young friend from America."

"Yes? One for the three-thirty?"

"We've got one for the three-thirty. He wants to know whether his buddy left a couple of suitcases here. Do you mind if he has a look round? We don't want to move anything. Just to look."

"Well, that's something that's still free in this country, Inspector, believe it or not. Come behind, will you?"

So they came behind. Each time they came behind. And each time the tiered luggage looked back at them, contemptuous and withdrawn. As detached as only other people's belongings can look.

From the likely places they moved on to the mere possibles, sobered and apprehensive. They had hoped for a diary, for personal papers. Now they would settle for even a sight of the suitcases.

But there were no familiar cases on any of the shelves.

This so staggered Tad that Grant had difficulty in dragging him away from the later ports-of-call. He went round and round the filled racks in an unbelieving daze.

"They must be here," he kept saying. "They must be here."

But they were not there.

As they came out on to the street, baffled, after their last bet had gone down the drain, he said: "Inspector—I mean, Mr. Grant—where else is there that you would leave luggage after checking out of a hotel? Have you those personal lock-up places?"

"Only limited-period ones. For people who want to park a case for an hour or two while they do something."

"Well, where *are* Bill's things? Why aren't they in any of the obvious places?"

"I don't know. They may be with his girl."

"What girl?"

"I don't know. He was young and handsome and celibate; he would have a fairly wide choice."

"Yes, of course. That's maybe what he did with them. Which reminds me." His face lost its discontented, purposeless look. He glanced at his watch. It was nearly dinner-time. "I've got a date with that girl in the milk-bar." He caught Grant's eye and looked faintly abashed. "But I'll stand her up if you think I can be any good to you."

Grant sent him away to meet his milk-bar sweetie with a slight sense of relief. It was rather like having a mournful puppy around. He himself decided to postpone dinner for a little and go and see some of his Metropolitan friends.

He dropped into the Astwick Street Police Station and was greeted with the identical phrase that he had been listening to all the afternoon and evening: "Hullo, Inspector, what can we do for you?"

Grant said that they might tell him who was on the Britt Lane beat just now.

The man on the beat was P. C. Bithel, it seemed; and if the Inspector wanted to see him he was at this moment in the canteen having sausage-and-mashed. His number was 30.

Grant found Number Thirty at a table by himself at the far end of the room. A French grammar was propped up in front of him. Looking at him, sitting there unaware, Grant thought how London policemen had changed in type in the short space of a quarter-century. He himself, he knew, was a departure from type; a fact that had been of great use to him on various occasions. P. C. Bithel was a dark, slight boy from County Down with a mat sallow skin and a kind, reassuring drawl. Between the French grammar and the drawl, Grant felt that P. C. Bithel was headed for great things.

The boy began to get up when Grant had introduced himself, but Grant sat down and said: "There's one small thing you might do for me. I'd like to know who cleans the windows of 5 Britt Lane. You might make a few inquiries when—"

"Mr. Lloyd's place?" the boy said. "Richards does them."

Yes, indeed, and indeed P. C. Bithel had a future; he must keep his eye on P. C. Bithel.

"How do you know that?"

"I pass the time of day with him here and there on my beat. He stables his barrow and things in that mews further along Britt Lane."

He thanked the budding Superintendent and went away to find Richards. Richards, it seemed, lived above his barrow. He was a bachelor ex-serviceman with a short leg, a cat, a collection of china mugs, and a passion for darts. There was nothing that P. C. Bithel, not long from County Down, did not know about his London beat.

At the corner of Britt Lane was the Sun, where Richards played darts, and it was to the Sun that Grant went. This was to be an altogether informal arrangement and it demanded an informal launching. He did not know the Sun or its proprietor, but he had only to sit still and behave himself and presently he would be invited to play darts, and from that to having a quiet one with Richards was only a step.

It was a step that took a couple of hours, as it turned out; but eventually he had Richards to himself in a corner with a pint. He was debating with himself whether to produce his card and use his official credentials for unofficial business, or to make it an affair of one ex-serviceman obliging another for a small consideration, when Richards said:

"You don't seem to have put on any weight with the years, sir."

"Have I met you somewhere?" Grant asked, a little annoyed that he should have forgotten a face.

"Camberley. More years ago than I like to think about. And you needn't worry about forgetting me," he added, "because I doubt if you ever saw me. I was a cook. You still in the Army?"

"No, I'm a policeman."

"No kidding! Well, well. I'd have said you were a dead cert for C.I.G.S. I see now why you were so anxious to get me into a corner. And me thinking it was my way with a dart that won you!"

Grant laughed. "Yes, you can do something for me, but it isn't official business. Would you take a pupil tomorrow for a small consideration?"

"To do any special windows?" Richards asked, after a moment's thought.

"Number 5 Britt Lane."

"Ho!" said Richards, amused. "*I'd* pay *him* to do *them!*"

"Why?"

"That bastard is never pleased. There's no hanky-panky about this, is there?"

"Neither hanky nor panky. Nothing is going to be abstracted from the house, and nothing upset. I'll go bail for that. Indeed, if it will make you any happier, I'll put the contract in writing."

"I'll take your word for it, sir. And your man can have the privilege of doing Mr. Flipping Lloyd's windows for nothing." He lifted his mug. "Here's to the old eyesright. What time will your pupil be coming along tomorrow?"

"Ten o'clock do?"

"Make it half-past. Your valentine goes out most mornings about eleven."

"That's very thoughtful of you."

"I'll get my early windows done and meet him at my place—3 Britt Mews—at half-past ten."

It was no use trying to telephone Tad Cullen again tonight, so Grant left a message at the Westmorland asking him to come to the flat as soon as he had had breakfast in the morning.

Then he at last had dinner, and went thankfully to bed.

As he was falling asleep a voice in his head said, "Because he knew that there was nothing to write on."

"What?" he said, coming awake. "Who knew?"

"Lloyd. He said, 'On what?'"

"Yes. Well?"

"He said it because he was startled."

"He certainly sounded surprised."

"He was surprised because he knew that there was nothing to write on."

He lay thinking about it until he fell asleep.

13

Tad arrived, very washed and shining, before Grant had finished breakfast. His soul was troubled, however, and he had to be coaxed out of a contrite mood ("Can't help feeling that I walked out on you, Mr. Grant") before he was any good to anyone. He cheered up at last when he found that there were definite plans for the day.

"You mean you were serious about window cleaning? I thought it was only a—a sort of figure of speech, maybe. You know, like, 'I'll be selling matches for a living if this goes on.' Why am I going to clean Lloyd's windows?"

"Because it is the only honest way of getting a foot inside the house. My colleagues can prove that you have no right to read a gas-meter, or test the electricity, or the telephone. But they cannot deny that you are a window-cleaner and are legally and professionally getting on with your job. Richards—your boss for today—says that Lloyd goes out nearly every day about eleven, and he is going to take you there when Lloyd has gone. He'll stay with you and work with you, of course, so that he can introduce you as his assistant who is learning the trade. That way you will be accepted without suspicion and left alone."

"So I'm left alone."

"On the desk in the big room that occupies most of the first floor there is an engagement book. A large, very expensive, red-leather affair. The desk is a table one—I mean that it doesn't shut—and it stands just inside the middle window."

"So?"

"I want to know Lloyd's engagements for the 3rd and 4th of March."

"You think maybe he travelled on that train, 'm?"

"I should like to be sure that he didn't, anyhow. If I know what his engagements were I can find out quite easily whether he kept them or not."

"Okay. That's quite easy. I'm looking forward to that window cleaning. I've always wondered what I could do when I get too old for flying. I might as well look into the window trade. To say nothing of looking into a few windows."

He went away, blithe and apparently forgetful that half an hour ago he was "lower than a worm's belly," and Grant looked round in his mind for any acquaintances that he and Heron Lloyd might have in common. He remembered that he had not yet rung up Marta Hallard to announce his return to town. It might be a little early in the day to break in on Marta's slumbers, but he would risk it.

"Oh, no," Marta said, "you didn't wake me. I'm halfway through my breakfast and having my daily dose of news. Every day I swear that never again will I read a daily paper, and every morning there is the blasted thing lying waiting for me to open it and every morning I open it. It upsets my digestive juices, and hardens my arteries, and my face falls with a thud and undoes five guineas' worth of Ayesha's ministrations in five minutes, but I have to have my daily dose of poison. How are you, my dear? Are you better?"

She listened to his answer without interrupting. One of Marta's more charming characteristics was her capacity for listening. With most of his other women friends silence meant that they were preparing their next speech and were merely waiting for the next appropriate moment to give utterance to it.

"Have supper with me tonight. I'll be alone," she said when she had heard about Clune and his recovered health.

"Make it early next week, can you? How is the play going?"

"Well, darling, it would be going a lot better if Ronnie would come up-stage now and then to talk to me instead of to the audience. He says it emphasises the detachment of the character to practically stamp on the floats and let the front stalls count his eyelashes, but I think myself it's just a hangover from his music-hall days."

They discussed both Ronnie and the play for a little, and then Grant said: "Do you know Heron Lloyd, by the way?"

"The Arabia man? Not to say know; no. But I understand he's almost as much of a hogger as Ronnie."

"How?"

"Rory—my brother's boy—was mad to go exploring in Arabia—though why anyone should want to go exploring in Arabia I can't imagine—all dust and dates—anyway, Rory wanted to go with Heron Lloyd, but it seems that Lloyd travels only with Arabs. Rory, who is a nice child, says that that is because Lloyd is so Arabian that he is *plus royaliste que le roi,* but I think myself—being a lowminded creature and a rogue and vagabond—that he is just suffering from Ronnie's trouble and wants the whole stage."

"What is Rory doing now?" Grant asked, skating away from Heron Lloyd.

"Oh, he's in Arabia. The other man took him. Kinsey-Hewitt. Oh, yes, Rory wouldn't be put off by a little thing like a snub. Can you make it Tuesday: the supper?"

Yes, he would make it Tuesday. Before Tuesday he would be back at work, and the matter of Bill Kenrick, who had come to England full of excitement about Arabia and had died as Charles Martin in a train going to the Highlands, would have to be put behind him. He had only a day or two more.

He went out to have a hair-cut, and to think in that relaxed hypnotic atmosphere of anything that they had left undone. Tad Cullen was lunching with his boss. "Richards won't accept anything for this," he had said to Tad, "so take him out to lunch and give him a thundering good one and I'll pay for it."

"I'll take him out all right and be glad to," Tad said, "but I'm damned if I'll let you pay for it. Bill Kenrick was my buddy, not yours."

So he sat in the warm, aromatic air of the barber's shop, half dive, half clinic, and tried to think of something that they could still do to find Bill Kenrick's suitcases. But it was the returning Tad who provided the suggestion.

Why, said Tad, not Agony-advertise for this girl.

"What girl?"

"The girl who has his luggage. *She* has no reason to be shy—unless she's been helping herself to the contents, which wouldn't be unknown. But Bill is a—was a better picker than that. Why don't we say in capital letters: 'BILL KENRICK'—to catch the eye, get it?—and then just, 'Any friend get in touch with Number what's-it.' Is there anything against that?"

No, Grant could think of nothing against that, but his eye was on the piece of paper that Tad was fishing from his pocket.

"Did you find the book?"

"Oh, yes. I had only to lean in and pick it up. That guy doesn't do any homework, it seems. It's the dullest list of engagements outside a prison. Not a gardenia from start to finish. And no good to us anyway."

"No good?"

"He was busy, it seems. Will I write out that advertisement for the papers?"

"Yes, do. There's paper in my desk."

"Which papers shall we send it to?"

"Write six, and we can address them later."

He looked down at Tad's child-like copy of the entries in Lloyd's engagement book. The entries for the 3rd and 4th of March. And as he read them the full absurdity of his suspicions came home to him. What was he thinking of? Was his mind still the too impressionable mind of a sick man? How could he ever have dreamed that Heron Lloyd could possibly have been moved to murder? Because that was what he had been thinking, wasn't it? That somehow, in some way that they could not guess, Lloyd had been responsible for Bill Kenrick's death.

He looked at the crucial entries, and thought that even if it were proved that Lloyd had not kept these particular engagements it would be fantastic to read into that absence any more than the normal explanation: that Lloyd had been indisposed or had changed his mind. On the night of the 3rd he had apparently attended a dinner.

"Pioneer Society, Normandie, 7:15" the entry read. At 9:30 the following morning a Pathé Magazine film unit were due to arrive at 5 Britt Lane and make him into number something-or-other of their Celebrities at Home series. It would seem that Heron Lloyd had more important things to think of than an unknown flyer who claimed to have seen ruins in the sands of Arabia.

"But he said, 'On what?' " said that voice in him.

"All *right,* he said, 'On what?' A fine world it would be if one was going to be suspected, if one was going to be judged, by every unconsidered remark!"

The Commissioner had once said to him: "You have the most priceless of all attributes for your job, and that is flair. But don't let it ride you, Grant. Don't let your imagination take hold. Keep it your servant."

He had been in danger of letting his flair bolt with him. He must take a pull on himself.

He would go back to where he was before he saw Lloyd. Back to the company of Bill Kenrick. Back from wild imaginings to fact. Hard, bare, uncompromising fact.

He looked across at Tad, nose to paper and pursuing his pen across the page with it as a terrier noses a spider across a floor.

"How was your milk-bar lady?"

"Oh, fine, fine," said Tad, absent-minded and not lifting his glance from his handiwork.

"Taking her out again?"

"Uh-huh. Meeting her tonight."

"Think she will do as a steady?"

"She might," Tad said, and then as he became aware of this unusual interest he looked up and said: "What's this all about?"

"I'm thinking of deserting you for a day or two, and I'd like to know that you won't be bored if left to your own devices."

"Oh. Oh, no; I'll be all right. It's time you took some time off to attend to your own affairs, I guess. After all, this is not trouble of yours. You've done far too much as it is."

"I'm not taking time off. I'm planning to fly over and see Charles Martin's people."

"People?"

"His family. They live outside Marseilles."

Tad's face, which had looked blank for a moment, grew animated again.

166

"What do you think you'll get from them?"

"I'm not doing any thinking. I'm just beginning from the other end. We've come to a blank wall where Bill Kenrick is concerned—unless his hypothetical girl-friend answers that advertisement, and that won't be for two days at the very least—so we'll try the Charles Martin end and see where we get from there."

"Fine. What about me coming with you?"

"I think not, Tad. I think you had better stay here and be O.C. the Press. See that all these are inserted and pick up any answers."

"You're the boss," Tad said in a resigned way. "But I sure would like to see Marseilles."

"It's not a bit the way you picture it," Grant said, amused.

"How do you know how I picture it?"

"I can imagine."

"Oh, well, I suppose I can sit on a stool and look at Daphne. What funny names girls have in this neck of the woods. It's a bit draughty, but I can count up the number of times people say thank you for doing other people service."

"If it's iniquity you're looking for, you'll find as much on a Leicester Square pavement as you will on the Cannebière."

"Maybe, but I like my iniquity with some ooh-la-la in it."

"Hasn't Daphne got any ooh-la-la?"

"No Daphne's very la-di-da. I have an awful suspicion that she wears wooden underwear."

"She would need it in a milk-bar in Leicester Square in April. She sounds a nice girl."

"Oh, she's fine, fine. But don't you stay too long away, or the wolf in me will prove too strong and I'll take the first plane out to Marseilles to join you. When do you plan to go?"

"Tomorrow morning, if I can get a seat. Move over and let me reach the telephone. If I get an early-morning service I can, with a piece of luck, get back the following day. If not, then Friday at the latest. How did you get on with Richards?"

"Oh, we're great buddies. But I'm a bit disillusioned."

"About what?"

"About the possibilities of the trade."

"Doesn't it pay?"

"I expect it pays off in coin but not any other way, take it from me. All you can see from outside a window, believe it or not, is your own reflection in the glass. What are the names of those papers you want me to address these things to?"

Grant gave him the names of the six newspapers with the largest circulations, and sent him away with his blessing to employ his time as he saw fit until they met again.

"I certainly wish I was going with you," Tad said once more as he was leaving, and Grant wondered if seeing the South of France as one big honky-tonk was any more absurd than seeing it as mimosa. Which was what it was to him.

"France!" said Mrs. Tinker. "When you've only just come back from foreign parts!"

"The Highlands may be foreign parts, but the South of France is merely an extension of England."

"It's a very expensive extension, I've 'eard. *Roonous*. When was you expectin' to be back? I got a loverly chicken from Carr's for you."

"The day after tomorrow, I hope. Friday at the latest."

"Oh. then it'll keep. Was you wantin' to be called earlier tomorrow mornin', then?"

"I'll be away before you come in, I think. So you can have a late morning tomorrow."

"A late mornin' wouldn't suit Tinker, it wouldn't. But I'll get me shoppin' done before I come in. Now you see and take care of yerself. No burning the candle at both ends and comin' back lookin' no better than when you went away to Scotland in the beginnin'. I 'ope it keeps fine for you!"

Fine indeed, Grant thought, looking down at the map of France next morning. From that height on this crystal morning it was not a thing of earth and water and crops. It was a small jewelled pattern set in a lapis-lazuli sea; a Fabergé creation. Not much wonder that flyers as a species had a detached attitude to the world. What had the world —its literature, its music, its philosophies, or its history— to do with a man who saw it habitually for the thing it was: a bit of Fabergé nonsense?

Marseilles, at close quarters, was no jeweller's creation. It was the usual noisy crowded place filled with impatient taxi-horns and the smell of stale coffee; that very French smell that haunts its houses with the ghosts of ten million coffee-brewings. But the sun shone, and the striped awnings flapped a little in the breeze from the Mediterranean, and the mimosa displayed its pale expensive yellow in prodigal masses. As a companion picture to the grey and scarlet of London it was, he thought, perfect. If he ever was rich he would commission one of the best artists in the world to put the two pictures on canvas for him; the chiaroscuro of London and bright positive blaze of Marseilles. Or perhaps two different artists. It was unlikely that the man who could convey the London of a grey day in April would also be able to paint the essence of Marseilles on a spring noon.

He stopped thinking about artists and ceased to find Marseilles either bright or positive when he found that the Martin family had left the suburb only the week before for parts unknown. Unknown, that was, to the neighbours. By the time that he had, with the help of local authorities, discovered that "parts unknown" merely meant Toulon, a great deal of precious time had been wasted, and still more was wasted in journeying to Toulon and finding the Martins among its teeming inhabitants.

But in the end he found them and listened to the little they had to tell. Charles was a "bad boy," they said, with all the antagonism of the French for someone who had apostatised from that supreme god of the French idolatry, the Family. He had always been a wilful, headstrong creature and (crime of crimes in the French calendar) lazy. Bone-lazy. He had gone away five years ago after a small trouble over a girl—no, no, he had merely stabbed her—and had not bothered to write to them. They had had no news of him in all those years except that a friend had run into him in Port Said about three years ago. He was doing pavement deals in second-hand cars, the friend said. Buying up crocks and selling them after he had tinkered with them a little. He was a very good mechanic; he could have been a very successful man, with a garage of his own and people working for him, if he had not been so lazy. Bone-lazy. A laziness that was formidable. A laziness that was a disease. They had heard nothing more of him until they had been asked to identify his body.

Grant asked if they had a photograph of Charles.

"Yes, they had several, but of course they were of Charles when he was much younger.

They showed him the photographs, and Grant saw why Bill Kenrick, dead, looked not too unlike the Charles Martin that his family had remembered. One thin dark man with marked eyebrows, hollowed cheeks and straight dark hair looked very like any other similar young man when individuality was quenched. They did not even have to have the same colour of eyes. A parent receives a message saying: Your son is dead as the result of a regrettable accident; would you please identify him as your son and arrange for the burial. The bereaved parent is presented with his dead son's papers and belongings and is asked to identify the owner as his son. There is no question in his conditioned mind; he accepts what he sees, and what he sees is what he expected to see. It would not occur to him to say: Are this man's eyes blue or brown?

In the end, of course, it was Grant who submitted to questioning. Why was he interested in Charles? Had Charles after all left some money? Was it that Grant was looking for the legal heirs, perhaps?

No, Grant had promised to look Charles up on behalf of a friend who had known him on the Persian Gulf coast. No, he did not know what the friend wanted of him. He understood that there was some suggestion of a future partnership.

In the expressed opinion of the Martin family, the friend was lucky.

They gave him Armagnac and coffee and little biscuits with Bath-bun sugar on them, and asked him to come again if he was ever in Toulon.

On the doorstep he asked if they had possession of their son's papers. Only his personal ones, they said: his letters. The official ones they had not bothered with or thought about. They were no doubt still with the Marseilles police, who had first made contact with them when the accident happened.

So a little more time was wasted in making friends with the Marseilles officials; but this time Grant spent no energy on conscientiously unofficial methods. He produced his credentials and asked for a loan of the papers. He drank a *sirop*, and signed a receipt. And he caught the afternoon plane to London on Friday afternoon.

He had two more days. Or one day and a Sunday, to be accurate.

France was still a jewelled pattern as he flew back over it, but Britain seemed to have disappeared altogether. Beyond the familiar outline of the western European coast there was nothing but an ocean of haze. Very odd and incomplete the map looked without the familiar shape of that very individual island. Supposing there never had been that island: How different would the history of the world have been? It was a fascinating speculation. An all-Spanish America, one supposed. A French India: an India without a colour-bar and so racially intermarried that it had lost its identity. A Dutch South Africa ruled by a fanatic Church. Australia? Who would have discovered and colonised Australia? The Dutch from South Africa, or the Spaniards from America? It was immaterial, he supposed, since either race would in a generation have become tall, lean, tough, nasal, drawling, sceptical and indestructible.

They dropped into the ocean of cloud, and found Britain again. A very mundane, muddy, and workaday place to have changed the history of a world. A steady drizzle soaked the land and the lieges. London was a water-colour of grey reflections with spots of vermilion oil paint where the buses plunged dripping through the haze.

All the lights were on in the finger-print department, although it was still daylight; and Cartwright was sitting just as he had last seen him—as he had always seen him —with a half-drunk cup of cold tea at his elbow, the saucer filled with cigarette butts.

"Something I can do for you this beautiful spring afternoon?" Cartwright said.

"Yes. There is one thing I want very much to know. Have you ever drunk the second half of a cup of tea?"

Cartwright considered this. "Come to think of it, I don't know that I ever have. Beryl usually takes my cup away and fills it up with fresh stuff. Something else off the cuff?" Or is this just a social call?"

"Yes, something else. But you'll be *working* for me on Monday, so don't let your sense of benevolence get out of hand." He put Charles Martin's papers on the table. "When can you do these for me?"

"What is this? French identity papers. What are you getting into—or do you want to keep it to yourself?"

"I'm just having one last bet on a horse called Flair. If it comes off I'll tell you about it. I'll pick up the prints tomorrow morning."

He looked at the clock and reckoned that if Tad Cullen was "dating" Daphne, or any other female creature, tonight, he would at this moment be dolling himself up in his hotel room. He left Cartwright and went to a telephone where he could talk unheard.

"We-e-ll!" said Tad joyously, when he heard Grant's voice. "Where are you talking from. Are you back?"

"Yes, I'm back. I'm in London. Look, Tad, you say you've never known anyone called Charles Martin. But is it possible that you knew him under another name? Did you ever know a very good mechanic, very good with cars, who was French and looked like Bill?"

Tad thought this over.

"I don't think I've ever known any mechanic who was French. I've known a Swedish mechanic and a Greek mechanic, but neither of them was in the least like Bill. Why?"

"Because Martin worked in the Middle East. And it is just possible that Bill got those papers from him before he ever came to Britain at all. Martin may have sold them to him. He was—is: he may be living—a lazy creature and probably very hard-up at intervals. Out there, where no one bothers very much about credentials, he might have tried to cash them."

"Yes; he might. Someone else's papers are usually more valuable than your own out there. To have around, I mean. But why would *Bill* buy them? Bill never did anything on the side."

"Perhaps because he looked a little like Martin. I don't know. Anyhow, you yourself have never run into anyone like Martin in the Middle East?"

"Not anywhere, that I can think of. What did you get out of the Martins? Anything worth while?"

"I'm afraid not. They showed me photographs which made it clear how much he would look like Bill if he was· not alive. Something that we knew already. And of course the fact that he had gone East to work. Any answers to the advertisement?"

"Five."

"Five?"

"All from fellows called Bill Kenrick."

"Oh. Asking what was in it for them?"

"You've got it."

"Not a word from anyone who knew him?"

"Not a peep. And nothing at the Charles Martin end either, it seems. We're sunk, aren't we?"

"Well—waterlogged, shall we say. We have one remaining asset."

"We have? What is that?"

"Time. We have forty-eight more hours."

"Mr. Grant, you're an optimist."

"You have to be in my business," Grant said, but he did not feel very optimistic. He felt flat and tired. He was within an ace of wishing that he had never heard of Bill Kenrick. Wishing that he had come down that corridor at Scoone just ten seconds later. In ten more seconds Yoghourt would have realised that the man was dead and would have shut the door and gone for help; and he, Grant, would have walked down the empty corridor and stepped down on to the platform unaware that there had ever existed a young man called Bill Kenrick. He would never have known that any-one had died on the train. He would have driven away with Tommy to the hills, and no words about singing sands would have disturbed his holiday. He would have fished in peace, and finished his holiday in peace.

In too much peace perhaps? With too much time to think about himself and his bondage to unreason. Too much time to take his own mental and spiritual pulse.

No, of course he was not sorry that he had heard of Bill Kenrick. He was Bill Kenrick's debtor as long as he lived, and if it took him till the end of his days he would find out what had changed Bill Kenrick into Charles Martin. But if only he could clear up this thing before he was swamped by that demanding life that was waiting for him on Monday.

He asked how Daphne was, and Tad said that as a female companion she had one enormous advantage over everyone he had ever known; she was pleased with very little. If you gave her a bunch of violets, she was as pleased as most girls are with orchids. It was Tad's considered opinion that she had never heard of orchids, and he, personally, had no intention of bring-ing them to her notice.

"She sounds the domestic type. You take care, Tad, or she'll be going back to the Middle East with you."

"Not while I'm conscious," Tad said. "No female is going back East with me. I'm not having any little woman round the house cluttering up *our* bungalow. I mean, my bun—I mean—" His voice died away.

The conversation became suddenly broken-backed and Grant rang off after promising to call him as soon as he had anything to report or an idea to share.

He went out into the wet haze, bought himself an evening paper, and found a taxi to take him home.

173

The paper was a *Signal*, and the sight of the familiar heading took him back to that breakfast at Scoone four weeks ago. He thought again how constant in kind the headlines were. The Cabinet row, the dead body of the blonde in Maida Vale, the Customs prosecution, the hold-up, the arrival of an American actor, the street accident. Even "PLANE CRASH IN ALPS" was common enough to rank as a constant.

"Yesterday evening the dwellers in the high valleys of Chamonix saw a rose of flame break out on the icy summit of Mont Blanc—"

The *Signal*'s style was constant too.

The only thing waiting for him at 19 Tenby Court was a letter from Pat, which said:

Dear Alan, they say you must have marjuns but I think marjuns is havers. waste not want not. this is a fly I made for you. it was not done in time before you went. it may not be any good for those english rivers but you better have it anyway your affectionate cousin Patrick.

This production cheered Grant considerably, and while he ate his dinner he considered alternately the economy, in capitals as well as in margins, and the enclosed lure. The fly exceeded in originality even that remarkable affair which he had been lent at Clune. He decided to use it on the Severn on a day when fish would take a piece of red rubber hot-water bottle, so that he could write honestly to Pat and report that the Rankin fly had landed a big one.

The typical Scots insularity in "those english rivers" made him hope that Laura would not wait too long before sending Pat away to his English school. The quality of Scotchness was highly concentrated essence, and should always be diluted. As an ingredient it was admirable; neat, it was as abominable as ammonia.

He stuck the fly above the calendar on his desk, so that he might go on being amused by its catholicity and warmed by his young cousin's devotion, and got thankfully into pyjamas and dressing-gown. There was at least one consolation for being in town when he might still be in the country: he could get into a dressing-gown and put his feet on the fender in the sure and certain knowledge that no telephone call from Whitehall 1212 would intrude on his leisure.

But he had not had his feet up for twenty minutes when Whitehall 1212 was on the telephone.

It was Cartwright.

"Did I understand you to say that you had had a bet on Flair?" said Cartwright's voice.

"Yes. Why?"

"I don't know anything about it, but I have an idea that your horse has won," said Cartwright. He added, very silky and sweet like a Broadcasting Aunt, *"Good night, sir,"* and hung up.

"Hey!" said Grant, and jiggled the telephone key. *"Hey!"*

But Cartwright had gone. And it would be no use trying to bring him to the telephone any more tonight. This amiable piece of teasing was Cartwright's comeback, his charge for doing a couple of buckshee jobs.

Grant went back to his Runyon, but he could no longer keep his attention of that strictly legit character, Judge Henry G. Blake. Blast Cartwright and his little jokes. Now he would have to go to the Yard first thing in the morning.

But in the morning he forgot all about Cartwright.

By eight o'clock in the morning Cartwright had sunk back into the great ocean of incidentals that bear us on from one day to the next, unremarkable in their plankton swarming.

The morning began as it always did, with the rattle of china and the voice of Mrs. Tinker as she set down his early-morning tea. This was the preliminary to four glorious minutes during which he lay still more asleep than awake and let his tea cool, so that Mrs. Tinker's voice came to him down a long tunnel that led to life and the daylight but need not yet be traversed.

"Just listen to it," Mrs. Tinker's voice said, referring apparently to the steady beat of the rain. "Stair rods, cats and dogs, reservoyers. Niagara also ran. Seems they've bin and found Shangri-la. I could do with a spot of Shangri-la myself this morning."

The word turned over in his sleepy mind like a weed in calm water. Shangri-la. Very soporific. Very soporific. Shangri-la. Some place in a film. In a novel. Some unspoiled Eden. Shut away from the world.

175

"According to this mornin's papers they never 'ave no rain at all there."

"Where?" he said, to show that he was awake.

"Arabia, so it seems."

He heard the door close and dropped a little further under the surface of things for the enjoyment of those four minutes. Arabia. Arabia. Another soporific. They had found Shangri-la in Arabia. They—

Arabia!

In one great whirl of blankets he came to the surface and reached for the papers. There were two, but it was the *Clarion* that came to his hand first because it was the *Clarion* whose headlines constituted Mrs. Tinker's daily dose of reading.

He did not have to search for it. It was there on the front page. It was the best front-page stuff that any newspaper had had since Crippen.

SHANGRI-LA REALLY EXISTS. SENSATIONAL DISCOVERY. HISTORIC FIND IN ARABIA.

He glanced over the hysterically excited paragraphs and discarded the paper impatiently for the more trustworthy *Morning News*. But the *Morning News* was almost as excited as the *Clarion*. KINSEY-HEWITT'S GREAT FIND, said the *Morning News*. ASTOUNDING NEWS FROM ARABIA.

"We print, with great pride, Paul Kinsey-Hewitt's own despatch," said the *Morning News*. "As our readers will see, his discovery had been vouched for by three R.A.F. planes sent to locate the place after Mr. Kinsey-Hewitt's arrival at Makallah." The *Morning News* had had a contract with Kinsey-Hewitt for a series of articles on his present journey, when that journey should be completed, and was now delirious with pleasure at its unexpected luck.

He skipped the *Morning News* on its own triumph and went on to the far soberer prose of the triumphant explorer himself:

We were in the Empty Quarter on scientific errands . . . no thought in our minds of human history either factual or legendary . . . a well-explored country . . . bare mountains that no one had ever considered climbing . . . a waste of time between one well and the next . . . in a land where water is life no one turns aside to climb precipitous heights . . .

176

attention caught by a plane that came twice in five days and spent some time circling low above the mountains . . . occurred to us that some plane had crashed . . . possible rescue . . . conference . . . Rory Hallard and I to search while Daoud went on to the well at Zaruba and brought a load of water back to meet us . . . no entrance apparent . . . walls like the Garbh Coire on Braeriach . . . giving up . . . Rory . . . a track that even a goat would baulk at . . . two hours to the ridge . . . a valley of astounding beauty . . . green almost shocking . . . kind of tamarisk . . . crumbled architecture reminiscent of Greece rather than Arabia . . . colonnades . . . paved squares and streets . . . oddly metropolitan . . . in the position of a small island in an ocean of desert . . . strip cultivation . . . monkey god in stone . . . Wabar . . . volcanic convulsion . . . Wabar . . . Wabar . . .

The *Morning News* had inset a neat outline map of Arabia with crosses in the appropriate place.

Grant lay and stared at it.

So *that* was what Bill Kenrick had seen.

He had come out of the shouting heart of the storm, out of the whirling sand and the darkness, and looked down at that green valley lying among the rocks. Not much wonder that he had come back looking "concussed," looking as if his mind were "still back there." He had not quite believed it himself. He had gone back to search; to look for, and eventually look at, this place that appeared on no map. This—*this*—was his Paradise.

This was what he had been writing about on the blank space of an evening paper.

This was what he had.come to England to—

To Heron Lloyd to—

To *Heron Lloyd!*

He flung the *News* away and leaped out of bed.

"Tink!" he called as he turned on the bath-water. "Tink, never mind breakfast. Get me some coffee."

"But you can't go out on a morning like this with just a cup of—"

"Don't argue! Get me some coffee!"

The water roared into the bath. The liar. The Goddamned smooth heartless limelight-hogging liar. The vain vicious murdering liar. How had he done it?

By God, he would see that he hanged for this.

"On what evidence?" said his inner voice, nasty-polite.

"You shut up! I'll get the evidence if I have to discover a whole new continent to find it? Poor boy! Poor boy!" said he, shaking his head over so sad a fate. "Sweet Christ, I'll hang for him myself if I can't kill him any other way!"

"Calm down, calm down. That's no mood to interview a suspect in."

"I'm not interviewing a suspect, blast your police mind. I'm going to tell Heron Lloyd what I think of him. I'm not a police-officer until after I've dealt personally with Lloyd."

"You can't hit a man of sixty."

"I'm not going to hit him. I'm going to half murder him. The ethics of hitting or not hitting don't enter into the matter at all."

"He may be worth hanging for but not worth being requested to resign for."

" 'I found him delightful,' said he, kind and patronising. The bastard. The smooth vain murdering bastard. The—"

From the wells of his experience he dredged up words to serve his need. But his anger went on consuming him like a furnace.

He flung out of the house after two mouthfuls of toast and three gulps of coffee, and went round to the garage at the double. It was too early to hope for a taxi; the quickest way was to use his car.

Would Lloyd have read the papers yet?

If he did not normally leave the house before eleven o'clock, then surely breakfast could not be until nine. He would like very much to be at 5 Britt Lane before Lloyd opened his morning paper. It would be sweet, consoling sweet, satisfying sweet, to watch Lloyd take the news. He had murdered to keep the secret his own, to ensure that the glory should be his, and now the secret was front-page news and the glory belonged to his rival. Oh, sweet Jesus, let him not have read about it yet.

He rang twice at 5 Britt Lane before his summons was answered, and then it was answered not by the amiable Mahmoud but by a large woman in felt slippers.

"Mr. Lloyd?" he asked.

"Oh, Mr. Lloyd's up in Cumberland for a day or two."

"Cumberland! When did he go to Cumberland?"

"Thursday afternoon."

"When do you expect him back?"

"Oh, they've just gone for a day or two."

"They? Mahmoud too?"

"Of course Mahmoud too. Mr. Lloyd he doesn't go anywhere without Mahmoud goes with him."

"I see. Can you give me his address?"

"I'd give it to you if I had it. But they don't bother with re-addressing when they go for only a day or two. Will you leave a message? Or will you call back, perhaps? They'll like as not arrive back this afternoon."

No, he would not leave a message. He would come back. His name did not matter.

He felt like someone who has braked too suddenly and been hit in the wind. As he went out to his car, he remembered that Tad Cullen would read the story in a few minutes' time, if he had not read it already. He went back to the flat and was met in the lobby by a relieved Mrs. Tinker.

"Thank heaven you're back. That American boy's been on the phone and goin' on somethink awful. I can't make 'ead or tail of what 'e thinks 'e's talkin' about. Ravin' mad, 'e is. I says: 'Mr. Grant'll ring you,' I says, 'the minute 'e come in,' but 'e can't leave the phone alone. Just puts it down an' picks it up again. I bin running backwards and forwards between the sink and the phone like a—" The telephone rang. "There you are! There 'e is again!"

Grant picked up the receiver. It was indeed Tad, and he was all that Mrs. Tinker had said. He was incoherent with rage.

"But he lied!" he kept saying. "That guy lied. Of *course* Bill told him all that!"

"Yes, of course he did. Listen, Tad . . . listen . . . No, you can't go and beat him to a jelly. . . . Yes, of course you can find his house for yourself; I don't doubt it, but . . . *Listen*, Tad! I've *been* to his house . . . Oh, yes, even at *this* hour of the morning. I read my papers earlier than you do . . . No, I didn't beat him up. I couldn't . . . No, not because I'm windy but because he's in Cumberland . . . Yes. Since Thursday . . . I don't know. I'll have to think about it. Give me until lunch-time. Do you trust my judgment on things in general? . . . Well, you'll have to trust it in this. I must have time to think . . . To think up some evidence, of course . . . It's customary . . . I'll tell

179

my story to the Yard, of course, and of course they will believe me. I mean, my story of Bill's visit to Lloyd, and Lloyd's lies to me. But proving that Charles Martin was Bill Kenrick is quite a different matter. Until lunch-time I shall be writing out a statement for the Yard. Come about one o'clock and we can have lunch together. In the afternoon I must turn the whole thing over to the authorities."

He hated the thought. This was his own private fight. It had been his own private fight from the very beginning. From that moment when he had looked down through the open compartment door on to the dead face of an unknown boy. It was a thousand times more his private fight since his meeting with Lloyd.

He had begun to write, when he remembered that he had not yet picked up the papers he had left with Cartwright. He lifted the receiver, dialled the number, and asked for Cartwright's extension. Could Cartwright possibly find a messenger to send round with those papers? He, Grant, was frantically busy. It was Saturday, and he was clearing up before going back to work on Monday. He would be very grateful.

He went back to his writing, and became so absorbed that he was conscious only in a dim way that Mrs. Tinker had brought in the second post: the noon one. It was when he raised his glance from the paper to search his mind for a word, that his eye fell on the envelope she had laid beside him on the desk. It was a foolscap envelope, rather stiff and expensive, well-filled, and addressed in a thin, angular cramped hand that managed to be at once finicking and flamboyant.

Grant had never seen Heron Lloyd's handwriting. He recognised it instantly.

He put down his pen cautiously, as if the strange letter was a bomb and any undue vibration might send it off.

He wiped his palms down the thighs of his trousers in a gesture he had not used since he was a child, the gesture of a small boy facing the incalculable, and put out his hand for the envelope.

It had been posted in London.

14

The letter was dated Thursday morning.

MY DEAR MR. GRANT,

Or should I say Inspector? Oh yes, I know about
that. It did not take me long to find out. My excellent
Mahmoud is a better detective than any of your well-
meaning amateurs on the Embankment. But I shall not
give you your rank, because this is a social communi-
cation. I write to you as one unique human being to
another worthy of his attention. Indeed, it is because
you are the only Englishman who had ever moved me
to even a momentary admiration that I present these
facts to you and not to the Press.

And because, of course, I am sure of your interest.

I have this morning had a letter from my follower,
Paul Kinsey-Hewitt, announcing his discovery in Arabia. The letter was sent from the *Morning News* office
at his request, to anticipate the publication of the news
tomorrow morning. A piece of courtesy for which I am
grateful to him. It is ironic that it should have been
the Kenrick youth who was responsible for bringing
to him, too, the knowledge of the valley's existence. I

saw a great deal of the Kenrick youth while he was in London and I could find nothing in him worthy of so great a destiny. He was a very commonplace young man. He spent his days flying a mechanical contraption mindlessly across deserts that men had conquered only with suffering and resolution. He was full of a plan whereby I should provide the transport and he should lead me to this find of his. But that of course was absurd. I have not lived my life and made a great name in the desert to be led to discovery by an instrument-watcher from the back streets of Portsmouth; to be a transport provider, a camel-hirer, for some other man's convenience. It was not to be thought of that a youth who by a climatic hazard, a geographical accident, had stumbled on one of the great discoveries of the world should be allowed to profit by it at the expense of men who had given their lives to exploration.

As far as I could judge, the young man's only virtue (why do you waste your interest on so dull a piece of human mass-production?) was a capacity for continence. In speech, of course; please don't misunderstand me. And it was important from my point of view that the tongue which he had held with so rare a continence should go on being unwagged.

Since he had arranged to meet another of his kind in Paris on the 4th (poor beautiful Lutetia, for ever raped by the barbarian), I had a little less than a fortnight to contrive this. I did not, in fact, need the fortnight. I could have achieved my end in two days if necessary.

I had once, when travelling to Scotland by night, stayed awake to write some letters and post them at Crewe when the train would reach its first stop. I had thought then, as I sat looking at the platform after getting rid of my letters, how easy it would be to leave the train unobserved. The attendant stepped out to receive late-joining passengers and then went away on affairs of his own. There was a long wait at a quite deserted platform while luggage was loaded into the distant vans. If one had managed to travel so far unaccounted for, one could step off the train and no one would ever know that one had been on it.

That memory was the first of the two props for my inspiration.

The second was my possession of Charles Martin's papers.

Charles Martin was my mechanic. He was the only European and the only technician (what an appropriately deplorable word!) ever employed by me. I engaged him for the least successful of my expeditions, the semi-mechanised one, because my Arabs (though learning rapidly, alas!) were not skilful with machinery. He was a repellent creature, interested in nothing but internal combustion and the avoidance of his share of camp duties, and I was not sorry when he died in mid-desert. We had by that time found the vehicles a liability rather than a help and had decided to abandon them, so Martin had already outlived his usefulness. (No, I had nothing to do with his death; Heaven in this insance did its own scavenging.) No one asked for his papers, and since the journey was from coast to coast we never returned to the town in which I had engaged him. His papers lay in my baggage, a matter of no interest to me or to anyone else, and came back to England with me.

I remembered them when it was necessary to silence the Kenrick youth. Kenrick looked not too unlike Charles Martin.

It was Kenrick's plan to go back to his Carter-Paterson occupation in the East until such time as I should join him there, and we should then set out on our expedition together. He came to see me at Britt Lane very often, to discuss routes and plume himself on the prospect in front of him, and it amused me to see him sit there and babble his nonsense when I had so strange a translation prepared for him.

He had arranged to go to Paris by the night-ferry on the 3rd. He "collected" ferries, it seemed. He would go many miles out of his way to be punted across a stream which he could have crossed by a bridge a few yards from where he was standing. The Dover ferry was to be his two-hundredth, I think. When he told me that he had booked a berth on the train-ferry I telephoned, as soon as he had gone, and booked a berth to Scoone in the name of Charles Martin for the same night.

When I next saw him I suggested that since I was going to Scotland on the same evening on which he was leaving for Paris, he should leave his luggage (he had only two suitcases) in the cloak-room at Victoria, dine early with me at Britt Lane, and see me off at Euston.

He was always delighted to fall in with any suggestion that I was moved to put to him, and he agreed, as I knew he would, to this. We dined, on a rice and cutlets and apricots dish that Mahmoud has taught Mrs. Lucas to make (it needs long cooking so that the dish is impregnated with the flavour of the apricots), and Mahmoud drove us to Euston. At Euston I sent Kenrick to pick up my sleeper ticket while I went ahead. By the time Kenrick rejoined me, I had found my compartment and was waiting on the platform for his arrival. If by chance he wondered why I was travelling as Charles Martin I had the excuse of my fame to account for an incognito. But he made no comment.

I felt that the gods were on my side when I saw that the attendant was Old Yoghourt. You will not know Old Yoghourt. He had never in the whole course of his career been known to take an interest in any passenger whatever. His chief object when on duty being to retire to his own unsavoury compartment at the earliest possible moment and go to sleep there.

We had less than five minutes before the train was due to depart. We stood talking for a little with the door half closed, Kenrick facing the corridor. Presently he said that he had better get out, or he might be carried to the Highlands. I indicated my small overnight case, which was lying beside him on the bunk, and said: "If you open my case you'll find something in it for you. A keepsake till we meet again."

He bent over, with an almost childish eagerness, to unfasten the two locks. The position was perfect. I took from my pocket the most satisfactory weapon ever devised by man for the destruction of his unsuspecting enemy. Primitive man in desert countries had neither knife nor rifle, but he made the sand serve. A rag and a few handfulls of sand, and a skull would crack like an egg-shell; very neatly it would crack, without blood or fuss. He gave a small grunt and fell forward over the case. I shut and locked the door and looked to see if his nose was bleeding. It was not. I dragged him off the berth and bundled him under it. This was my only miscalculation. One half of the

184

space under the berth was occupied by some permanent obstruction, and thin and slight as he was his knees could not be pushed back out of sight. I took off my coat and flung it on the berth so that it hung over and hid his legs. As I arranged the folds in a manner at once concealing and suitably casual, the whistle went. I put the outward half of my ticket to Scoone, together with my sleeper ticket, on the small shelf below the mirror where Yoghourt would see it, and walked down the corridor to the lavatory. No one had interest for anything but the moment of leave-taking. I shut myself into the lavatory and waited.

About twenty minutes later I heard the successive closing of doors that meant that Yoghourt was making his rounds. When I heard him in the compartment next door, I began to wash, noisily. He tapped at the door a few moments later and asked if I were the passenger in B Seven. I said that I was. He announced that he had found my tickets and taken them. I heard him go through to the next coach and begin his door-slamming, and I walked back to B Seven and locked myself in.

After that I had three uninterrupted hours to make all perfect.

If you ever want to be sure of uninterrupted peace, my dear Mr. Grant, buy yourself a sleeper ticket to the North of Scotland. There is nowhere in this world where one is so safe from interruption as one is in a sleeping compartment once the attendant has done his round. Not even in the desert.

I retrieved Kenrick from below the bunk, rubbed his head on the edge of the wash-hand basin, and laid him on the bunk. An examination of his clothes showed a gratifying cosmopolitanism. His underclothes seemed to be dhob-washed, his suit made in Hong Kong, and his shoes in Karachi. His watch was a cheap metal one with neither name nor initials.

I removed the contents of his pockets and substituted Charles Martin's pocket-book and its contents.

He was still alive, but he stopped breathing as we were running through the yards at Rugby.

From then on I dressed the set, as they say in the theatre. And I don't think that I missed anything, did I, Mr. Grant? The details were perfect, even to the crushed hairs in the wash-hand basin and the dusty palms of his hands. In the case that I was leaving behind were old clothes of my own, well-worn and washed, and of a type that he was in the habit of wearing; and such Frenchness as I had been able to supply from my own store: a novel and a Testament. The case also, of course, contained the all-important bottle.

Kenrick had an extraordinarily hard head. I refer to the matter of drink, of course, not to the results of sand-bagging. I had plied him with whisky at dinner, and had offered him a stirrup-cup of such dimensions that any other man would have blenched at the prospect. He did indeed look at the half-tumbler of neat whisky a little doubtfully, but, as I have said, he was always anxious to please me and he drank it down without protest. He remained sober or to all appearances sober. But both his blood and his stomach would be whisky-sodden when he died.

So was his compartment when I had finished with it. As the lights of Crewe began to go by, I put the final touch. I laid the half-full bottle on the floor and rolled it to and fro over the carpet. As the rain slowed down I unlocked the door, shut it behind me, walked away down the train until I had several coaches between me and B Seven, stood looking in a casual, interested way at the traffic on the platform, stepped, still casual, down on to that platform and strolled along it. In hat and coat I did not look like a passenger, and no one took any notice of me.

I came back to London on the midnight train, arriving at Euston at half-past three, and was so exhilarated that I walked all the way home. I walked as if on air. I let myself in, and was sleeping peacefully when Mahmoud came to call me at seven-thirty and to remind me that I had an appointment to entertain Paris representatives at half past nine.

It was not until you called to see me that I knew about the scribbled words on the newspaper that had been in his coat pocket. I admit that I was for a moment dismayed that I should have overlooked anything at all, but I was instantly comforted by the venial nature of the slip. It did not in any way detract from, nor endanger my unique achievement. I had let him keep his deplorable rag as a piece of set-dressing. That it proved to have Kenrick's handwriting on it would not be of interest to authorities who had accepted the young man as Charles Martin.

The following evening, at the rush hour, I drove myself to Victoria and retrieved Kenrick's two cases from the cloak-room. I took them home, removed from them all maker's marks and any identifying articles, sewed them both up in canvas, and sent them with their contents to a refugee organisation in the Near East. If you ever want to get rid of anything, my dear Mr. Grant, do not burn it. Post it to a remote island in the South Seas.

Having seen to it that the admirably reticent tongue of the Kenrick youth would stay reticent, I looked forward to enjoying the fruits of my labours. Indeed, yesterday I had assurance of sufficient backing for my new expedition, and had planned to fly out next week. The letter from Kinsey-Hewitt this morning alters all that, of course. The fruits of my achievement have been taken from me. But no one can take from me the achievement itself. If I cannot be known as the discoverer of Wabar, I shall be known as the author of the only perfect murder ever perpetrated.

I cannot stay to be a candle-holder at Kinsey-Hewitt's triumph. And I am too old to have more triumphs of my own. But I *can* light a blaze that will make the candles on the Kinsey-Hewitt altar look small and pale and uninteresting. My funeral pyre will be a beacon to light all Europe, and my achievement in murder a tidal-wave that will sweep Kinsey-Hewitt and Wabar into the waste-paper baskets of the world's Press.

This evening, at dusk, I light my own pyre, on the highest slope of the highest mountain in Europe. Mahmoud does not know this. He thinks we are flying out to Athens. But he has been with me for many years and would be very unhappy without me. So I am taking him with me.

Good-bye, my dear Mr. Grant. It grieves me that someone of your intelligence should be wasting his talents in that rather stupid establishment on the Embankment. It was clever of you to discover that Charles Martin was not Charles Martin but someone called Kenrick, and I salute you. What you are not clever enough to discover is that he did not die by accident. What no one would ever be clever enough to discover is that I am the man who killed him.

Please take this letter as a mark of esteem and *pour prendre congé*. Mrs. Lucas will post this on Friday morning.

H.C. HERON LLOYD

Grant became aware that Mrs. Tinker was showing Tad Cullen into the room, and that she must already have been in without his noticing because the envelope from the Yard was lying beside him on the desk.

"Well?" said Tad, his face still thunderous. "Where do we go from here?"

Grant pushed over the pages of Lloyd's letter for him to read.

"What's all this?"

"Read it."

Tad took the thing up doubtfully, looked for a signature, and then fell on the manuscript. Grant put his thumb in the envelope from Cartwright and broke it open.

When Tad had finished he looked up with a shocked face and stared at Grant. When at last he spoke, what he said was, "I feel dirty all over."

"Yes. It is an evil thing."

"Vanity."

"Yes."

"That's the crash that was in the evening papers last night. The crate in flames on Mont Blanc."

"Yes."

"So he would have got away with it after all."

"No."

"No? He had thought of everything, hadn't he?"

"They never think of everything."

"They?"

"Murderers. Lloyd forgot so obvious a thing as fingerprints."

"You mean he didn't do that job in gloves? I don't believe it!"

"Of course he did it in gloves. Nothing he touched in the compartment would have any print of his. What he forgot was that there was something in the compartment that he had handled before."

"What was that?"

188

"Charles Martin's papers, the Testament, and the French novel." Grant flipped them with his finger-tip where they lay on the desk. "They are covered with Lloyd's prints. They never think of everything."

15

"You look like a bridegroom," Sergeant Williams said in great satisfaction, pump-handling Grant on Monday morning.

"Well, I'd better go and have rice thrown at me, I suppose. How is the old man's rheumatism this morning?"

"Oh, fairly good, I think."

"What is he smoking? A pipe? Or cigarettes?"

"Oh, a pipe."

"Then I'd better go in while the barometer is still high."

In the passage he encountered Ted Hanna.

"How did you run into Archie Brown?" Hanna asked, when he had greeted him.

"He's writing a Gaelic epic in the hotel at the place where I was staying. And his 'ravens,' by the way, are foreign fishing-boats."

"Yes?" said Hanna, stiffening into interest. "How do you know?"

"They got together at a party. It was the old 'have-a-cigarette-no-no-keep-the-packet' routine."

"Sure it *wasn't* cigarettes?"

"Quite sure. I picked his pocket in the course of one Grand Chain and unpicked it next time round."

"Don't tell me you've been *country dancing!*"

"You'd be surprised at the things that I've been doing. I'm a little surprised myself."

"Your holiday seems to have done you good," Hanna said. "I've never seen you so on top of the world. You're positively purring."

"As they say in the far North, I wouldn't call the King my cousin," Grant said, and meant it.

He was happy not because of the report that he was going to give Bryce, not even because he was his own man again; he was happy because of something young Cullen had said to him at the airport that morning.

"Mr. Grant," Tad had said, standing very straight and solemn and making a formal little speech of leave-taking like a well-brought-up boy, "I want you to know that I'll never forget what you've done for me and Bill. You couldn't bring Bill back to me, but you've done something much more wonderful: you've made him immortal."

And indeed that was just what he had done. As long as books were written and history read, Bill Kenrick would live; and it was he, Alan Grant, who had done that. They had buried Bill Kenrick six feet deep in oblivion, but he, Alan Grant, had dug him up again and set him in his rightful place as the discoverer of Wabar.

He had paid back the debt he owed that dead boy in B Seven.

Bryce greeted him amiably, and said that he was looking well (which didn't count, because he had said that at their last interview) and suggested that he might go down to Hampshire in answer to an appeal from the Hampshire police which had just come in.

"Well, if it's all the same to you, sir, I'd like to get the Kenrick murder off my chest first."

"The what?"

"This is my written report on it," Grant said, laying in front of Bryce the neat bundle of quarto pages that was the product of his pleasant Sunday at home.

As he laid the thing down he remembered in a vague, surprised way that what he had planned to lay in front of Bryce was his resignation.

What odd notions occurred to one on holiday.

He was going to resign, and be a sheep farmer or something, and get married.

What an extraordinary idea. What a most extraordinary idea.